DATE DUE

FEB 0 6 2001
FEB 2 7 2001
MAR 1 0 2001
MAR 2 3 2001
APR 2 0 [illegible]
MAY 0 9 2001
JUN 1 5 2001
DEC 1 8 [illegible]
JAN 3 0 [illegible]
MAR 1 4 2003
JAN 2 4 2005
FEB 2 3 2005
DEC 2 7 [illegible]

MAR [illegible] 2007
OCT 2 8 2009
DEC 0 1 [illegible]
NOV 0 9 [illegible]
JUL 1 3 [illegible]
NOV 0 2 [illegible]
FEB 1 3 2014
NOV 2 9 2014
AUG 2 1 2015
NOV 0 [illegible]
NOV 0 5 2016
JUL 0 5 2017

FEB 0 2 2017
OCT 1 9 2018
JAN 2 4 2019

DISCARD

GAYLORD

PRINTED IN U.S.A.

6/00

AKER & TAYLOR

M

Trow, M. J.

Lestrade and the guardian angel

Lestrade and the Guardian Angel

Lestrade and the Guardian Angel

Volume VIII in the
Lestrade Mystery Series

M.J. Trow

A Gateway Mystery

JOSEPHINE COUNTY LIBRARY
GRANTS PASS, OREGON

Copyright © 1999 by Regnery Publishing

All rights reserved. No part of this publication may be reproduced or transmitted in any form or by any means electronic or mechanical, including photocopy, recording, or any information storage and retrieval system now known or to be invented, without permission in writing from the publisher, except by a reviewer who wishes to quote brief passages in connection with a review written for inclusion in a magazine, newspaper, or broadcast.

Library of Congress Cataloging-in-Publication Data

Trow, M.J.
Lestrade and the guardian angel / M.J. Trow
p. cm. — (Lestrade mystery series ; v. 8)
ISBN 0-89526-267-3
I. Title. II. Series: Trow, M.J. Sholto Lestrade mystery series ; v. 8.
PR6070.R598L475 1999
823'.914—dc21 99-41315
CIP

Published in the United States by
Regnery Publishing, Inc.
An Eagle Publishing Company
One Massachusetts Avenue, NW
Washington, DC 20001

Originally published in Great Britain

Distributed to the trade by
National Book Network
4720-A Boston Way
Lanham, MD 20706

Printed on acid-free paper
Manufactured in the United States of America

10 9 8 7 6 5 4 3 2 1

Books are available in quantity for promotional or premium use. Write to Director of Special Sales, Regnery Publishing, Inc., One Massachusetts Avenue, NW, Washington, DC 20001, for information on discounts and terms or call (202) 216-0600.

The character of Inspector Lestrade was created by the late Sir Arthur Conan Doyle and appears in the Sherlock Holmes stories and novels by him, as do some other characters in this book.

The past is the only dead thing that smells sweet.

Early One Morning, Edward Thomas

1

Alpha

Harry Bandicoot straightened himself with a groan, leaning gratefully on the scythe. To his right and left, his tenants toiled under the August sun, leather-gaitered and steel-sickled to mow down the golden corn. Across the field the reaper clanked and rattled on its furrow, the great black horses lifting their iron hoofs as one, straining sinew and shoulder. Bandicoot caught the nearest rein, throwing the scythe to a labourer, and hauled himself on to the harvester.

'Warm work, sir,' the driver called, passing him a jug. Bandicoot nodded, swigging gratefully. His eyes crossed as it reached those parts other jugs could not and the driver noticed.

'It's the Missus's,' he explained.

'Yes, I thought it must be,' scowled Bandicoot, and remembering his upbringing and his status, 'Good brew, Jack, good brew. Give my compliments to the Missus.'

Jack grinned broadly, tugging on his forelock, and cracked the horses into the furrow again.

'Rider comin', Mr Bandicoot,' a young voice called. The squire looked up to the top of the harvester, shielding his eyes from the glare of the sun. 'From the 'All, I'd say.'

He looked across in the direction of the pointing finger and saw a horseman galloping across the meadow and clashing through the stream.

'Can you make out who it is, Jem?' Bandicoot asked the boy.

'It do look like Tom Wyatt,' the boy called back, cupping his hands to shout over the grinding of the machine.

Bandicoot climbed still higher so that he stood beside the driver and saw that young Jem was right. The groom was lashing Bandicoot's bay for all he was worth and was standing in the stirrups as he took the crest of the hill and burst through the corn.

'You'll flatten it, you bloody idiot!' Jack bellowed, but Bandicoot's hand on his shoulder quietened him.

'You know Tom better than that, Jack,' the squire said. 'He'll have his reasons.'

Wyatt was yelling now, plunging through the harvest field and waving hysterically. He drew rein within inches of the plodding blacks who threw up their heads and looked at him.

'You look flushed, Tom,' Bandicoot greeted him, taking in the groom's open waistcoat and matted hair. 'What's the matter?'

'It's Mrs Bandicoot, sir,' Wyatt gasped, kicking himself free of the stirrups. 'She's started.'

'Started what?'

There was a silence in which all eyes turned to the squire. Jack, the driver, tugged on the squire's belt with one hand and began to light his pipe with the other. 'Whelping, sir,' he whispered, 'beggin' your pardon an' all.'

'Good God! She's three weeks early!' Bandicoot stood bolt upright like a recently castrated calf and leapt in one fluid movement into the saddle of the bay. It was as well it had been recently vacated by the groom.

'Carry on, Jack,' Bandicoot shouted, and drove his heels into the animal's flanks, crashing back through the devastation caused by the groom.

'That I will, sir,' Jack chuckled and threw his jug down to Tom Wyatt. The groom pulled off the stopper.

'Your Missus's?' he asked.

Jack nodded, and the groom replaced the stopper.

Squire Bandicoot hurtled through the stream, his legs straight in the stirrups, his head low to miss the branches. The two miles felt like twenty as he thrashed the bay's neck with his reins. The animal swerved on the gravel and then he was weaving between the gnarled old trees of the orchard, ducking and bobbing. The swans flapped noisily from the lake as his hoofbeats frightened them and he saw a flurry of activity on the terrace ahead. Another groom caught the lathered, snorting bay as Bandicoot leapt from its back, running like the Old Etonian he was up the slope.

'Oh, sir,' wailed the hysterical girl on the terrace as he arrived.

'What is it, Maisie?' He held her heaving shoulders and attempted to sound calm.

'It's bad news, sir,' she sobbed.

Bandicoot stared at the tearful eyes and the red, throbbing nose.

'What? What?' he shouted.

'It's Grizzle. She's . . . she's dead,' and the maid sank to her knees, sobbing uncontrollably.

Bandicoot looked helplessly around him. It was something he had been doing now for more than thirty years. He was quite accomplished at it. It was with exquisite relief he welcomed the arrival of Miss Balsam, as gnarled as any of the trees he had just ridden past and a little riper, to boot.

'Tsk, girl,' she snarled at the maid, who bobbed up, curtsied to the squire and left, wailing.

'Grizzle? What's happening, Nanny Balsam?'

'Grizzle?' Miss Balsam repeated. 'Oh, that tiresome child. I think she must be referring to the frog of the same name.'

'A frog, Miss Balsam?' Bandicoot couldn't understand it. Everyone had been sane when he left the Hall that morning. What could have happened since?

'A pet, I understand.' Miss Balsam was shepherding the squire to a chair on the terrace. 'Cook accidentally trod on it this morning. I am, as you know, trained in resuscitation, but I fear I drew the line at *Rana temporaria*. Had it been *Rana esculenta*, of course . . .'

'Miss Balsam!' Bandicoot was near to breaking point. 'Letitia . . .'

'. . . is doing very nicely without you, thank you very much,' and she pushed him bodily into the wicker. 'Men!' She clicked her tongue.

'Has she . . . ? Is she . . . ? I must go to her!' He stood up.

'Never!' Miss Balsam's five foot one bowled over Squire Bandicoot's six foot two with all the force of her sensibilities and her sex. 'What goes on in that room', she wagged her finger at the leaded window above, 'is no business of yours.' Then calmer, 'You've done your part. Now let Lettie do hers.'

She patted his bewildered curls. 'You need an amontillado,' and she swept indoors.

Bandicoot fumbled for his hunter. 'Half-past three,' he said aloud, and began to pace the terrace. He looked up at the window to see shadows and reflections flitter this way and that. He heard no sound inside but the occasional roar of Miss Balsam. 'Towels!' interspersed with 'Hot water!'

'Beggin' your pardon, sir.' A voice caused Bandicoot to spin round to see the red-nosed Maisie standing with a glass of sherry wine on a tray of Bandicoot silver. 'Your armadillo, sir,' she sniffed.

'My . . . ? Oh, I see. Thank you, Maisie . . . and I'm very sorry about your frog.'

The tray clashed loudly on the terrace and the maid hauled up her petticoats and rushed away howling.

An iron-grey head poked itself through the leaded panes. 'Be quiet down there!'

Bandicoot sat down and sipped his sherry as quietly as he knew how. With all his other worries, the last thing he wanted was to cross Miss Balsam now. He watched the sunshine ripple on the waters of the lake and old Wiggins trailing the far bank with his nets, trawling for pike. One of them would get him, one of these days, and old Wiggins would take his place in the trophy room of Bandicoot Hall, framed and glazed with the rest. The swans had come back now, gliding in on silent wings to ruffle the still surface of the water. From the reeds to his left, Grizzle's relatives kept up their watery lament, throaty organs swelling in the afternoon stillness.

Then he heard an alien sound and it took him a while to place it. It was a slap, of skin on skin, followed by a cry, sharp, surprised, indignant. It wasn't little Emma, whose six-month noise had a more worldly tone to it. Bandicoot dropped his glass and dashed through the French windows, tearing back the heavy velvet, hurtling across his study and through the hall. Servants appeared from nowhere, anxiously peering after the Master, as he bounded up the stairs three at a time. There was a second slap as he reached the landing and another appalled noise joined the first. But Bandicoot did not hear it. Only his own heart thumped and banged in his ears. Raised to the scrum and the Wall Game, the Old Etonian lowered his shoulder for the charge. No footling time wasting with the niceties of door handles for him. Time was of the essence. And he knew that it and something else waits for no man.

In the event, Miss Balsam obligingly opened the doors for him so all Bandicoot had to do was to trip neatly over Joris, the cat, and catch his nose a sharp one on the bedstead.

'Harry!' Letitia looked at him in some alarm, blood trickling over his lips and all.

'Letitia!' he shouted back and saw, flanking his pink, radiant wife, two other heads, smaller, wrinkled like little old men.

'Harry,' she said, 'I'd like you to meet Ivo,' she lifted the little old man on her right arm, 'and Rupert,' she lifted the little old man on her left arm.

Bandicoot stood there.

'Like this, Mr Bandicoot,' said Miss Balsam, placing the squire's arms just so, 'hold them like this.'

He took first one little wrapped bundle, then the other.

'Hello, old man,' he said to Ivo, 'Hello,' to Rupert.

They both looked at him blearily, each with one eye open. Letitia beamed proudly. 'Before you take them to see the horses, Harry,' she said, 'could I hold them for a while?'

'Oh, my darling, of course,' and he very carefully handed them back. He was about to assert himself as Master of the House and kick out the roomful of women, when he turned and saw they had gone. All save Miss Balsam, who handed him a cigar. 'Noisome things, of course,' she smiled, 'but fitting at times like these,' and she hurried away, dabbing her eyes. On the landing, Miss Balsam rested against the double doors, her work done. How many babies, she wondered, had she helped into the world? And why, oh why, did they not stay as innocent as the little boys inside?

Bandicoot sat gingerly on the counterpane. 'My dearest,' he said, 'how are you?'

'Fine, Harry,' she smiled, looking lovingly at her three men.

He smoothed her cheek. 'It's funny,' he said. 'All the way up here from the fields, all I could think of was Sarah Lestrade and poor old Sholto. What if, I thought. What if?'

Letitia caught for a moment the eyes wet with tears. 'Harry Bandicoot!' she said sharply. '*Floreat Etona*. We loved Sarah. And we love Sholto. And most of all we love their little Emma.

But we have our own children now. They'll grow together. Emma and the boys. Brothers for her. A sister for them.'

'You're right,' he smiled, sniffing hard. Then, springing to his feet, 'I must send Sholto a telegram.'

'In a moment, Mr Bandicoot,' she said softly.

He knelt again, resting his head on her breasts between the boys. 'In a moment, Mrs Bandicoot . . .'

2

Odd Fellowes

Her Majesty's carriage disappeared in a flutter of flags, the rattling wheels and jingling harness drowned in a deluge of cheering. Queen's weather shone down on the Queen's day. It had been meticulously planned, this Diamond Jubilee, and the Home Secretary himself sat braced and upright in his Whitehall office, surrounded by telephones, wires, constables with reputations for running. Her Majesty had made it clear that nothing must go amiss. At the recent coronation of His Imperial Majesty the Tsar three thousand peasants had been trampled in the rush. It must not happen here. It could not, Mr Keir Hardie had retorted in the Commons. Thanks to the Independent Labour party there was not a single peasant in England.

From the Home Secretary to the Commissioner of the Metropolitan Police, ashy grey under the gusting plumes of his cocked hat, sitting his horse with the obvious discomfort of a lifetime's martyrdom to haemorrhoids. Still, he had made his pile. He must sit on it. His strained, flinty eyes watched for the blue helmets in the crowd, edging it, ringing it, the white gloves flying up to salute as the royal cortège passed. From the Commissioner to the Assistant Commissioner, and to the Superintendents and so on down to the Inspectorate, that unsung body of men who now mingled with the great, cheering, radiant British public along the royal route. Those in braided patrol jackets and peaked caps like Athelney Jones, bobbing up and down on his river launch, were obvious enough. Others, like Sholto Lestrade, straw-boatered in his lightweight serge, were scarcely distinguishable from real people. Only the parchment skin gave it away, and the tired eyes and the look that was weary of the world.

From his window overlooking Whitehall, Mr Gladstone took in the scene, the scrawny turtle neck craning out of the upright collar, the eyes wild and dancing. He summoned his private secretary.

'Please convey to Her Majesty my heartfelt congratulations on Her Jubilee,' he said in his impeccable Lowland Scots, 'and may I be the first to suggest to Her Majesty that there could not be a finer moment for Her Abdication.'

Gladstone's wild eye caught a commotion in the surging crowds below. Immediately behind the Queen's carriage a scuffle had broken out. In the mêlée a man with parchment skin and a face that was weary of the world was struggling with another. They pirouetted into the trotting cavalcade of the Life Guards and the straw-boatered man somersaulted neatly off the right shoulder of the black stallion caracoling in a hopeless attempt to avoid him. Gladstone saw the Queen glance back: seeing the man roll upright again and hop around clutching a crushed foot, she commented to the Princess of Wales in her carriage that she was rather amused and would confide the fact to her journal. How kind of the man to provide this thoughtful entertainment for her. And how clever of him to know that such slapstick never failed to delight her. Her view had been a little impeded, however, as she had had to turn round. Perhaps his timing could have been better.

Sergeant Dixon had been on the Front Desk at the Yard, man and boy, for more years than he cared to remember. Rumour had it he had been a sergeant when Inspector Lestrade had arrived as a rookie. Rumour had it he had been a young constable in Sir Robert Peel's three thousand back in '29. Rumour had it he had joined the Bow Street Runners under Magistrate Fielding on account of how he already owned a red waistcoat and that was really the only entry requirement. But that, as most men tacitly admitted, was silly. The Runners had been established in 1748 and they only took men who were young and fit. Dixon was already over the hill by then.

So the sergeant had seen the Sights. All of them. Or so he

thought. But even his omniscient jaw fell slack at the apparition which greeted him in the foyer of the Yard that summer evening. A huge officer of the Life Guards in full dress uniform, complete with helmet and cuirass, stood before him, towering over him like a lamp standard.

'Evening, sir.' Dixon found himself saluting. 'Can I be of service?'

The Life Guard looked him up and down. 'Sorry,' he said through his chin-chain, 'should have enlisted years ago. Anyway, we've already got a mascot. Lestrange in?'

'Beg your pardon, sir?' Dixon was never at his best on the twilight shift.

'Sergeant Lestrange. Is he in?'

'If you mean Inspector Lestrade, sir, yes, he is.' Dixon was trying hard to remember to close his mouth after each word. He reached for the machine-with-wires on the wall. 'Who shall I say . . . ?'

'Don't bother.' The officer strode for the stairs, dragging his sword across Dixon's polished floor. 'I'll find him.'

'I'm afraid you can't . . .'

But the officer had gone, clattering up the staircase three at a time. Dixon wrestled manfully with the gadgetry which whirred and clicked at him.

'Dew?' he screamed down the tube.

'Do what?' a confused voice retaliated.

'Is that Constable Dew?'

'How dare you, Dixon! This is Assistant Commisioner Frost and you've got your wires tangled again. Get a grip, man, or I'll have your stripes. What will I have?'

'My stripes, sir,' and he clutched his ear as his superior rang off with more venom than was usual. As he replaced the receiver, a plainclothesman wafted through the hall.

'Dew!' Dixon barked.

'Hello, sarge,' the constable beamed back.

'Hello my arse! Get in that lift!' He ushered the flustered constable through the metal grilles, slamming them shut.

'What's up, sarge?'

'You are!' shouted Dixon, pressing buttons like a thing possessed. 'Third floor. Tell Mr Lestrade there's a ten-foot soljer on his way up.'

'On his way up?' Dew shouted down through the floor boards.

'That's right,' Dixon bellowed to the receding cage. 'I can still see his spurs, so 'is 'ead must be outside the guv'nor's office by now.'

But the officer was faster than Dew. Legs were after all made before lifts.

'Oswald Ames,' he introduced himself, 'Second Life Guards. Oh my God . . .'

He unhooked his chin-chain and swept off the glittering helmet, to crash down heavily and unasked on to the leather-backed chair.

'Of all the horses in all the Jubilee processions in the world, you had to walk into mine.'

Across the paper-strewn desk from him sat a parchment-faced man in an old lightweight serge. His eyes were tired, his face was world-weary. And his foot was resting on a stool, swathed in bandages.

'Forgive me for asking,' said Ames, 'but why is that stool swathed in bandages?'

'You can't get the staff nowadays,' the other man answered.

His door swung back. 'Mr Lestrade,' gasped Constable Dew, 'there's a ten-foot soldier on his way . . . up . . . to . . .'

'Captain Ames,' Lestrade read the pips on the man's shoulder cords, 'this is Constable Dew. Despite all appearance he makes an excellent cup of tea. Will you join me?'

'Tea? Is it Kokew Oolong?'

'It'll just be a jiffy, sir,' Dew was at pains to promise. He hustled through to the adjoining closet. Having made one *faux pas* already, he was not anxious to make another.

'Have you come to apologize or to press charges, Captain?' Lestrade asked.

'Neither, actually. Didn't realize you were the johnny one collided with today. Couldn't really see what happened. Sun was glancing off the Old Girl's tiara. Couldn't see a bally thing.'

'Well.' Lestrade began to unwrap his foot from the stool. 'There I was, minding everyone else's business in the crowd, when I felt my pocket being picked. I grabbed a hand and the fellow and I had a bit of a set to. Unfortunately it spilled out into your path. The rest you know.'

'I see. Well, fortunes of war. Not too badly crushed, are you?'

'No, no.' Lestrade winced. 'Nothing that three months in a sling won't cure.'

'Good. Good.' Ames unhooked his sword and rested it against the desk. 'Does your chappie do a bit of tartaring? Got some caviar on the old tunic this morning. Got a bash with Bertie tomorrow. Can't go looking like something the cat's brought in.'

'Quite.' Lestrade smiled quietly. 'Dew,' he called to the closet.

A macassared head appeared round the door. 'Sir?'

'How are you at cleaning drink stains off serge?'

'Melton.' Ames reminded him of the quality of the material.

'How are you at removing Melton stains off serge?'

'I'll have a go, sir.' Dew was the stuff the Yard was made of. Granite.

'On second thoughts, one had better stick to one's batman.'

'As you will, Captain.' Lestrade leaned back, resting his hands on his waistcoat. 'Now, you and I, I'm sure, have had an exceedingly long day. I wonder if . . .'

'Oh, my dear fellow, of course. Remiss of me. The purpose of my visit.'

Lestrade beamed.

'I understand you're on the case.'

'Case?' Lestrade leaned forward.

'Yes.' Ames did the same. 'Isn't that what you detective johnnies call it?'

'Er . . . yes . . . we do,' affirmed Lestrade, and eying the daunting pile of paperwork, 'Which one exactly?'

'My dear fellow.' Ames was amazed. '*The* case. Archie Fellowes.'

'Fellowes?'

'Brother officer. Army and Navy Club. Tragic. Quite tragic.'

'Ah!' Bells were clanging in Lestrade's brain. He ferreted among the papers. 'Yes. Captain Archibald Anstruther Fellowes. Second Life Guards. Found in the river at Shadwell Stair two days ago.'

'Quite. Utterly tragic. You *are* on the case?'

'Well, it's really a matter for the River Police. Inspector Jones . . .'

'Tosh!' Ames stood up to his full six foot eight and rammed

on his helmet. 'One has it on good authority that you are the best there is, Lestrade.'

'That's very flattering . . .'

'Flattering my numnah! It's a fact. Archie was a chum. Sorry he's gone. Can't be natural. Must be sorted. Not in keeping, y'see.'

'What isn't?'

'Suicide. Chaps in the Life Guards don't do it. And if they do, they use this,' he hooked up his sword, 'or their Webleys. They don't just jump in the bally river. Not dignified, y'see. Must be sorted. Good night.'

And he scraped a lump out of the door frame on his way out.

'Has he gone, sir?' Dew appeared with steaming mugs.

Lestrade listened as the sword clattered away down the stairs.

'I think so,' he said.

'I didn't understand most of that conversation, sir,' Dew admitted.

'Quite, Walter. That's why you're a constable. Where's that idiot who bandaged my foot?'

A pallid face appeared around a pile of paperwork.

'Sir?'

'Ah . . . Constable Lilley, isn't it?' Lestrade began unwrapping the swathes. 'I think you must have been reading your St John's Ambulance first-aid book upside down. What do you know about Shadwell?'

The pallid face became blanker. 'It's in London, sir.'

'So it is.' Lestrade fixed the young man with an odd faraway look in his eyes. 'At dawn tomorrow morning, you and Dew will meet me at the church of St Paul in that godforsaken part of Stepney and we'll do some sleuthing. Or rather we'll talk to Inspector Jones which sadly is not the same thing.'

The lighters and barges were already steaming their way across the river when the three policemen arrived. The constables, Dew and Lilley, helped the straw-hatted inspector aboard the Metropolitan Police Launch *Calliphora Vomitoria* to meet its 'Captain', who stood with his arms locked fore and aft around his great hulk.

'He looks like Nelson, sir,' Lilley whispered in some awe to Lestrade who transferred his weight to Dew at that moment.

'Before or after the sniper got him?' Lestrade asked. 'Besides, he's got too many eyes and arms and things.'

'Morning, Lestrade!' Inspector Jones bellowed. 'Cast off!'

'It's an old knitting term,' Lestrade explained to the green constable. 'Morning, Jones. You know Constable Dew.'

Jones grunted.

'This is Constable Lilley.'

He grunted again. 'To what do I owe the pleasure? Oh, hurt our foot, have we?' He noted Lestrade's discomfort as he hobbled gratefully to a chair bolted to the aft deck. The engines roared into life, coughed and died.

'Tickle it, man!' Jones roared to someone Down Below. He reverted to the question of Lestrade's foot, 'In what did you put that?'

'It was a chance meeting with a cavalry charger,' Lestrade explained, 'which brings me neatly to the purpose of my visit.'

'And I thought you'd come for some tips on police work.'

The engines roared again. 'Bring her head round!' Jones thundered. Dew and Lilley looked about them wondering where the lady was to whom the inspector was referring.

'Captain Fellowes,' Lestrade shouted above the din.

'Ah, yes. What about him?' Jones, ever the sensitive policeman, sensed intrusion.

'He was on my desk last night,' said Lestrade.

'Good God!' Jones knelt beside him, not the easiest of manoeuvres for a man with his hands stuffed in his waistcoat. 'How is that possible? When I saw him last he was on a slab in the mortuary.'

'I was speaking metatarsally, Athelney.' Lestrade thought he'd better humour his man. Years bobbing up and down on bilge water had obviously taken their toll.

'Oh, I see.' Jones stood up. 'But it's my case, dammit. He was found in my river.'

The constables, Jones's and Lestrade's, pricked up their ears. A fight between superiors was always good for a laugh.

'But presumably he landed in your river having jumped from my land.'

'Since when is Shadwell *your* patch?'

'Since when is the Thames yours?' Lestrade countered.

Jones bridled and stared fixedly at the prow. 'Keep her head round!' he snarled to a constable at the helm behind him.

Dew and Lilley exchanged glances.

Lestrade tried a different tack, with the wind this time. 'A man is dead, Athelney,' he said as quietly as he could above the throb of the Reardon Wesleys. 'I don't know why the case should have come my way, but it has and I've got to do something about it. Perhaps we can work together?'

Jones snorted in time to his pistons. 'Rowlocks!' he retorted.

'All right.' Lestrade leaned back in the chair with the air of a man who knows when he's beaten, 'What's it to be?'

Jones looked at the scarred, yellow face beneath the scarred, yellow boater. 'I've got a son coming up to age in a year or so . . .' he said.

'Go on.'

'Get him in at the Yard.'

'Come on, Athelney. You know I can't do that. Any more than you can.'

'I can't,' Jones reminded him, 'because I'm stuck out at Woolwich Reach half my bloody life. But you, you're in the old Opera House itself. On terra forma you can do some good . . .'

'Well, I could have a word with Abberline I suppose . . .'

'Not good enough.' Jones remained obdurate.

Lestrade blew outward until his moustache ends rose. 'All right then. I'll see Frost.'

Jones beamed. 'When?'

'How old's your boy?'

'Seventeen this month.'

'When the time comes, then.'

'We found him there.' Jones pointed to the scummy water slapping against the green encrusted pier poles.

'Who?' Lestrade had lost track of the conversation.

'Captain Fellowes. Your Tinbelly.'

Lestrade peered over the side. All he saw was his own reflection. 'You checked the place, of course?'

'Of course,' Jones told him. 'We found three kettles, a bedstead, some old bronze thing the British Museum is having a look at and more dogshit than you'll find in Battersea.'

'What about the body?'

Jones disappeared into the cabin behind him, thumping a constable as he passed. 'Watch your helm, Soulou.'

'Dew, get your bearings.' Lestrade called his constable to him. The man fumbled in his pockets. 'I mean, where are we, man?' He steadied himself on the deck.

'All engines stop,' he heard Jones bellow.

The constable scanned the horizon. 'I can't see much behind this pier thing, sir,' Dew confessed.

'That's the Stair, laddie,' Jones told him, re-emerging. 'The Highway, behind those wharfs. The Narrow, to starboard.' All eyes except Dew's looked right. 'New Basin, to port.' All eyes except Dew's looked left.

'He'd been in the water for two days, I'd say,' Jones explained, checking the notes he'd brought from the cabin. 'Some of his skin was coming away. What with the weather and all, a few more hours and he'd have been unrecognizable. If he'd swollen up much more he could have floated out to Erith. Then the herrings could have had him.'

There was no sound on the river now but the gentle lapping of the waters and the gentle vomiting of Constable Lilley over the side.

'Any other damage?' Lestrade asked.

'Better ask the coroner.' Jones shrugged.

'Well, I was hoping for an answer,' Lestrade said.

'Point taken.' Jones produced a hearty beef sandwich from his patrol jacket pocket. 'Elevenses. Any of your chappies . . . ?' but the colour of Constable Lilley made him aware of the futility of the question. 'He was pretty battered around the head,' Jones munched, 'but he would be. It's my guess he went in somewhere around Kew, perhaps Mortlake, and probably got stuck a few times. Chiswick Eyot's a bastard for that. Not to mention Oliver's Ait.'

'Now, Athelney, for the big one. Did he jump or was he pushed?'

Jones shrugged. 'You're the policeman,' he said.

Lestrade smiled broadly. 'Can I have that in writing? Thanks for your help, Inspector. Put me and my lads ashore, will you? Where is the good Captain now? Branch Road?'

Jones nodded.

'Come on Dew, Lilley, get me up these stairs, will you? We've got a body to view. It's all right, Lilley, you can stay outside.'

Sholto Lestrade circled the bloated remains of Captain Archibald Fellowes, holding the boater over his nose to avoid some, at least, of the smell of Thames water and formaldehyde. Beneath the green-white skin, flaking off the frame, he could vaguely discern a once handsome face, the moustache drooping over the tight, blue lips. He was, as Jones had told him, battered around the head, but it wasn't particularly pretty. The coroner was not in that morning, still sleeping off, as was most of London, the exhilaration of the Queen's Jubilee. But Lestrade had seen the Sights before. He knew that Jones was right. Those blows were caused after death, not before. Pier poles, anchor chains, stone corners and bridge supports had all taken their toll. The mortuary attendant had provided Lestrade with the clothes the deceased had been wearing when found. A lightweight suit, brown laced shoes, all bearing Savile Row labels, and oddly for a man in civvies, a medal. What was particularly odd about it was where it had been worn. Not pinned to his lapel, apparently, but wedged between his teeth.

'Between his teeth?' Lestrade repeated, unsure of his hearing.

'That's right,' the attendant told him, picking his nose thoughtfully. 'Held there by rigor mortis – and his gold fillin's.'

Lestrade looked again at the gong in his fist – a bronze four-pointed star with the legend 'Ashanti' and the date '1896'.

'Last year,' he murmured to himself.

'That's right,' the attendant agreed.

The inspector flipped the medal over. 'From the Queen,' he read.

'That's right,' the attendant agreed again.

Lestrade replaced his boater and tucked the medal in his pocket.

'That's evidence,' said the attendant, wiping the contents of his nose on his sleeve.

'That's right,' said Lestrade and, collecting Lilley from the outer office, he and his constables made for the light.

* * *

In the hansom on the way back to the Yard, Walter Dew was less than his placid self.

'What's the matter, Dew?' Lestrade was a noticing sort of inspector. 'Cat got your truncheon?'

'I'm sorry, sir,' Dew confided. 'I've got to come out with this.'

'Close your eyes, Lilley, you're of tender years.'

'I'm afraid I . . . picked something up, sir.'

Lestrade's eyebrows disappeared under the rim of his boater. 'That's what comes of loitering with intent in the Haymarket of an evening. Mrs Dew will have to know, of course . . .'

'No.' Dew blushed as only the lovesick can. 'From the corpse, I mean.'

'Have a rinse when you get to the Yard. I'll have a word with Dixon. He'll let you use the sergeants' slipper baths.'

'No, I mean evidence, sir. I found some evidence. In the lining of the deceased's pocket.'

'Really?' Lestrade was secretly impressed, but he wasn't going to let it show. 'Fluff?'

'I don't know, sir. I don't think I've ever seen wet fluff. Here it is.'

Lestrade examined the particles in Dew's palm, not easy in a jolting hansom with a second policeman's nose nuzzling against his own. The inspector leaned back. 'You may have bandaged my foot yesterday, Lilley, but I still hardly know you. Perhaps you could keep your nose out of Constable Dew's hand until we're all better acquainted?'

'Yes, sir. Of course, sir.' Lilley knew a rebuke when he heard one and he spent the remainder of the journey bolt upright.

'Fluff, be damned,' said Lestrade. 'They're seeds.' He jabbed the ceiling of the cab with his crutch. 'Kew Gardens, driver, and if you get there before dinner time, the constable here will give you a tip.'

'I will be able to claim all this on expenses, sir?' Dew checked, emptying all his pockets as he did so.

'Of course, Walter.' Lestrade hobbled manfully through the shrubbery. 'Usual thing. Forms in triplicate. Reimbursement next Christmas, assuming there's no R in the month. Don't forget the tip.'

'Kempton Park, three o'clock,' Dew muttered to the growler on his perch. 'Stingy Inspector, one hundred to one.'

'Yeah, I heard that one,' the growler growled and he and his cab rattled into the distance.

'Right, we'll try the Palm House first.'

'Must we, sir?' Lilley halted the policemen's progress.

'Is there a problem, constable?' Lestrade paused by a cedar of Lebanon to rest his leg.

'It's just that I'm not keen on heat, sir. It must be in the eighties now.'

'Mother frightened by a radiator, was she? All right, you wait here. Dew, open that door.'

The two of them entered a veritable jungle, verdure dripping everywhere. The place seemed deserted and Lestrade was just getting used to his trousers clinging clammily to his legs when a gnarled old head appeared out of the undergrowth.

'Good morning, gentlemen,' it said. '*Elaeis guineensis*.'

'Sholto Lestrade, Scotland Yard. This is Constable Dew. Are you in charge here, Mr Guineensis?'

The gnarled old head looked a trifle quizzical. 'Ah, I see. No. *Guineensis* is the plant you are looking at. My name is Bush. And please, no jokes. I have been a horticulturalist for the past forty years, man and boy. It does become a little wearing.'

'I'm sure,' commiserated Lestrade, watching the vapour condense on his hatbrim. 'I wonder if you might help us with our enquiries?'

'I'll certainly do my best, but I wonder if we might walk this way? I have my measurements to take.'

Lestrade and Dew obeyed to the letter, although creeping through the foliage with a crutch was not the easiest manoeuvre the inspector had ever performed. More than once the lianas coiled round his ferrule and he got a mouthful of John Innes. Still, it was all part of life's rich tapestry.

'It's quite a way,' Bush apologized. 'We'll take my trap.'

They helped the inspector aboard and rattled south-east with Constable Lilley jogging through the goose droppings behind. Lestrade and Dew were grateful for the fresh air of an English summer and to be able to leave the tropics under glass.

'Up there.' Bush pointed to the top of an ornate Chinese

pagoda. 'I have to measure my *Widdringtonia whytei* and this is the best vantage point.'

'Excuse me, sir,' gasped Lilley, 'but how high is that?'

'The pagoda?' Bush dismounted, rolling down his shirt-sleeves. 'One hundred and sixty-three feet.'

Lilley paled significantly. 'I wonder if you'll excuse me on this one, sir?' he said to Lestrade.

'Another problem, constable?' Lestrade seemed to have been this way before.

'It's height, sir. I don't really . . .'

'Mother frightened by a tallboy, eh? Dew, Mr Bush, could you assist me, please?'

It was half an hour later after much grunting and sweating that the three men arrived at the top.

'What a view!' the poetic Dew was heard to exclaim.

Bush leaned across with a tape measure attached to the pagoda's rim and began jotting hieroglyphics down in his notebook, tapping overhanging leaves and branches now and then.

'Now,' he said, 'how can I help?'

'Dew.' Lestrade snapped his fingers.

'Sir?' The constable was awestruck by Greater London stretching before him.

'Forgive my constable,' said Lestrade. 'He hasn't been this far north before.'

'With respect, sir, I have.' Even Dew had a certain amount of dignity. 'The Monument is, I believe, higher than this.'

The other two looked at him. 'The evidence, constable?' Lestrade reminded him.

'Ah, yes, sir. Of course,' and he fumbled in his pockets.

'Ah.' Bush held it up to the light, sniffed it, measured it and returned it to Dew. 'Well, of course I'm no expert, but I'd say it was fluff. Probably from someone's pocket.'

Lestrade had climbed a long way for nothing. 'But surely, there are seeds in it?' he said.

'Are there?' Bush focused his gnarled old spectacles on the end of his gnarled old nose. 'Oh yes, *Cedrela odorata*.'

'Er . . .' Lestrade had never got beyond the First Declension in his Latin at Mr Poulson's Academy.

'Bastard Cedar,' Bush explained.

'Now then, sir.' Dew knew when his guv'nor was being insulted.

'Go on,' Lestrade ignored him.

'One of the family *Meliaceae*. Native to the West Indies and South America. It is sometimes called the Barbados Bastard Cedar. It has a smell offensive to insects. Your wardrobe is probably lined with it. So are your cigar boxes.'

'And are these trees found growing outside the West Indies and South America?' Lestrade asked.

'Only one other place in the world,' Bush confided.

'Where might that be, sir?' Dew had his notebook at the ready.

Bush crouched for a moment, as though lining his eye up on the pagoda's rail. 'Just there,' he said. 'Half-way between the flagstaff and King William's Temple.'

Lestrade and Dew exchanged glances.

'May I ask why this interest in *odorata*, Mr . . . ?' Bush enquired.

'I'm afraid I'm not at liberty to divulge that, Mr Bush. Dew, before we take our leave of your view, cast your eyes over there.'

The constable followed the inspector's finger to the sun dazzling on the river. 'That's Brentford Dock. Mr Bush, is that path along the bank open to the public?'

'Like the rest of the Gardens, yes, it is.'

'Tell me, is there any way of knowing who visited the Gardens, say within the last week?'

'Well, there is a visitors' book at the Dutch House, but there's no compulsion to sign it. Nor indeed any compulsion to visit the Dutch House.'

Lestrade cupped his hands and shouted down to his man on the ground. 'Lilley, was your mother ever frightened by a windmill?'

The constable shook his head slowly, uncertainly.

'A clog?'

The same response.

'What about cheese?'

'I don't think so, sir, but could you ask me these questions from down here? I don't really like looking up.'

'Where is this Dutch House, Mr Bush?'

The horticulturalist pointed north.

'That way, Lilley. A building called the Dutch House. You're looking for a visitors' book. Any familiar names – in fact any names at all for the last week, write them down. Mother wasn't frightened by a pencil, was she?'

Lilley trotted along the Pagoda vista while an increasingly large crowd had gathered to gaze up at Lestrade as though he were something at Hyde Park Corner.

'You're making a spectacle of yourself, Dew. Get me downstairs.'

It was some days later that Inspector Lestrade received another visitor at the Yard. It came as a refreshing change. The heat of July was stifling and the open windows meant that the stench of Inspector Jones's river was worse than a horse fair on a bad day. At least the prevailing wind was away from Billingsgate and the Yard was always grateful for small mercies. The Fellowes case had ground to a halt after a promising start. Constables Dew and Lilley had expended tanneries of shoe-leather in their attempts to track down the names in the visitors' book at Kew Gardens. They had come up with a barrister, fourteen spinsters on a Spinsters' Outing from Skegness, eight shop assistants and assorted gentlemen friends, a vicar and an alcoholic who thought the Dutch House was a pub and complained in the book of the quality of the beer. No one knew a Life Guards officer named Fellowes and no one remembered seeing a moustachioed gentleman wearing the Ashanti Star. There was nothing else for it. Lestrade would have to visit the Knightsbridge Barracks and pursue his enquiries there. And he was just planning precisely this venture when the door opened to reveal a handsome lady in a frothy summer dress and parasol. She had blonde hair immaculately twined under her broad, feathered hat and she smiled as the inspector bobbed with difficulty to his feet.

'Sholto.' She kissed his cheek and held him for a moment. 'You've hurt yourself.'

'It's nothing,' he said. 'Where's my jacket?'

She hit him deftly with her parasol. 'Tsk, tsk, I've seen men in their shirt-sleeves before, you know. I have been married to Harry Bandicoot for some time now.'

He held her hand. 'How is Harry?' he asked.

She sat down suddenly, sweeping off her hat and arranging her dress. 'There's something wrong, Sholto.'

He leaned back in his chair. 'Could you stand a cup of Walter Dew's tea?' he asked.

'I think so,' she said.

'Then while I try to get myself sitting comfortably, you may begin.'

3

The Trouble With Harry

Assistant Commissioner Nimrod Frost was not a man to suffer fools gladly. Still less inspectors. He looked over his pince-nez at Sholto Lestrade.

'Leave?' he said.

'Yes, sir.' Lestrade stood his ground, on the carpet though he was.

'What of Archibald Fellowes?' Frost reminded him.

'He's dead, sir.'

'Indeed he is!' Frost slammed down his Bluebird with all the power his sixteen stone could muster. 'And I have a letter here, Lestrade.' He launched himself upright, waving it under what was left of the inspector's nose. His voice fell to a confidential whisper. 'It's from His Highness the Prince of Wales.'

'Ah.' Lestrade felt he knew what was coming.

'You may or may not be aware that His Royal Highness is Colonel of the Life Guards. He is particularly anxious that the business of Captain Fellowes be cleared up and quickly.'

Frost circled Lestrade a few times, so that the chandelier shook.

'You *are* working on the case?'

'The body was found in the river, sir.'

'Meaning?'

'The river is Inspector Jones's province, sir.'

'Don't try that one on me, Lestrade, I'm too long in the tooth for it. Athelney Jones couldn't solve his way out of a paper bag. But that isn't why I had the case passed to you.'

'Ah,' said Lestrade. He was feeling non-committal this morning and to say more might have incriminated him.

Frost lurched back into the padded chair which groaned and buckled under him. '*This* is why.' He shook the letter again. 'For some reason known only to God and the Prince of Wales, His Royal Highness has asked that you should be placed in charge of enquiries.' Frost leaned forward, his shoulders momentarily blotting out the sun. 'What's all this about, Lestrade? I didn't know you moved in such exalted circles.'

'Let's just say, the Prince and I enjoyed a quiet cigar together once.'

Frost eased himself backwards. 'Really?' His eyebrows crept skyward.

'At the Commissioner's Ball, sir, back in . . . let me see . . . '91, I believe.'

Frost's lips twisted into a sneer. He was a self-made policeman, from Grantham, the only inhabitant of that town ever likely to come to any good, and he resented 'contacts' and privilege with all the bitterness of a Socialist, though he would have cut off his right hand rather than admit it. He was also a Mason, but that was *de rigueur* at the Yard in those or any other days.

Lestrade was not going to add that he had also nearly fought a duel with the Prince's son and had once dallied amorously with the Countess of Warwick, at that time the Prince's paramour. It all seemed rather incestuous, looking back, and he didn't think Assistant Commissioner Frost, from Grantham, would understand.

'This being the case,' Frost went on, 'with a direct command from your future king, how is it you are applying for leave?'

'It's a personal matter, sir,' Lestrade told him. 'A friend of mine . . .'

'A friend?' Frost sneered. 'Inspectors of the Metropolitan Police do not have friends, they merely have suspects.'

'A friend of mine', Lestrade persisted steadily, 'needs my help. If you are asking me whether I should put my friend's request above my future king's, the answer must be an emphatic "perhaps".'

'You are presumptuous, Lestrade! What's to prevent me from writing to His Royal Highness and acquainting him of this situation?'

Lestrade stared resignedly ahead. 'Nothing, sir. Nothing at all.'

Frost tapped irritatedly on his desk top. 'You have precisely twenty-four hours to sort this . . . friend . . . out. In the meantime, who have you got to continue the Fellowes case?'

'I'm not sure it is a case, sir. It could still be suicide. Or an accident. Fell off a footpath while balance of mind – or body – was disturbed.'

'Who have you got?' Frost repeated.

'Er . . . Walter Dew, sir.'

Frost sank dejectedly in the chair. 'As I feared . . . very well, I'm giving you a new man. A Constable Skinner. He's recently joined the Yard, Lestrade, under Abberline. But he's rather unique among Metropolitan constables.'

'Unique, sir?'

'Yes, he has a brain. You'll find him in the West Wing. Brief him before you go. Good morning.'

'Sir.' Lestrade turned to go.

'And Lestrade . . .' Frost stopped him. 'Twenty-four hours, mind. After that, I dock your pay and you're on suspension. Savvy?'

Lestrade smiled at the purple features scowling across the desk at him. 'Perfectly, sir,' he said.

Lestrade gave Constable Leonard Skinner precisely ten minutes to digest his report on Archibald Fellowes. During this time, Letitia Bandicoot was downing the umpteenth cup of Walter Dew's tea in the corridor laughingly known as Lestrade's outer office. The inspector eyed the constable. The newcomer was a large man and he wore spectacles, never a good sign in Lestrade's book.

'Well?' Lestrade snapped, one hour of his twenty-four appreciably eaten into already.

The constable looked up from Lestrade's copperplate to its author. He took in the jaundiced skin, the scarred cheeks and forehead, the nose without a tip and the patient, tired eyes.

'It's not bad, sir,' Skinner said.

'I beg your pardon?' The inspector's jaw hung slacker than was usual.

'A little heavy on the gerundives, perhaps, and I fear you have split three infinitives. But I particularly like the use of hendiadys in line thirty-eight . . .'

'What the devil are you talking about, constable?' Lestrade was nonplussed.

'The report, sir. You asked my views on it.'

'I meant its contents, man! What do you think of the Fellowes case?'

'Ah, I see. Well, I'm afraid I didn't read the last section, sir, the coroner's report and so on.'

'Why not?' Lestrade raised an eyebrow in much the same manner that Frost had done moments earlier.

'Blood, sir. I don't really care for the violent side of life.'

'Indeed?' Lestrade leaned forward, dunking his tie nicely into his tea. 'Then why did you sign on to be a constable?'

'Oh, I didn't, sir. That is, I did, but I wanted to be a sort of back-room boy, you know, working on ciphers and codes and forgeries and so on.'

Lestrade sat back with a glazed expression and his glaze met that of Constable Dew, who coughed politely. 'I've got the station wagon here to take you and Mrs Bandicoot to the station.'

'Now there's an example,' Skinner went on. 'Contable Dew's last sentence was a triumph of bathos. He used the word "station" twice.'

All three policemen looked at each other.

'The use of the second "station" was anti-climacteric; redundant . . .'

'. . . which is, I suspect, what you will be come morning,' nodded Lestrade. 'It's all clear to me now.'

'Oh, good,' smiled Skinner, on another plane entirely. 'What is?'

'The reason for Chief Inspector Abberline's smile when I met him a few moments ago and told him I had been ordered to take you off his hands. It all makes perfect sense.' He sighed and reached for his boater. 'Over there,' he said to Skinner, 'is a pile of personal papers belonging to the late Captain Fellowes. Your job is to sift through them by tonight. And Skinner . . .'

'Sir?'

'We are looking for reasons for the man's sudden death, not his style of written English. Savvy?'

'Ah.' Skinner's eyes lit up. 'From the French *savior*; to know. And more closely, from the Spanish *sabe usted*. I had no idea you were such a linguist, Inspector.'

'And I had no idea you were such a . . .'

'Sholto!' Letitia Bandicoot's head popped round the door. 'Shall we go?'

Lestrade threw a spare collar into his battered Gladstone. 'Keep this man supplied with tea, Walter. If he talks to you, there's a dictionary here somewhere . . .'

It was early evening by the time Inspector Lestrade groped his way through the dolomitic conglomerate crevice that was Wookey Hole. He had left Letitia with Harry at Bandicoot Hall and grabbing Harry's trap, had jolted across country, rattling under Glastonbury Tor, hurtling around the George and Pilgrims' Corner on one wheel and grinding at last to a halt at the cave entrance.

Harry had been no more helpful than Letitia had been. But both of them had a profound sense of unease and Letitia had taken the reins in her hands and gone to the Yard and to Sholto Lestrade. And since the body of Richard Tetley had been found in the Hole, it was natural that it was here Lestrade should start his enquiries. He and Harry went back a long way and if Harry or Harry's wife asked for help, that was enough for him. The trouble with Harry was that he had an astonishing sense of duty and of loyalty and of honour. The late Richard Tetley had taken the Dower House some months before and had therefore become a tenant in an odd sort of way. And Harry looked after his tenants. He mowed with them when they mowed his corn. He laughed with them when they laughed and he helped to bury them when they died.

Caves were not Lestrade's favourite places. He kept his boater on in case a monstrous brood of vampire bats should suddenly sweep out of the darkness. He clutched the lantern Harry had thoughtfully lent in one hand and he clutched his crutch in the other. One could never be too careful in caves. Dolomitic conglomerate was soft, Harry had told him as a guide to

Wookey, but Lestrade's shins soon told a different story as he tapped his way into the innermost recesses of the pudding stone. At first, the wooden walkways and duckboards placed there for the curious among the summer visitors helped him, but they soon gave way to slippery, green channels and he raised the lantern to gaze in awe on the giant rock formations, jutting primevally from the ancient dark.

'Watch out for the witch!' a voice boomed nearby. Or was it far away? It roared and ricocheted with a thunderous echo that made Lestrade drop his lantern and his crutch.

'Sorry, old boy. Just my idea of a joke,' the voice boomed on. 'Over here. To your right.'

Lestrade floundered till he found the lantern and steadied himself on an outcrop while trying to relight it.

The owner of the voice emerged beneath a lurid green light. 'Bulleid.' He extended a hand.

'Who is?' Lestrade wondered how the cave's occupant could pick out an ocular deficiency at that distance. Perhaps if you lived in caves, you became more proficient at these things.

'I am,' the green face said. 'Arthur Bulleid. Archaeologist.'

'Ah.' Lestrade reached forward to the outstretched hand, and fetched himself a sharp one on something hard and groin-height in front of him.

'That was a stalagmite.' Bulleid smiled. 'Place is riddled with 'em. Mind how you go.'

Lestrade wondered through his tears whether this man knew Sergeant Dixon at the Yard, whose favourite phrase that was. 'You said something about a witch?' he asked.

'Just my little joke,' guffawed Bulleid again. 'She's up there. See?' He pointed to a projection of rock, twisted and gnarled into the profile of a grotesque old hag. 'The Mother-in-law of Wookey. Now, let me see. You are . . . ?'

'In pain.' Lestrade sank gratefully on to a rock ledge only to rise again with a further feeling of distinct discomfort.

'No, I wouldn't sit down. There are puddles everywhere. Besides, never know when you'll find a flint implement – and believe me, they're damned sharp, some of them. Are you an archaeologist or one of those damned tourist chappies?'

'Neither,' said Lestrade. 'I'm a policeman.'

'Good Lord.' Bulleid squinted at him through the lantern's

green gleam. 'So you are. You've come about old Tetley, no doubt.'

'You found him, I gather?'

'That's right, Mr . . . er . . . ?'

'Lestrade, Scotland Yard.'

'Oh, the Yard.'

'You know our work?'

'No. But I did read a pamphlet on the body they found when they were building the Opera House, which was later occupied by your chaps.'

'Yes. Quite. Now, about Tetley . . .'

'He was over here,' Bulleid said, leaving Lestrade to stagger like a straw-hatted crippled mole in the darkness behind him. At a point where the slimy floor of the cavern widened, Bulleid suddenly crouched, pointing to an area cordoned off in blue ribbon. 'Here,' he said, scratching instinctively with his trowel.

'Is this cordon yours, sir?' Lestrade asked.

'Good Lord, no. Local constabulary put it there. Annoying really. I was hoping for a fascine. Or at least some crannogs.'

Lestrade wondered why the man hadn't brought his sandwiches, but it seemed impolite to ask.

'You found him two days ago?'

'Yes. Shortly after midday.'

'He was lying here?' Lestrade did his best to crouch, but one-legged, it did not come easy and he gave it up as a bad job.

'That was the damnedest thing. Someone had laid him out as though for burial.'

'With his hands across his chest, you mean?'

'Yes, but rather after the manner of the Pharaohs, as though in a sarcophagus.'

'Can you think why that should be?' Lestrade asked, wondering if the latter were some kind of trance.

'Well, Tetley was an Egyptologist. Rather fitting, I suppose.'

'An Egyptologist, sir?'

Bulleid perched himself on a stalagmite. 'He had excavated tombs in Upper Egypt, Mr Lestrade. Thebes, Luxor. It was at Luxor he found the tomb of Amenhotep. It was the find of the century.'

'Was it?' Lestrade was doubly in the dark.

'You must have heard of it. Happened back in . . . let me see

. . . '91. Yes, that would be it. Made old Tetley's career, of course.'

'How old was he?'

'Fifty or so. Between you and me, he wasn't much of an archaeologist. Like that Schliemann chappie, only British of course. Bit of a showman.'

'What did you do when you found the body?'

'Damned near filled my breeks, I don't mind tellin' you. I mean, fossilized remains, Etrurian excrement, mummified fingers, all that's in a day's work. But this one was a threat fresh.'

'How fresh, would you say?'

Bulleid rummaged in his rucksack for a cigar. 'Well, he was still warm, if that's any help. Smoke?'

'No, thank you. Did you see anyone else – in the cave or nearby?'

'Old Spiggot, the guide.'

'He works here?'

'In a manner of speaking,' puffed Bulleid. 'Shows people round for sixpence a throw.'

'And was there anyone here that morning?'

'There may have been. You'll have to ask him. The arrangement is that he keeps them to the lower levels in the mornings only. I have free run of the place in the afternoon. Good Lord.' He snapped shut his hunter with its luminous dial. 'Is that the time? I'm due at the Bandicoots.'

'So am I. Shall we?'

But Lestrade did not go to Bandicoot Hall. Time was short and there were pressing questions to be asked if he was to put Harry's mind at rest about the demise of Richard Tetley. He borrowed Harry's trap and sped through the lovely summer's evening to the quaint little cottage where lived Old Spiggot, the guide. Bearing in mind the old boy eked out a living in the days of his dotage by talking his way around the cave at Wookey, he was about as articulate as a Billingsgate slab. But what he lacked in bonhomie was compensated for by his wife, Old Mrs Spiggot. She was in the process of talking the hindleg off Harry's horse, when Lestrade took pity on the animal and whipped it south-east in the direction of the Dower House, home of the former Richard Tetley, deceased.

The Old Spiggots, for all the lady's loquacity, were not much help. Tuesday had been a typical day. Old Spiggot must have shown a dozen or so people the cave. No, he'd noticed no one in particular. There was a rather weasly man with a bad cough and a woman with an outsize ear trumpet who kept knocking Spiggot's hat off, but nothing untoward. Spiggot had been a bit annoyed to find Mr Tetley there too early – the arrangement was specifically for twelve midday and Old Spiggot had definitely heard the bells of Wells striking eleven as he arrived.

The Dower House on the Bandicoot estate was less opulent than the Bandicoots', but older – an Elizabethan edifice on the classic 'E' plan, with curling brick chimneys, redundant now in the warmth of summer. The place was a silent silhouette against the sunset when Lestrade reined in on the gravel drive. He was shown in by an equally silent silhouette of a butler who checked Lestrade's credentials and ushered him reverently into a parlour where Richard Tetley lay in a silk-lined coffin.

'A glass top,' Lestrade commented, admiring the rich mahogany and gilded fittings. 'Isn't that rather unusual?'

'I believe it is an American custom, sir,' the butler intoned. 'Mr Tetley spent several years in the United States. After Egypt, it was his second love.'

'I see. Tell me . . . er . . .'

'Hickok, sir.'

'. . . Hickok, was Mr Tetley married?'

'To his work, sir.'

'Quite,' sighed Lestrade, knowing that feeling well. But he heard the grandfather in the hall chime nine and his twenty-four hours were running out. 'Was there a woman in his life, Hickok?'

The butler turned the colour of mildew. 'Oh, no, sir,' he whispered. 'I had the honour to serve Mr Tetley for thirty years. Never in that time has there been . . . a . . . woman.'

Lestrade circled the room, letting his fingers play for a while on the Egyptian figurines on the sideboard.

'Anubis,' Hickok said as Lestrade stared at a marble carving.

'Really?' Lestrade knew a thing or two about art. He had once met Mr Alma-Tadema. 'Looks more like a jackal. Was Mr Tetley in the habit of going to the cave at Wookey regularly?'

'Of recent weeks, sir, yes. He was, I believe, working with a Mr Bulleid.'

'Yes, I've met him. Another archaeologist.'

Hickok sniffed disapprovingly. 'If you say so, sir.'

'Mr Bulleid says so.' Lestrade smiled. 'Do I gather you don't approve, Hickok?'

The butler pulled himself upright so that his starched shirt-front creaked. 'I am a gentleman's gentleman, sir. The son and grandson of a gentleman's gentleman. It is not my place to disapprove.'

'I see.' Lestrade reached for a cigar, caught the butler's quivering nostril, for which he duly apologized and put the cigar away. 'Have the local constabulary been here?'

'We have!' A voice made him turn. 'And we've returned.'

A large, ruddy man in a Panama and shirt-sleeves stood grinning between two constables. 'Lestrade of the Yard, is it?' he asked archly.

'You've heard of me?' Somewhere Lestrade too had an ego.

'No. But I met Mr Arthur Bulleid earlier and he told me you were in the area. This would be the logical place to find the long nose of the Yard. I also met Mr Harold Bandicoot.'

'Harry,' Lestrade corrected him.

'He may be Harry to you, Inspector, but to me he is a potential suspect.'

'I mean he was christened Harry. And what do you mean "suspect", Inspector . . . er . . . ?'

'*Chief* Inspector,' the ruddy-faced man felt compelled to correct *him*. 'Guthrie. Somerset Constabulary. Hickok, get out!'

The grandson of a gentleman's gentleman bowed and left while Guthrie's constables flanked the door.

'Gives you the creeps this place, doesn't it?' Guthrie reached for a cigar.

Lestrade looked disapprovingly and quivered his nostril until Guthrie put it away.

'All this,' the chief inspector went on, 'all this old stuff.'

'Egyptology.' Lestrade limped to the mantelpiece. 'Anubis.' He picked up the figure.

'I thought you said it was a jackal, sir,' a constable said to his guv'nor.

Guthrie's look said it all. 'Remind me to put you back on the horse troughs at Weston tomorrow, Cherill.'

'Very good, sir.' The chastened constable saluted.

'What is your interest in the case, Lestrade?' Guthrie asked, reclining on a *chaise-longue* crafted in the manner of Upper Egypt. 'Egyptology, is it?'

'Mr Tetley was a friend of Mr Bandicoot,' Lestrade said.

'. . . who is a friend of yours?'

'Quite so,' Lestrade nodded. 'Why is he a suspect? And what is the crime?'

'The crime', guffawed Guthrie, 'is lying in that box. People don't just keel over and die in caves, Lestrade, even if they do suffer from hydrophobia. Mr Tetley was in the prime of life. A resilient fifty-three. Not unlike my good gentleman self, in fact.'

'Murder, then?' Lestrade probed his man.

'Of course. At the moment by person or persons unknown.'

'But you suspect Harry Bandicoot?'

'I suspect *everyone*.' Guthrie nodded sagely.

Lestrade hobbled over to the coffin. 'You've checked the body?'

'Of course.'

'Cause of death?'

Guthrie got to his feet. 'Now, look, Lestrade. I'm not one of your Yard rookies, y'know. You've got no offical jurisdiction in this case. None whatever.'

'The Yard's writ runs everywhere,' Lestrade countered.

'Only when it's been called in by the Chief Constable of the County. And that hasn't happened yet, has it?'

Lestrade was forced to concede it had not. 'Even so, I would like to have your views on what you find. Or to examine the corpse myself.'

'Over his dead body!' Guthrie roared.

'The coroner's report, then.' Lestrade held his ground. He had met blustering chief inspectors before.

'This is rural Somerset, Lestrade, not smart-alec London. You'll be lucky if you see it at all.'

'You realize you are hampering police in the pursuance of their duties?'

'I know my duty, Lestrade. Until the Yard gets the all-clear, neither you nor anyone else from your High and Mighty

Division gets a smell in here. The funeral's tomorrow and I'll be closing this room now. Hickok!'

The gentleman's gentleman duly appeared.

'This room is to be locked. Now. I will personally return at eight in the morning to see it unlocked. In the meantime, I shall take charge of the key. Mr Lestrade is just leaving.'

The inspector took his hat and brushed past the chief inspector. He heard the door click behind him and made for the waiting trap. On the way, his hand just happened to fall against the harness of the chief inspector's vehicle and the surprisingly stiff breeze that had risen from nowhere happened to catch the hames and lift them just sufficiently for the horse to wander away in the darkness.

As he cracked his whip, he heard the bewilderment of the Somerset Constabulary behind him.

'Damn you, Cherill, you can't even harness a horse, man. I won't put you on the troughs tomorrow. I'll put you in them! And why did you have to choose a black one? Where is the bloody thing?'

Lestrade tugged on the right rein and whipped the horse in the darkness past the wing where Richard Tetley lay. The house was dark and dead now, except for a slight glow in a downstairs room . . .

A slight breeze lifted the leaves in Letitia's hanging arrangement on the verandah. Lestrade had had dinner and now enjoyed a cigar in the stillness of the night. Far across the lake the nightjars hunted in the low woods and a single ghostly owl followed the line of the water, skimming the giant elms that guarded Bandicoot Hall.

'It was good of you to come, Sholto.' Harry poured them another brandy. 'I didn't want to trouble you.'

'It was no trouble, Harry.' Lestrade blew smoke rings to the sky. 'But I've been little help, I'm afraid.'

'It wasn't that I knew Tetley well, nor even liked the man, but he was a tenant, you see.'

'Did he have any enemies, Harry? Anyone who would want to see him dead?'

'You'd better ask Bulleid. Tetley was hardly ever at home.

We rode to hounds once or twice, bagged a few pheasant, but his real love was archaeology. I'll see the Chief Constable, Sholto. I'm not happy leaving this to Guthrie. He has the finesse of an elephant on heat.'

'I'm prepared to forego your Indian reminiscences, Harry. Did he owe money?'

'Guthrie? I wouldn't be surprised.'

'No. Tetley.'

'I wouldn't know, Sholto.'

'I know.' Lestrade held up his hand. 'Gentleman don't ask. You'd have made a tolerable copper, Harry, but you'd never have got far because you don't gossip about people.'

'Sorry, Sholto.'

'Mr Bandicoot, sir!' a voice called from the shrubbery.

'Tom?' Harry was on his feet.

'It's the Superintendent, sir. You'd better come quick!'

'The Superintendent?' Lestrade hobbled upright.

'My horse,' Harry shouted. 'Help yourself to the brandy, Sholto. I might be gone a while,' and he followed the groom into the gloom.

'Young man!' A voice like a bass drum caught his ears.

'Good evening.' Lestrade found his chair again.

'Don't get up,' the voice said. 'You must be Inspector Lestrade.'

'Yes, Mrs . . . er . . .'

'Miss,' the voice was firm, 'Miss Balsam.'

'Ah, yes. Letitia's nanny.'

'Letitia's, yes. And now I supervise the children's nanny.' She sat down on Harry's chair. 'Yes,' she said, her grey eyes twinkling in the light from the French windows, 'yes, I can see it.'

Lestrade glanced down, but all was well. 'Indeed?'

'Emma. She has your nose, poor dear.'

'That's kind of you, Miss Balsam. The rest of her is, I would imagine, like her mother.'

'You would imagine?' Miss Balsam sat upright. 'When did you last see your daughter, Mr Lestrade?'

'I assume you've been on the premises, Miss Balsam. And yet we've never met. You must know, I have not seen her since she was born.'

Miss Balsam sat back, shaking her raddled old head. 'A great tragedy,' she said. 'It is true we have never met, but I am often away on business. I had hoped you would have visited your child in my absence. Now, young man,' she said, 'this murder.'

'What murder, Miss Balsam?'

She poked him with a window hook that was minding its own business on the verandah. 'Don't play the innocent with me, Inspector Lestrade. I've known too many little boys. And for all they grow into nasty, horrid men, they don't lose one basic inability.'

'Really?'

'Their inability to tell Nanny Balsam a lie. Now, what theories do you have?'

'Miss Balsam.' Lestrade tried dignity as a first approach. 'I am an Inspector of Scotland Yard. I cannot divulge . . .'

'Tosh and fiddlesticks. Richard Tetley was a dreadful old reprobate. It was his only vice which killed him.'

'His only vice?' Lestrade's ears began to prick up. He still had some hours of his Frost-given twenty-four left.

'He was a thief, Mr Lestrade.'

'A thief?' Lestrade sat up. 'You mean he stole things?'

'Not that I'm one to gossip, you understand,' Miss Balsam assured him.

'No, no, of course.' Lestrade blew smoke rings on the night air. 'You have proof, of course?'

'Let's just say I know things. Goodnight, Mr Lestrade,' and she smiled disarmingly and rose.

'Nanny. It's long past your bedtime.' Letitia floated through the French windows. 'You'll catch your death. And, little Nan, you've had a busy day.'

'Yes, time for Bedfordshire,' Miss Balsam said. 'I have enjoyed our little chat, Mr Lestrade. *A bientôt*, as the French say,' and Letitia shepherded her away.

'Has that mad old besom gone?' A harsh whisper rasped from the wisteria.

'Who's that?' Lestrade called.

'Bulleid. I was walking in the grounds to get rid of some of Letitia's buck venison. Capital dinner, what?'

'Capital indeed, Mr Bulleid.'

'You know she's mad, don't you?'

'Letitia?' Lestrade found it hard to believe.

'Miss Balsam. The twice I've met her she seemed totally doolally. Talked about how important it was not to overpraise a child. Bad luck, apparently. And how all her babies but one cried at the font.'

'I don't follow,' Lestrade confessed.

'My dear boy, do you think I did? She obviously noted my lack of comprehension and harangued me for half an hour on the subject of children and superstition. Two hundred years ago, they'd have burnt her. Mind you, if I catch her near a candle, I might do it myself. You got off lightly.'

Lestrade poured the archaeologist a brandy. 'You heard her accusation, then – about Tetley being a tea leaf?'

'Balderdash!' he snorted. 'Here's gold in your trowel,' and he quaffed the glass. He leaned forward to Lestrade. 'It's the curse, you see.'

'The curse? But surely, Miss Balsam is too old . . .'

'No, no, man. The Curse of the Pharaohs. That's what killed Richard Tetley.'

Lestrade smiled. 'I thought you didn't believe superstitions, Mr Bulleid.'

'That Balsam woman's folklore gibberish, no, I don't. But the testimony of the spade, Lestrade. It never lies.'

'I think you'd better explain that, Mr Bulleid.'

'Very well. I'm a Celts man myself. Some years ago I discovered the Lake Village at Glastonbury. Ninety wattle and daub huts in a settlement extending to three and a half acres. Tetley was altogether a more . . . shall we say, exotic, archaeologist. He loved fame, the bright lights, foreign travel. The only reason he rummaged around at Wookey is that it was on his doorstep so to speak. I gather from Harry that the Yard is not always welcome on forays into alien territory, eh?'

'One can encounter certain difficulties, yes.'

'Chief Inspector Guthrie?'

'He is the difficulty I had in mind, yes,' Lestrade admitted.

'Perfect swine.' Bulleid produced an ornate briar and began to fill it. By the smell, the tobacco was probably third century BC. 'Which is why I didn't tell him about this.'

He groped in a pocket and brought out a piece of marble, dark green in colour and as smooth as glass.

'What is it?' Lestrade asked.

'It's an amulet. Of the time of Amenhotep. But it's rather a curious one. It's the scarab, don't you know.'

Lestrade didn't know.

'The beetles of death. Actually, it's the symbol of Khepri, the sun-god and as such a talisman of creation. But among archaeologists, it has a more sinister reputation. As it is found adorning the dead, it has come to be associated with the dead.'

'And this is one of Tetley's?'

'Well, it might be, but . . . I certainly found it on his body.'

'You said "but" . . .' Lestrade was a stickler for unfinished sentences.

'Well, Tetley let me have a look at his inventory. He was very thorough. I don't recall seeing a scarab among his souvenirs. Yes. It was wedged between his teeth.'

Lestrade rose to his foot. 'Between his teeth?' he repeated.

'Bizarre, what? What do you make of it?'

'I'm not sure . . . yet.'

'Well, you can't arrest a ghost, Lestrade.' Bulleid helped himself to more of Bandicoot's brandy.

'A ghost?'

'The Curse of the Pharaohs. Anyone who touches the graves of the kings risks death. Look at young Jones.'

'Jones?'

'Oscar Myron Jones III. Came from a good family in Indiana.'

'Indiana? Let's see, that's . . .'

'America, Lestrade. The colonies. Still, let's not be bigoted about this. Young Oscar had a very promising career ahead of him and he worked with Tetley on the Amenhotep dig.'

'What happened to him?'

'He died.'

'Oh?'

'The curse, y'see. Twenty-four he was. Still, they buried him in Luxor. He'd have liked that.'

'Tell me, Mr Bullied.' Lestrade joined the archaeologist in a replenished glass. 'Did anyone else on that dig die?'

'I'm talking about ten years ago, Lestrade. There were hundreds of niggers on the job, of course, as well as Tetley, young Jones. At the time, it was the biggest dig in the world. I seem to remember there was a third member of the expedition. A woman. She had something to do with the Jeromes.'

'The Jeromes? Didn't they write *Three Men in a Boat*?' Lestrade was ever the man of culture.

Bulleid looked at him oddly. 'Different branch,' he concluded. 'Jenny Jerome knew her well. Y'know, Lady Randolph Churchill.'

'Churchill?'

'Do you know her?'

'I believe I've met her son, Winston.'

'Ah, shame. Man's a dolt. Not, I fear, a chip off the old block. But as I was saying, Lestrade, you can't arrest a ghost. Mark my words, some pretty strange things happen in the East.'

'The giant rat of Sumatra,' Lestrade mused, suddenly some miles away.

'Eh?' Bulleid clamped again on the pipe-stem.

'Oh, nothing,' Lestrade smiled. 'Just a story for which I hope the world will never be ready.'

Bulleid leaned closer to him. 'It's the hand of Amenhotep, Lestrade,' he whispered, 'reaching from the grave. That', he tapped the scarab, 'is his calling card.'

'You realize your withholding of this constitutes obstructing the police with their enquiries?' He raised an eyebrow in Bulleid's direction.

'And I thought I'd done you a favour!' Bulleid snorted.

'So you have, sir,' Lestrade assured him, 'so you have.' And he put it in his pocket.

'By Jove's beard!' Bulleid shouted. 'Look at the time. I must get back to my hotel. I'm staying at the George in Glastonbury. Beds are damned lumpy, but the coffee's good. I hope we meet again, Lestrade.' He clasped the inspector's hand. 'And good luck with this business. It's nasty, very nasty. I couldn't face my lunch the day it happened for half an hour or so. Toodlepip!'

And he marched off to say his farewells to the Bandicoots.

Lestrade sat awhile in thought, ruminating. It was probably Letitia's buck venison. The night air had turned chill and he had many miles to go before he slept.

'Sholto,' a warm voice called to him from the drawing-room.

'Letitia, thank you for an excellent dinner. I'm sorry I was late for it.'

'Don't be silly. You wouldn't be here at all if I hadn't come to see you. Harry is so much happier now you're here. Can you help?'

'I don't know,' he said. 'I shall need to see the coroner's report. But I've stumbled on something.'

'Oh, do be careful, Sholto.' Letitia knew Lestrade's habits of old.

'Do you believe in the Curse of the Pharaohs?' he asked her.

'What?'

'That a man dead for thousands of years can reach beyond the grave and commit murder.'

She stopped and looked at him. 'Is it the brandy?' she asked sagely.

He patted her hand tucked into the crook of his elbow. 'I expect it is,' he said, 'and now I must be going. Or Assistant Commissioner Frost will have my guts for garters. Is there someone to drive me to the station?'

'I'll take you,' Letitia said. 'But first . . . You haven't seen your daughter.'

He held her hand. 'Letitia . . .'

'You haven't seen her in three years, Sholto. Not since you brought her to us, a babe in arms. You didn't even come when our boys were born.' She held up her hand, ready for the explanation. 'I know,' she said, 'I know. Crime and tide waits for no man.'

'Letitia . . .' he said again. 'I'm afraid.'

She looked into the sad, dark eyes. 'You?' she said. 'You, who have faced East End roughs and bullets and swords and death itself? She's asleep, Sholto. What harm can a little girl do you?'

She led him quietly up the stairs, though by virtue of the crutch, the progress was a little slow. They entered the twilit nursery where the night light lent a greenish glow that shone on the huge dolls' house and the dappled rocker. The boys, sturdy now in their nightdresses, lay together, snoring quietly. In another bed, on a feather pillow edged with lace, lay Emma Lestrade, now Emma Bandicoot, her golden hair curling round her cheeks, the middle fingers of her left hand resting gently on her slightly parted lips.

'There.' Letitia nuzzled her head against Lestrade's shoulder.

'There she is. What is it that frightens you? That wasn't so bad, was it?'

And he held her to him, kissed her swiftly and slid down the stairs, in haste so that she couldn't see his face, jarring his foot on every riser.

Lestrade limped across the cobbled courtyard and eased himself up the steps.

'Mr Lestrade, sir.' Sergeant Dixon was still shaving in the outer office. 'Morning, sir. Can I get you something?'

'About three years' leave, sergeant. And a new leg. But right now, I'd settle for a cup of tea.'

'Leave it to me, sir. Would you like a Peake Frean?'

'A what? Oh, I see. No thanks. My stomach would rebel. What time is it?'

'Nearly five-thirty, sir.'

'Anybody in yet?'

'I don't think Skinner's gone home, sir.'

Lestrade looked up in alarm. 'But I left him here yesterday morning,' he said. 'Send the tea up, will you?'

He swung his leg into the lift and whirred and clanked to his floor. Sure enough, Constable Skinner sat at his desk, in exactly the same position as when Lestrade had seen him last.

'Well, Skinner, what news on Captain Fellowes?'

'Ah.' The constable stood up. 'He had smallpox as a child, sir.'

Lestrade collapsed gratefully into his chair, freeing his tie and collar and unbuttoning his waistcoat. 'Good Lord, no.'

'He attended St Ethelred the Unready Preparatory School in Buxton.'

'He was lucky to survive all that, wasn't he?'

'Indeed, Inspector, he was.' Skinner adjusted his pince-nez, an odd accessory for a young man. 'But survival at Charterhouse was, I suspect, more difficult for him. How he obtained a commission, I can't imagine.'

'Sandhurst?' Lestrade suggested.

'Indeed, but I was referring to the rather vulgar moral tone of the place . . . not particularly *comme il faut*.'

'Yes, of course.' Lestrade smiled through gritted teeth. 'Tell me, constable, when are we going to get to anything vaguely connected with the captain's death? Only I shall be retiring in twenty years or so, and I would like to make some headway by then.'

'Well, if I may posit a hypothesis, sir?'

'If you must,' Lestrade sighed. 'And then let's have some ideas.'

'The Ashanti medal. Fellowes was a member of a special field unit, drawn from various regiments. They were trained for a secret mission, and would be what I believe the Boers of Natal call Kommandoes.'

'If this is secret,' Lestrade took the steaming mug from the constable who entered, hotfoot from Sergeant Dixon, 'how do you know about it?'

'Ah.' Skinner rummaged through the mountains of paper. 'Captain Fellowes' diary. All military men over thirty commit their experiences to paper. So that when they become famous, their memoirs are ready for publication.'

'So you're ruling out suicide?' Lestrade checked. 'A man who writes for prosperity is not likely to kill himself.'

'Unless he were trying to choke himself to death, I think suicide highly unconvincing, sir.'

'So do I, constable. Am I warming to you, or is it because I've had no sleep all night?'

'Fellowes was a hero, sir. At least if we believe his diary.'

'Is there a reason why we shouldn't?'

'Memoirs are particularly suspect material for the historian, Inspector. My uncle is Regius Professor at Oxford. Take Francis Place, for instance . . .'

'You take him, Skinner. One case at a time is enough for me. What does the diary say?'

'Oh, various details of embarking and so forth. He mentions the Fetish Tree being destroyed January before last . . .'

'The Fetish Tree?' Lestrade's mind was drawn irresistibly to Kew Gardens and the seeds found on Fellowes' suit.

'It was at Koomassie, sir, a place of annual sacrifice of slaves.'

'Does it have any significance?' Lestrade asked.

'Within the tribal structure of the Ashanti, sir, the place of slaves is an anomalous one. Certainly, as a survival of an ancient culture . . .'

'I mean, what has it to do with Fellowes?'

'Nothing, sir.'

Lestrade nodded. 'Get on with it, Skinner.'

'But the Bowl of King Prempeh has.'

'Oh?'

'The Bowl was used for sacrifices. It was also at Koomassie, which means, in the Ashanti tongue, the City of Death. Sir Francis Scott who led the expedition brought it back last year. The Bowl is probably of Moorish origin, with lions' heads in bas relief . . .'

Lestrade leaned forward. 'I've been up for thirty-six hours, Skinner,' he grated. 'What has this to do with Fellowes?'

'Well, sir, it seems that he and the rest of his Kommandoes got to Koomassie well ahead of the main British Expeditionary Force. They were evidently spotted by Prempeh's cohorts and Fellowes and another officer named Hely became detached from the detachment.'

'That makes sense,' shrugged Lestrade.

'They were captured, tortured and, thanks to Fellowes' heroism, escaped. Unfortunately Hely was killed in the mêlée. Fellowes rejoined the unit.'

Lestrade waited. 'And that's it?'

'Nearly, sir. Look at the handwriting.'

Lestrade did. Pages of averagely neat lines. 'Well?' he said.

'Do you notice anything?'

'Don't tell me; his spelling's poor. Well, St Ethelred's, Charterhouse, what can you expect?'

'No, no. The slope of the letters. A sound cursive hand, but here, on these pages, it slopes *so*,' he riffled further on, 'and here, *so*.'

'Change of pen,' Lestrade concluded.

'Change of fact.'

'What?'

'I have studied graphology, sir – the science of interpretation of human characteristics from modes of writing – and I believe Captain Fellowes is lying in these pages.'

'As you say,' said Lestrade. 'Suspect material. If a man can't blow his own trumpet, so to speak, who will do it for him?'

'I'm not sure it's as simple as that, sir. I believe Fellowes had something very positive to hide.'

Constable Lilley arrived at that moment with Dew at his elbow. Both men were visibly shaken.

'Gentlemen.' Lestrade noted it. 'What's the matter?'

'You'd better walk this way, sir,' Dew said.

'If I could walk that way, Dew, I wouldn't need this damned crutch. Still, as Shakespeare said, "Lead on, Macbeth".'

Skinner groaned.

'If I stay here much longer, I'll be as mad as Constable Skinner. Go home, man,' Lestrade said to him. 'You clearly need more sleep than I do.'

4

Victim of the Witch

The three policemen stood below the massive stone beast. Yards from them the Palace of Glass glinted in the summer sun and the strains of Handel floated across the water.

'Ugly.' Lestrade was grim-faced.

'But you haven't seen it yet, sir,' Walter Dew said.

'I was referring to the monster.' Lestrade cocked his head in the direction of the giant reptile that crouched craftily in the shrubbery. 'What have you dragged me all the way down here to see?'

The three policemen met several more and uniformed, gloved hands shot helmetwards at their arrival. The inspector in the centre shook Lestrade's hand. 'Sholto,' he said, 'good of you to come. Your man found you, then?'

'My man?'

The inspector nodded at the pallid Lilley.

'Oh, of course. You live here, don't you, constable?'

'Not on the Hill, sir,' Lilley answered. 'I couldn't afford the rent.'

'No, of course not. Well, Arnold, what have we got?'

'I hope you enjoyed your breakfast, Sholto. You'll probably see it again in a minute. Down here.' The inspector led the inspector through a gap in the rhododendron bushes near the lake. All avenues here were guarded by constables and roped by the inevitable cerulean cordon. Lestrade always admired the thin blue line. She lay on her back on the dry grass of summer, dead, sightless eyes staring at the sky. Her face was a mask of blood and there were splatters of it across the leaves and over her dress.

'Who found her?' Lestrade crouched there, turning the battered head slightly from side to side.

'Do you mind if I sit this one out, sir?' Walter Dew had never been the same since the Ripper case.

'All right, Walter, but remember you're booked for the Mazurka.'

'In answer to your question, Sholto,' the inspector crouched beside him, 'one of the groundsmen. Half-past five this morning.'

'And?'

'I've had a word. He's clean as a constable's whistle.'

'She's been dead . . . what? Twelve, thirteen hours?'

'I'd say so.'

'That makes it last night, somewhere between ten and midnight. Any sign of a weapon?'

'None.'

'Anything on here last night?' Lestrade stood up and craned to see the Palace at his back.

'Thursday night,' the inspector said. 'Fireworks all month. That would have drowned any noise.'

'It would also have meant the place was swarming with people. Was the groundsman any help there?'

'He said this particular part of the park wasn't used much.'

Lestrade nodded. 'Do we know who she is?' he asked.

The inspector shook his head. 'Well-to-do, though, wouldn't you say?'

Lestrade would.

'Sir.' A constable was dragging a painted lady through the cordon.

'What's this?' the inspectors asked simultaneously.

'Sorry, Arnold,' Lestrade demurred. 'Your patch.'

'Thank you, Sholto. What's this?'

'Don't you mean who?' the girl flounced.

'Now then, Liz,' the constable snarled. 'None of your lip.'

'Are you acquainted with this young lady's lips, constable?' the inspector asked.

'Ain't 'e, though!' Liz giggled, much to the discomfiture of the blushing bobby.

'She has some information, sir. I thought you should hear it.'

'Go on . . . madam.' The inspector stiffened.

''Ere, what's going on?' Liz made an attempt to push past him to the clearing of carnage.

'Better you don't know.' Lestrade held her shoulders.

'Ooh, you're a strong un, aren't yer? Got nice 'ands. I go for 'ands, I do.'

'Yes, quite.' It was Lestrade's turn to stiffen. 'What's this information you have?'

'What's it worff?'

'Now look . . .' the inspector began.

'Arnold, Arnold.' Lestrade patted his arm. 'Sometimes a policeman has to do what a policeman has to do. Dew, Lilley.'

'Sir?' The plainclothesmen stepped forward.

'Give this young lady the contents of your pockets.'

Dew and Lilley frowned at each other, but the coppers duly tumbled into her tight little fist and disappeared down her cleavage and into her fol-de-rols.

'Careful, my dear.' Lestrade led the girl away. 'Constable Dew is a married man. Now, what can you tell us?' He gestured behind him for the others to stay where they were.

''Ere, you got a gammy leg?' She noticed him hobble.

'Just a limp,' he smiled.

'Well, we can't have you limp, can we?' she grinned and pinned him against a tree.

'Madam.' Lestrade extricated himself. 'Perhaps another time. What of last night?'

'Spoilsport!' She dropped her skirts again. 'There's a woman dead over there, ain't there?'

'There is,' Lestrade told her.

'Green dress, with white ribbons?'

'That's right. I didn't think you'd seen the body.'

'I 'aven't, guv'nor. I seen 'er last night. Still walking around in it.'

'Are you sure? There must have been lots of ladies here last night.'

'Yeah, but not many wiv a bloke what was dragging her through the bushes.'

'A bloke? What time was this?'

'Lord love you, guv. I dunno. If you want to know the time, ask a policeman. Only me and the police, we don't get on, see.'

'Not even you and Constable Whatsisname?' Lestrade teased her.

'Nah. I just says 'ello to 'im, on 'is rounds. 'E's a Miltonian, see. Can't afford me on 'is pay. Now you, you probably could . . .'

'I'm a Miltonian too.' Lestrade knew the vernacular of the East End.

'Ah, yeah, but you're a proper gent. Nice suit. And such nice 'ands . . .'

'This bloke. The one with the lady in the green dress. Can you describe him?'

'Er . . . let's see. Tall, big moustache. Topper and cape.'

'Did he carry a cane?'

'A stick fing. Wiv a knob on the end – whoops, begging your pardon.'

'Granted,' sighed Lestrade. 'You say he was dragging her through the bushes?'

'Yeah. She was carrying on something cruel. She looked too posh for a working girl, but I could be wrong.'

'Did you hear anything she said?'

'Er . . . no, not really. Oh, wait. She called 'im a funny name. Now, what was it? Oh, yeah. Looney. That's it. Bloody silly name that, ain't it?'

'Would you know this Looney if you saw him again?' asked Lestrade, sensing an Irish connection.

'Nah. After a while they all look the same, guv'nor. I shuts me eyes and finks of England.'

'Yes,' smiled Lestrade. 'There'll always be one, won't there? Leave your address with your constable, Liz. I may need to talk to you again.'

'Ooh, I hope so, dearie.' She flicked his tie. 'I can tell you're good-natured,' and she flounced away.

'Well, Arnold,' Lestrade called. 'A word in your ear.'

The inspectors strolled together by the lake in the midday sun.

'How do you see it, Sholto?'

'With difficulty at the moment, Arnold. A young lady. Mid-thirties, perhaps a little younger. Cause of death, blunt instrument to the head, some time around midnight last night. We have a witness,' he waved in Liz's direction, 'albeit a rather dubious one, who claims to have seen her in the company of a man whose description could fit half of London, apparently dragging her into the bushes.'

'Ah. A client, perhaps? Things got too rough?'

'Had she been interfered with?' Lestrade hadn't liked to check in case he upset Constable Dew's sensibilities. There was no fear of upsetting Constable Lilley as he had kept well upwind of the lady since his arrival.

'No. At least, not recently.'

'A married woman then?'

Arnold chuckled. 'You cynic, Lestrade.'

Lestrade stopped. 'Was she wearing a ring?'

'No jewellery at all.'

'But the clothes are fine.'

'Oh, she was wealthy, all right,' Arnold said. 'Or at least, her provider was.'

'So you're still clinging to the prostitute theory?'

'Seems most logical. She may have been a Seven Dials doxy but her fancy Dan set her up in fineries and kept her in the manner to which she was certainly not born but may have become accustomed.'

'But no jewellery?' Lestrade was obstinate.

'Robbery,' Arnold conjectured. 'A client was a prig, out for a good time. Tailed her and helped himself to her swag.'

'But she hadn't been touched, Arnold. You said so yourself.'

'All right. So he didn't tail her. But the rest fits.'

'According to our friend,' Lestrade watched as Liz wandered the park in search of new work, 'the gent was a toff. Topper, cape and knobkerrie. Not your average thief, Arnold.'

'I wouldn't take her word for much, Sholto.'

'Perhaps not,' he agreed. 'Does the name Looney mean anything to you?'

Arnold looked blank – his favourite expression.

'Get the lady over to the morgue, will you? I'll look in on her later.'

'Other fish to fry?' the inspector asked as Lestrade hailed his constables.

'When is there not, Arnold?' he asked. 'When is there not?' and he hobbled away.

* * *

They were not that helpful at the Knightsbridge Barracks. Captain Ames was away on leave. It was after all the Twelfth tomorrow and no self-respecting cavalry regiment could expect to have more than a skeleton of officers for the next couple of weeks. The duty officer was a very young subaltern. He had not known Captain Fellowes personally, but understood he had covered himself with glory in the Ashanti War. As to Lestrade's rather fatuous question whether he was a strong swimmer, the subaltern really had no idea. He was not a Marine.

The War Office were even worse. A severely correct clerk in pince-nez told him that as it was Friday, he must really wait until the following week. Surely, it was common knowledge that War Office personnel worked no later than mid-afternoon on Fridays? Had the world gone mad? When Lestrade had attempted to pull rank and asked for the man in charge, he was told that that would be Sir Bolitho Hector, but he was currently unavailable as tomorrow was the Twelfth and there were, after all, priorities. In any case, the information the inspector required, viz. the details of a campaign less than two years old, were highly confidential. When could he call back? In twenty-eight years.

So it was that Lestrade lay dozing fitfully in his old leather chair, stirring occasionally as the scratching of Constable Dew's pen jarred with the dream whirling in his brain. He stood on the edge of an abyss, leaning down into a chasm so deep, so dark. He could not see the bottom, but he had this overwhelming urge to fling himself down.

'Jump to it, Lestrade!' A barked order sent his feet hurtling off the desk top and he focused to see the less-than-welcome features of Chief Inspector Abberline. 'Ho, ho,' crowed Abberline, not one of Nature's gentlefolk, 'a sleeping policeman.'

'Mr Abberline,' Lestrade said through gritted teeth, 'how nice. Is there something I can help you with? Your coat, perhaps? The *Times* crossword?'

'Now, then, Lestrade.' Abberline refused to be ruffled this fine summer's evening. 'None of your attempts at wit. I really haven't the time. I got a telegram from that idiot Arnold Boreham. Boreham by name and Boreham by nature, eh?' Abberline sniffed his gardenia ostentatiously.

'I always found Inspector Boreham to be a first-rate policeman, sir,' Lestrade observed.

'If you say so, Lestrade. You must have found him on a good day. The telegram was opened in error of course,' Abberline assured him.

'It just happened to fall near your kettle as it was boiling,' Lestrade smiled.

Abberline didn't. 'I'll pretend I didn't hear that. The deceased in the shrubbery was one Marigold de Lacy, formerly of Mawson Gardens, Chiswick. He found a ring of hers near the body. It fitted. Boreham's obviously tied to his patch in Sydenham and would you break the news to her husband?'

'Her husband?'

'Yes. And a word of warning, Lestrade.' Abberline leaned nearer. 'I know you of old. Your fondness for trampling over the Establishment's flower beds, untying the old school tie. The de Lacys came over with the Conqueror, you know. You see that you show some respect.'

Number Forty-three, Mawson Gardens was an opulent villa, facing south-west. As Lestrade stood with Constable Lilley on the broad flight of steps that led to the front door, he glanced back and saw above the houses the Chinese pagoda and Lebanon cedars of Kew. He was in his forty-third year and knee-deep in murder. Well, what was new? He wouldn't really have it any other way.

The door was opened by the man, Manfred, who checked Lestrade's credentials and showed the Yard men into the library. While they waited, Lestrade scanned the tomes – Debrett's and Burke's took pride of place and he took the opportunity of showing Lilley what a book looked like. An imposing man of indeterminate years joined them before long. He sported a clipped, military moustache and an elegant dinner jacket.

'I was on my way out, gentlemen,' he said. 'I trust this will not take long. My man informs me you are from Scotland Yard.'

'Inspector Lestrade,' said Lestrade. 'Constable Lilley. You are Mr de Lacy?'

'Howard Luneberg de Lacy, at your service.' The man gave a

Hunnish bow by clicking his heels. Lestrade was puzzled. Abberline had said this man's family had come over with the Conqueror. Surely the Conqueror was French, not German? Perhaps he'd misunderstood all those years before at Mr Poulson's Academy for the Sons of Nearly Respectable Gentlefolk.

'I'm afraid I have some grave news, Mr de Lacy,' Lestrade said, 'concerning your wife.'

'Marigold? Has there been an accident?' De Lacy put down the top hat.

'Should there have been, sir?' Lestrade asked.

'Don't play games with me, man!' de Lacy snapped. 'You said your news was grave.'

'Your wife is dead, sir.'

De Lacy sat down. 'I see,' he said. 'What happened?'

'Her body was found in Crystal Palace Park early this morning,' Lestrade told him.

'Sydenham? But that's not possible.'

'Really, sir? Why not?'

'My wife was visiting friends in Somerset, Inspector. What would she be doing in Sydenham?'

'Watching the fireworks, sir?' Constable Lilley's rejoinder was hardly useful. Both men looked at him.

'There must be some mistake.' De Lacy poured himself a drink. He did not offer one to anybody else.

'I'm afraid we have positive identification,' Lestrade said.

'Oh?'

'A ring was found some yards away, I understand. It fitted the . . . your wife perfectly and her name is inscribed inside.'

'That could be coincidence,' de Lacy persisted.

'Yes, sir, it could be, assuming that she had been to the park recently. Unless of course, you've had some jewellery stolen?'

De Lacy shook his head.

'It's my unpleasant duty to ask you to accompany me to the mortuary to identify the body.'

'Impossible, Lestrade. I'm on my way to *Die Fledermaus*.'

'I would suggest you didn't leave the country at the moment, sir. Formalities, you understand.'

De Lacy looked oddly at Lestrade, as though he didn't understand at all.

'It must wait until morning, whatever the formalities.'

'If you insist, sir.' Lestrade was less than pleased.

'I do. Good evening, gentlemen. Manfred will show you out.'

'One moment, Mr de Lacy. Could I have the name of the friends your wife was visiting?'

'Certainly.' De Lacy picked up his topper and cane. 'Bandicoot. Mr and Mrs Harry Bandicoot of Bandicoot Hall, Huish Episcopi.'

It was true that Assistant Commissioner Frost was not an easy man to persuade. And a corpse floating at Shadwell Stair and another in a cave at Wookey bore little resemblance to each other. It took all Lestrade's powers to make him accept that the medal in the mouth of one and the scarab in the mouth of the other stretched the laws of coincidence a little far and, with Frost's insistence that he keep expenses to a bare minimum and a reminder that he didn't approve of Inspectors of the Metropolitan Police who were prima donnas ringing in his ears, Lestrade went west.

And so it was that he stood on the green below the great arches of the abbey ruins, the sun glowing on the mellow stone. High on the tor above him rose another tower, more solid, more sinister than the ruins he walked among. For a moment he heard a whisper in the grass, some long-forgotten sigh that echoed down the dear, dead days.

'*Hic jacet Arturus Rex*.' A voice disturbed his solitude, and he tripped over an ancient slab at his feet.

'Balch,' the voice said again, extending a hand to haul him upright.

'Pardon?' Lestrade was back in his usual state, utter confusion.

'Herbert Balch. Are you Mr Lister?'

'The same,' lied Lestrade. 'How did you find me?'

Balch chuckled. 'They told me at the George you had arrived. A stranger in our town has but two places to visit, Mr Lister – the abbey ruins or the tor. I hoped you'd choose the ruins. Less far to walk, you see.'

'You don't care for walking, Mr Balch?'

'Ah,' Balch grinned, 'I'm the local postman, Mr Lister. It's what you might call an occupational hazard.'

'I was rather expecting Mr Bulleid,' said Lestrade.

'Gone,' said Balch, dusting the inspector down. 'To Camelot.'

'Camelot?' Lestrade felt the ground slipping away from beneath him again.

'Cadbury Hill. Mr Bulleid believes it may be the site of King Arthur's legendary castle.'

Lestrade had never realized King Arthur had lived in Birmingham, but he wasn't in a position to dispute it.

'That's his grave, they say.'

Lestrade looked down. 'Bulleid?' A sudden panic seized Lestrade. Corpses were bobbing up in the sea of slaughter eddying red around him.

'No, Arthur. As I said a moment ago – here lies King Arthur.'

'Ah.' Lestrade whipped out the pince-nez he had lifted from Skinner's locker for the occasion. He put them on. He looked no more professional than before, but he persevered. 'Quite.'

'Of course, they hanged him, you know.'

'King Arthur?'

'The last abbot of Glastonbury. He refused to surrender the place to His late Majesty Henry the Eighth and they hanged him for it.'

'I see.' Lestrade looked up at the colossal stones.

'Can you start tomorrow?' Balch asked.

'Delighted,' beamed Lestrade.

'Would you allow me to buy you supper at the George tonight? Professor Dawkins will be there and Miss Truefitt.'

'Will they?' Lestrade was getting in deeper and deeper. 'Splendid. Shall we say eight?'

'Eight it is,' and Balch shook his hand warmly and left Lestrade to the solitude of the ages. It gave him time to worry that the fides he had sent by telegram to the local Clerk of Works might not be as bona as all that. He was posing as an archaeologist in an attempt to unravel the mysterious death of another archaeologist. What had Bulleid called it, rather ominously? The testimony of the spade?

The pig was capital. The port was excellent. The company impossible. Professor Boyd Dawkins took off his pince-nez as often and as resolutely as Lestrade and this at least gave the inspector some hope that he too was behaving like a real archaeologist. Dawkins was an old man who clearly was unimpressed by Bulleid's techniques, preferring the Pitt-Rivers system to anything flashily achieved by Schliemann. He also spent much of the evening talking about hyenas.

Miss Truefitt was another matter. A lady of perhaps twenty-five, she explained that her grandfather had worked with Fiorelli at Pompeii. Lestrade assumed he was an ice-cream salesman until the lady began to discuss erosion, debris and bedrock. Then he didn't have a clue what she was talking about. She was a dazzling-looking woman, however, with a fine mouth and glittering fingers which played incessantly with her wine glass. She sat next to Lestrade and as the evening wore on and the dining-room emptied, he felt a certain pressure on his good knee below the table cloth. After a while, he felt the unmistakable squeeze of fingers on the same knee and, clear his throat though he might, the light pressure continued. There was nothing in the face or conversation of Miss Truefitt to betray why only one hand now toyed with her wine glass.

'You know the cave, of course?' Dawkins asked and it needed a nudge from the hand on his thigh to make Lestrade realize he was being addressed.

'Indeed,' he said, possibly his first truth that night.

'How should we proceed?' Dawkins went on.

'I . . . er . . . well, we'd better . . .' It was the moment of truth.

'Now, Professor.' Miss Truefitt came to Lestrade's rescue. 'Mr Lister has not seen Arthur Bulleid's notes. And after all, *you* are the renowned excavator of the Hyena Den.'

Dawkins was old enough and silly enough to blush and take his spectacles off. 'Well, then, I suggest we move outward from the Den towards Glencot . . .'

'"Where Alph, the sacred river, ran, Through caverns measureless to man . . ."' Balch suddenly interrupted.

Lestrade took the opportunity to remove his knee, but the leg of the table was a powerful obstacle and he bit hard on his port glass as the whole structure trembled. Miss Truefitt smiled at him and continued to examine the weave of his trousers.

'Balch,' the Professor said quietly, 'I know you believe the Axe runs deeper . . .'

'It must, Professor. Ever since I first took up a trowel at your knee, I have been sure of it. There are subterranean chambers there, Mr Lister. Mr Bulleid was coming to believe it, I know. So was Mr Tetley.'

'Ah, yes.' Lestrade saw the chance he had been waiting for. 'What a tragedy. Did any of you know him?'

'I delivered his letters for some weeks before my promotion to counter service,' said Balch.

'Egyptologist,' snorted Dawkins, pouring himself more port. 'Too flashy, these Egyptologists. Not true scientists at all.'

'But he worked at Wookey,' said Lestrade.

'He gatecrashed at Wookey,' retorted Dawkins. 'You've seen the type, Lister. Johnny-Come-Latelies who let some other fool do the digging and then steal all the glory for themselves.'

"Steal the glory"; the phrase echoed round the vast emptiness of Lestrade's head. Nanny Balsam had said Tetley was a thief.

'All the same,' Dawkins pursued the point with the tenacity of a miffed warthog, 'a murder, in Somerset, of a prominent archaeologist. Shocking! What are the police doing about it, that's what I'd like to know.'

'The local constabulary are in charge,' Miss Truefitt said. 'An Inspector Guthrie. Perfect pig of a man. Has the sloping forehead and pronounced eyebrow ridges of *Homo Neanderthalensis*.'

Lestrade wondered where he had seen them before.

'They say', she leaned towards Lestrade, lowering her eyelids, 'That a chap from Scotland Yard was investigating the crime, but Guthrie sent him packing.'

'Tut, tut.' Lestrade put his spectacles on quickly and shook his head. 'Did you know Tetley, Miss Truefitt?'

She ran her fingers higher up his thigh and purred. 'No. He wasn't my type, Mr Lister . . . of archaeologist, I mean,' and she fluttered her eyelashes at him.

'They say they found a scarab in his mouth,' Lestrade said.

Miss Truefitt sat upright and withdrew her hand, much to Lestrade's relief. Dawkins and Balch blinked at each other.

'Damned Egyptologists!' Dawkins snorted, quaffing his port.

'I didn't read that in the papers,' Balch said, with a frown.

'Er . . . no . . . Arthur Bulleid told me.'

'Oh? When did you see him?' For a postman turned amateur archaeologist, Balch had a mind like a razor.

'Er . . . the other week,' Lestrade went on. 'That's when he asked me to join this dig.'

'Yet he didn't mention that he was going to Cadbury? How odd.'

'Yes.' Lestrade drained his glass quickly. 'Isn't it?' He rummaged in his pocket for the half-hunter. 'Good Lord. Is that the time? I have been travelling much of the day . . .'

'Of course.' Miss Truefitt rose with him. 'Are you staying here at the George, Mr Lister?'

'Er . . . Yes, I am.'

'Well,' she beamed, 'what a coincidence. So am I. Goodnight, gentlemen. Shall we say nine in the morning?'

'Nine in the morning,' the men chorused and they made their various exits.

Lestrade should not have been surprised at the knock on his door in the wee, small hours. He lit the candle with much fumbling and fussing and peered through the heavy velvet which shrouded his bed.

'Who is it?' he whispered. He could see nothing but the reflection of the flame on the distorted medieval glass of the latticed windows.

'Valentina Truefitt,' the voice said.

'It's late, Miss Truefitt,' Lestrade protested.

'It's never too late,' she said and before he knew it, the door was opened and closed and she stood there in the candlelight, his and hers.

'Tell me,' she said, 'is that regulation at Scotland Yard?'

Lestrade glanced down frantically. He hoped she was referring to his nightshirt. 'Scotland Yard?' he tried to bluff it out.

She sat on the bed and placed her candle on a cabinet. 'I too was intrigued by the death of Richard Tetley,' she told him. 'That's how I know Inspector Guthrie. The silly man prides himself as a paragon among policemen – suspecting no one and everyone, giving nothing away. Within a few moments he had told me all he knew. And I'd only gone to him to report a lost dog.' She crossed the rug to him and ran her finger up his arms. 'I have that effect on most men.'

He broke away. 'Miss Truefitt . . .'

'Inspector Guthrie was incensed by the arrival of an Inspector Lestrade.' She turned to face him, with wide, angelic eyes. 'A man, I gathered from the talk at the station, who had a pronounced limp and the tip missing from his nose.' She flicked it playfully.

'Good Lord,' he said.

'What they didn't tell me at the station,' she said, 'was that Inspector Lestrade had such lovely eyes.'

Their lips closed together in the candlelight and he held her to him. Her hair smelt like fresh flowers as she swayed there, running her fingers the length of his spine.

'Miss Truefitt.' He came up for air.

'Vallee,' she said.

'What?'

'Call me Vallee.'

'We hardly know each other . . .'

'Oh, Mr Lestrade . . .'

'Call me Inspector,' he said.

'I do so hate the silly little conventions society imposes. I was brought up at my grandfather's knee in digs all over the world. I have handled more corpses than you, Inspector. I am not only a woman of this world but of many others. We are creatures of pleasure, Inspector. Men and women. Why should we be bound by pettiness and the fatuous little rules they make out there?'

She forced him backwards so that his head smacked awkwardly against one of the posts of the bed. Undaunted, she hauled him upright and pinned him under her on the mattress.

'Tomorrow,' she said, 'you and I will be up to our haunches in palaeolithic droppings. I because it is my life's work and you because . . . because I assume you must play out this charade in order to catch a murderer. But tonight . . . tonight belongs to us . . .'

She pressed still further and he squeaked as her hand found its way up his nightshirt.

'I really don't think . . .' he was still protesting.

'Probably not,' she said, holding her free hand over his

mouth, 'but that's no fault of yours. You're a policeman. Now, where were we?'

'Who do you suspect, Miss Truefitt?'

'Vallee,' she whispered, letting her long hair cascade over him like a warm tent. 'If I tell you, will you stop talking, just for a moment?'

He nodded.

'Balch,' she said. 'Never trust a digging postman.'

'What was his motive?'

'You heard him tonight.' She rolled sideways and pulled up his nightshirt. 'Ooh,' she purred, 'so it wasn't your truncheon. He's obsessed with the cave. The Great Hole of Wookey. But he's an amateur, Inspector. A beginner. Richard Tetley was a professional. Years of experience in Egypt and elsewhere. Boyd Dawkins summed it all up. Tetley, Balch feared, would take over the excavations at Wookey. He'd rob him of his moment of fame. Now . . .' She wriggled closer. 'Now it's our moment.'

Lestrade gulped. 'So be it,' he said. 'Miss Truefitt,' he lifted her earnest face, 'be gentle with me!'

The little party wound their way among the stalactites, out of the glare of the September sun. They picked their way past what was left of Guthrie's blue cordon where Richard Tetley had lain, another corpse for the cave. Another sacrifice for the gods. Another victim of the witch. Their voices echoed as they spoke, to be drowned out now and then by the rush of the air in the caverns, the clashing cymbals described, as Balch lovingly told Lestrade, by Clement of Alexandria.

'There she is,' said Balch, taking off his pack and jacket. 'The Great Witch.'

Lestrade looked up again to the yawning formations overhead and saw the legendary creature outlined in stone, who guards the head waters of the Stream of Sorrow.

'"Her haggard face was foull to see; Her mouth unmelt a mouth to bee; Her eyne of deadly leer . . ."' Balch was in his element, leering even more madly than the witch might have done before a local parson turned her to stone.

'Shall we get on?' Dawkins brushed past him. 'I assume you're familiar with all this, Lister?'

Lestrade looked with mounting horror at the paraphernalia arranged carefully above the line of peat-brown water ahead.

'We thought you'd like the honour, as it's our first day.'

'Honour?'

'Of diving, man. I'm too long in the tooth. Balch here can't swim and you wouldn't ask Miss Truefitt, surely?'

Lestrade smiled stupidly at them. 'But, I . . .'

'Now, now.' Miss Truefitt began to haul off his jacket and tie. 'You're the obvious choice. Just remember to watch your footing and keep pulling on the line every thirty seconds. It'll be dark down there,' she pressed briefly to him, 'but I know how capable you are in the dark,' she whispered.

Lestrade found himself being thrust into a diving suit of vast proportions. It smelt revoltingly of indiarubber, but worse was to come. Balch and Miss Truefitt began buckling a metal corselet over his shoulders.

'Get your hands in the air, Mr Lister.' Balch hooked lead weights on to Lestrade's chest and back. 'You probably won't need these, but we don't really know how deep the water is or what you'll meet.'

'Er . . . what am I looking for, exactly?' He hoped his voice wasn't trembling as much as his body was.

'Palaeolithic remains. Bones, shards. Evidence of civilization, Lister.' Dawkins busied himself with the airline and the pump.

'That noise.' Balch lifted a finger. 'The clashing cymbals. It's probably the Axe gushing out down there somewhere. There must be other chambers, Mr Lister, going who knows how many miles underground.'

'Miles?' Lestrade's voice was scarcely audible and he was sure the thudding of the mighty Axe was his own heart, drowning in hopelessness. Balch lifted the great copper helmet and screwed it shut around Lestrade's neck. He opened the grilled porthole at the front.

'All right?' he beamed.

Miss Truefitt blew him a kiss. 'Be careful,' she said.

And Lestrade turned to the water.

'Come on, Lister,' Dawkins said. 'He who hesitates is lost.'

Lestrade heard nothing but the sound of his own breathing as he waded into the black water. The lights of the company's torches danced and dazzled on the beaten copper. Miss Truefitt saw the eyes wide with disbelief and the moustache floating on water as Lestrade's lead-lined boots parted company with the ground and he slid headlong into the gloom. Balch fed out the line inch by inch, foot by foot. Dawkins operated the pump.

'Now?' said Balch as the bubbles subsided.

'Now!' snarled Dawkins and turned off the pump. Simultaneously, Balch fed out the line quickly and let go of it. Miss Truefitt ran forward. 'What are you doing?' she screamed. 'You'll kill him.' Her words ricocheted round the cave.

'He's an impostor, Valentina,' Dawkins said. 'You heard him last night. He's no more an archaeologist than I'm a police inspector.'

'That's no reason to kill him.' Miss Truefitt wrestled with the controls and the air thudded through the pipe again. 'Herbert, grab that line.'

'We're not going to kill him, Valentina,' Balch said. 'Just frighten him a little. The police should be here soon.'

'The police are here already,' growled Miss Truefitt and, wading into shallow water, she grabbed the line and hauled it in. Balch added his weight to the problem and hauled with her.

'Now then, now then!' An Inspectorial voice echoed above their frantic splashings. 'What seems to be the trouble?'

The struggling company turned to see Chief Inspector Guthrie and a clutch of constables from the Somerset Constabulary. 'Lend a hand there, you men!' he ordered and the bobbies hauled the apparition from the deep.

'What is it?' Guthrie crouched beside the prone form.

'It's the impostor I told you about,' said Balch, feverishly unbuckling straps and weights.

'He's a policeman,' Miss Truefitt told the company.

'Is he now?' said Guthrie, wrenching the helmet sideways. There was a loud cracking noise and it came away. 'Lestrade!' he snarled.

'He told us his name was Lister,' Dawkins offered the explanation.

'I'll have his badge for this,' Guthrie went on.

'For God's sake, help him.' Miss Truefitt straddled the unconscious inspector, pushing violently on his ribs.

'Now then, miss, I'm sure you're very fond of the inspector, but now is not the time and place. Constable, you went on that life-saving course. Get on top of him.'

'I'm a married man, sir,' the constable objected.

'That *is* an order, constable.' Guthrie rocked back on his heels, looking fixedly ahead. The bobby complied and assumed the position astride Lestrade which Miss Truefitt had just vacated.

'You say he was posing as an archaeologist, Mr Balch?' Guthrie asked. 'Do you know why?'

'To investigate the death of Richard Tetley,' Miss Truefitt interrupted. 'I think you'd better ask Mr Balch here about that, Inspector.'

'What do you mean?' The digging postman was outraged.

'You just tried to kill Inspector Lestrade. I saw you!' Miss Truefitt screamed.

'Has he succeeded, constable?' Guthrie asked the bobby pumping at Lestrade.

'No, sir. He's coming round. Mind you, he's swallowed enough peat to start an allotment.'

'Attempted murder, then,' beamed Guthrie, though there was something in his eyes which betokened disappointment.

'Murder, my trowel!' snapped Dawkins. 'Look here, Inspector or whatever you are. I am a distinguished archaeologist. Mr Arthur Bulleid who recently vacated these diggings is another. Likewise Mr Balch. Along comes some idiot who clearly doesn't know a posthole from his kneecap and who claims to be one of us. Archaeology is a precise science, Inspector. We can't have buffoons cluttering up the place. He could have ruined years of work. Destroyed vital evidence. He might have been a newspaperman!' Dawkins turned pale at the thought.

'Worse,' sighed Guthrie, 'he's from Scotland Yard. But you're probably right about destroying vital evidence. Besides, he was expressly working unofficially. I warned him off last week. I accept that you intended to scare him a little, no more. But you will be careful in future, won't you?'

'Of course.' Dawkins and Balch looked a little shamefaced.

A groan told the company that Lestrade had returned, however briefly, to the land of the living.

'He must be rushed to the hospital,' entreated Miss Truefitt.

'Yes, indeed,' Guthrie smiled. 'Wells is the nearest. Lift him up, men. And take your time with your rushing, won't you?' He tilted his bowler at Miss Truefitt and made for the entrance by which he had come. 'Have a nice dig,' he shouted.

Letitia Bandicoot sat with her hands clasped in front of her in the waiting-room at St Wifrid's. Scattered on the table before her were back numbers of the *Lancet*, but urticaria in the under-fives held no fascination for her, so she stared at the wall. Nanny Balsam on the other hand *was* concerned to know the prevalence of ringworm in the Chiltern Hundreds or at least found this preferable to the hospital's excruciating taste in wallpaper. Both women stood up, however, at the arrival of the man in the white coat.

'Mrs Bandicoot?' he addressed Nanny Balsam.

'Yes?' said Letitia.

'Ah.' The man transferred his grip to the younger hand. 'Dr Higgs. Thank you for coming. You are . . . ?' He turned back to Miss Balsam.

'Annoyed at being kept waiting,' she beamed icily.

'I'm . . . sure the doctor has many duties, Nanny,' Letitia chided her.

'I'm sure he has.' Miss Balsam looked over her pince-nez at him. 'And one of them is punctuality. I detest sloppiness in children, Dr Higgs, and I doubly detest it in adults. Where is Mr Lestrade?'

'I think I should tell you, ladies,' the doctor ignored Miss Balsam's jibes as the ramblings of the elderly deranged, 'that Inspector Lestrade is not the man you knew.'

'What happened exactly?' Letitia asked. 'I only discovered he was here from Mrs Lemonofides who is a personal friend and is a Visitor here.'

'Indeed, indeed,' the doctor gushed. 'A gracious lady. Well, as far as I can ascertain, Mr Lestrade is suffering from acute oxygen deprivation.'

'If you mean shortage of breath, young man, say so,' Miss Balsam admonished him. 'And isn't that usually fatal?'

'Eventually, ma'am. But in the meantime, I fear that Mr Lestrade has become a vegetable.'

Miss Balsam's spectacles hurtled from the bridge of her nose only to be saved from destruction by the twin salvation of her ample bosoms and the chain around her neck. Mrs Beeton's Household Management had simply not prepared her for this.

'May we see him?' Letitia asked, gripping Nanny's arm.

'Of course. But . . . I had to prepare you.' Dr Higgs led the ladies along the corridors, offensive in their institutional green and cream, until they came to the double doors marked 'Stephen Ward' and they entered. Wizened old men hauled on their bedclothes at the arrival of the ladies. One of them remained oblivious, struggling as he was with a hacking cough.

'That's enough of that!' Miss Balsam caught his feet a sharp one with her handbag as she sailed majestically past his bed. Sure enough, it was. He stopped immediately.

They came to Lestrade's bed. The inspector lay on his side, one arm hooked over his face.

'Sholto,' Letitia said softly. No response.

'Mr Lestrade.' The doctor tapped his shoulder lightly. Nothing.

'He's sleeping, dear,' said Miss Balsam to Letitia. 'We'll come back later.'

'May we stay, doctor?' Letitia asked. 'Just for a while?'

'I fear it will be useless,' Higgs sighed, 'but of course you may. I'll see that a nurse brings you some chairs.'

The doctor went about his business as Letitia closed to the wreck on the bed, craning forward for some semblance of recognition, some sign of hope. Miss Balsam examined the charts at the bottom of the bed.

'You're reading those upside-down,' Lestrade growled from the canopy of his nightshirted arm.

'Sholto!' Letitia squealed.

'Sshh!' he hissed and the familiar blunted nose protruded from the covers.

'You're all right,' whispered Letitia.

'As all right as I ever will be. What are you doing here?'

'A friend of mine is a hospital Visitor. She recognized your name and remembered my talking of you.'

Miss Balsam leaned over him. 'The doctor thinks you're a vegetable, Mr Lestrade.'

'An opinion others have shared, Miss Balsam,' Lestrade

mumbled. 'Let's keep it like that, shall we? Letitia, can you get me out of here, released into your custody, so to speak?'

'I don't know.' Letitia sat up. 'Why don't you just walk out of the door? What's the reason for all this subterfuge?'

Lestrade looked around the bed, wondering which of the appliances was the subterfuge. He wished now he'd been to that first-aid lecture.

'I don't know,' he came clean, 'but with a summons against me from the Somerset Constabulary, a murderer and two attempted murderers afoot only a few miles away, I thought it best to lie doggo and bide my time. Temporary derangement can be useful.'

'I don't understand any of this, Sholto,' Letitia confessed.

'All in good time. Now, be a dear and work your feminine wiles on Dr Higgs. There's much to be done.'

Letitia did as she was told while Miss Balsam scurried hither and yon bringing screens to hide Lestrade's embarrassment as he rummaged for his clothes. When the nurse came to intervene, Miss Balsam told her to go away and even threatened the back of her hairbrush if the order was not instantly obeyed. Lestrade was in the act of buttoning up his summer issue combinations when Miss Balsam's ancient head whizzed around the screen. The inspector's hands immediately sprang to his defence.

'You don't need to cover yourself up,' Miss Balsam assured him. 'I've handled dozens of little boys in my time.'

'Little boys, possibly, madam.' Lestrade's dignity was a little trampled.

'Well, in your case, there's clearly little difference,' and she vanished in search of Letitia.

Now, Letitia Bandicoot was a striking-looking woman, but when it came to striking, she was not in Nanny Balsam's league. She was getting nowhere with the obstinate Dr Higgs, who insisted that Lestrade was too ill to be moved. Very quietly, Miss Balsam shepherded Letitia out of Higgs's office and closed the door behind her. There were whispered exchanges, a high-pitched male shriek and the feverish scratching of a pen. Minutes later, Nanny Balsam emerged, beaming triumphantly, waving a piece of paper.

'This is the authorization we need. Come along,' and she swept Letitia away.

Autumn was coming to Bandicoot Hall. It coloured the leaves that shook in the breeze along the lake. It shone golden through the stained glass that threw its lights on the flagstoned floor. It whistled with the ghosts of minstrels in the gallery and it made the swallows gather in numbers to wing their way south.

Lestrade strolled beside the still waters with Letitia on his arm.

'But surely, Guthrie can't *actually* issue you with a summons?' she asked.

'No, I don't think he can,' chuckled Lestrade, 'but that won't stop him from trying.'

'Will you be in trouble at the Yard?'

'I'm used to the feel of carpet underfoot.' He patted her hand. 'Tell me, when is Harry due back from Yorkshire?'

Her face fell. 'A week or so. He claims it's business, but you know Harry. He's packed his Purdy, so he'll be stalking the moors for a while. He'll be sorry to have missed you.'

'I doubt that. Letitia, I'm sorry I can't help at the moment in the Tetley business. But perhaps you can help me. Where's Miss Balsam?'

'In the village, I believe. She's a law unto herself, Sholto, as you may have gathered at the hospital.' They laughed. 'Why?'

'Oh, it's nothing really. Something she said about Richard Tetley when I was here last.'

'What was that?'

He turned to face her. 'She said he was a thief. What do you suppose she meant by that?'

Letitia chuckled. 'I don't know, Sholto, but I wouldn't read too much into it. Nanny Balsam is the salt of the earth. Before she was my nanny she was nanny to some of the finest, oldest families in the land – and some of the newest. Did you know she's organized a Nannies' Convention?'

Lestrade stopped suddenly.

'I'm serious. A whole coven of them met at Cheltenham a couple of months ago. I couldn't imagine what had got into her at first, but she said she had her professional pride, that the

British Nanny was an institution. I thought it was very enterprising of her.'

Resisting the impulse to tell Letitia that Miss Balsam should have been *in* an institution, Lestrade laughed. 'Is she forming a Trade Union?'

'Sholto, Nanny Balsam is an eccentric from a long line of eccentrics. She's ever so slightly dotty. And we love her dearly, Harry and I, but you mustn't take what she says too seriously.'

'I'm not sure I take anything seriously any more.' He turned her towards the house. 'Oh, one other thing. Does the name de Lacy mean anything to you?'

'Howard and Marigold de Lacy?'

'Yes. Do you know him?'

'Not very well. I know Marigold, of course. We were at finishing school together.'

'I'm sorry.' Lestrade was grim-faced.

'Sorry?' She held his arm. 'Sholto. I don't understand. What's the matter?'

'My God, you don't know,' he said.

'Know what?' Letitia looked her most vulnerable when she was alarmed.

'I thought you'd have read it in the newspapers. Marigold de Lacy is dead, Letitia, over a week ago now.'

Letitia's hand involuntarily covered her mouth.

'I'm very sorry,' he said again. 'I hadn't realized.'

'Was it . . . an accident?' she managed.

'No, Letitia. I'm afraid it was murder.'

Letitia sat down heavily on the terrace seat, 'Oh, my God. Poor, poor Marigold. I can't believe it. Harry will be heartbroken.'

'Harry will?'

'Oh, it's silly really. He met Marigold shortly before we were married. I could tell he was smitten with her and she with him. I used to tease him mercilessly about it; that she was the other woman and so on. He won't believe it either. What happened?'

Lestrade sat down beside her and looked out across the darkening waters of the lake. 'I'm afraid I can't tell you,' he said, 'but you can tell me something. Was Marigold de Lacy due to visit you last week, say on Thursday?'

'Visit us? Good Lord, no. At least, nothing had been arranged. Harry was in London . . .'

'I thought you said Yorkshire.'

'Yes, Yorkshire, but he had some business in the City first. She may have been coming on spec.'

'Is that usual?'

'No, it isn't. Sholto, I haven't seen Marigold de Lacy since her wedding. Why should she have suddenly come to visit me last week? And why should anyone want to kill her?'

Lestrade stood up. It was late. And he had a train to catch.

'When I have those answers,' he said, 'I might also have her murderer.'

He saw himself out.

5

Jenny

'Your telegram said an accident.' Nimrod Frost moved his elephantine girth a little to the left and blotted out the sun.

'That's correct, sir.' Lestrade stood to attention, the bowler in the crook of his arm, his hair carefully macassared in compliance with Winter Regulations. September was nearly over. The Frosts – Jack and Nimrod – would soon be upon him.

The Assistant Commissioner turned to the inspector with the truculence of the grossly overweight. 'You look bloody well on it.'

'Don't let this rugged exterior fool you, sir,' Lestrade said. 'I haven't been feeling myself recently.'

'Apparently not.' Frost whisked a piece of paper under his nose and then under Lestrade's. 'Attar of Roses, wouldn't you say?'

Lestrade hadn't a clue whose Attar it was, but he wasn't going to show his ignorance to Frost. Not, that is, unless he had to.

'It's a letter from a V. Truefitt who claims to be an archaeologist and who claims to know you.'

Lestrade's colour drained.

'Tell me,' Frost lurched around his desk, 'is this Truefitt a female?'

'Yes, sir.' Lestrade didn't care for the angle of Frost's eyebrow. It had an accusatory tilt to it.

'Thank God for that at least. Nothing odd about Miss Truefitt. Except that she claims that the murderers of Richard Tetley were a Professor Boyd Dawkins and a postman called Belch.'

'Balch,' Lestrade corrected him.

'Do I assume from that remark you do not think Miss Truefitt is correct?'

'No, sir.'

'And is she correct when she claims that these gentlemen also tried to kill you?'

'No, sir. It was all a misunderstanding. I merely met with an accident.'

'And then,' Frost reached over his stomach to lift a second letter from his desk, 'there is this letter from a Dr Higgs of Wells in Somerset who claims he was bludgeoned by a deranged old biddy to release you from his care.'

'Ah.' Lestrade's face fell. 'Does he say how she did it, sir?'

Frost read between the lines. 'No doubt there are some things better left unsaid, even by the medical fraternity. According to Higgs, your mind has gone due to respiratory failure.' Frost produced an acid grin. 'Nice to have it confirmed.'

'That was a misunderstanding, sir.'

'And then, of course,' the Assistant Commissioner reached for a third letter, 'Chief Inspector Guthrie of the Somerset Constabulary does not use scented notepaper. His prose is colourful enough. Let me see – no warrant, blah, blah, blah; impersonating an archaeologist (very badly) blah, blah; wasting police time, blah; using a police vehicle viz. and to wit blah . . . Need I go on? Or is that enough blah for one morning?'

'Another . . .'

'Misunderstanding? Quite, Lestrade. But which of the three do you wish me to accept? Are you the unwitting victim of a murder attempt? Are you a vegetable? Are you guilty of interfering without authority in the case of another Constabulary? Or are you in fact suspended for two weeks without pay? Good morning.'

'Sir, I . . .'

'Good morning, Lestrade!' Frost's fist landed among the jumping debris of his desk and the inspector sensed the conversation was at an end.

He turned on his heel and hobbled to his office in the labyrinth of the converted Opera House. Constable Skinner was, as usual, buried in paperwork.

'Good morning, sir.' He struggled to his feet.

'Is it?' Lestrade barked. 'Where's Dew?'

'Er . . . down there, sir.'

Skinner pointed to the curious sight of two plainclothes policemen lolling on the rail overlooking the river.

'Got anything for me?' Lestrade asked the bespectacled bobby.

'I'm still working on the Fellowes diary, sir. I fully expect a breakthrough in two or three months. Faster, if only I could find my spectacles!'

'Good. Good. Well, don't let me disturb your concentration. Oh, by the way,' he reached into his pocket and found Skinner's glasses, 'borrow mine.'

Lestrade crammed some papers into the battered Gladstone in his locker and took the stairs rather than the lift. He stepped out into the weak sun of September. He felt strangely free, suddenly. And startled coppers going about their business noticed him skipping through the Embankment archway.

'Now then Dew, Lilley.' He clapped them both on the shoulder.

'Sir!' Both men leapt upright.

'As you were, gentlemen.'

They lolled again. Lilley was the colour of the tripe dangling out of Dew's sandwiches.

'Sandwich, sir?' Dew offered.

'No, thanks, constable. I've got a few years in me yet.' He squeezed between them to rub shoulders with the other constable.

'Well, Lilley, how's it going?'

The constable looked more vacant than usual. 'He was dead, sir.'

Lestrade looked at Dew, who was making silent grimaces in Lilley's direction.

'Well, you shouldn't eat them.' Lestrade assumed the sandwiches were to blame. 'Who's dead, constable?'

'Mr de Lacy, sir.'

Lestrade straightened. 'De Lacy? Howard Luneberg de Lacy?'

Lilley nodded, then turned sharply to stare at the river sparkling in the morning.

'All right, lad.' Lestrade patted his shoulder. 'Feel like talking about it?'

Lilley didn't. But his guv'nor was asking. He cleared his

throat and began. 'Well, sir, I went round to Mr de Lacy's house the next morning, while you was off to Somerset.'

'And?'

'His man told me he'd come back late the night before and had left instructions he wasn't to be disturbed.'

'What did you do?'

'I disturbed him, sir.'

'Good man,' Lestrade said. 'You'll go far.'

'I said I had my orders and the gentleman was to accompany me to the mortuary to identify his wife.'

'What then?'

'The gentleman's manservant refused to assist, so I knocked on the door. It opened under my knock and I went in.' Lilley was shaking.

'Easy does it, lad.' Lestrade was as gentle as he knew how. It was not long ago he was talking as gently to Walter Dew as he stood quivering outside Miller's Court in the days of the Ripper.

'Mr de Lacy was lying in bed, sir, staring at the ceiling. There was . . . blood over his pillow.'

'What did you make of it?'

'I thought it must have been a brain heritage, sir.'

'I see. What then?'

'I . . . er . . . I don't know, sir. I fainted.'

Lestrade's eyes narrowed and his moustache twitched.

'Dew. Were you involved in this?'

'No, sir. Two constables from "B" Division did the honours. Sealed off the room and sent for us. Mr Abberline . . .'

'Damn!' Lestrade's fist rang on the rail so that passers-by with perambulators looked at him. 'Where's the body now?'

'Still at Mawson Gardens, sir. Mr Abberline didn't want him moved until he had a chance to look him over.'

'When was this?'

'Day before yesterday, sir. Mr Abberline had an aunt he had to show round the City. Gave instructions Mr de Lacy wasn't to go anywhere until he returned.'

'An aunt, eh?' Lestrade was talking to himself. 'Then we may not be too late. I'll wager, gentlemen, Mr Abberline's aunt has flaming red hair and a backside like a Davenport. *And* I'll bet she's seen the sights before. Don't giggle, Dew, that's bloody unprofessional.'

'You there!' An overweight voice caused all three to look up to a window high among the trees across the road.

'Mr Frost.' Lestrade waved cheerily.

'You're lolling!' Frost roared. 'Dew and Whoever-You-Are. The Criminal Investigation Department doesn't loll. And you, you're suspended!' He slammed the window shut.

Lestrade pointed to the Gladstone in his hand. Dew and Lilley looked around, wondering to whom Frost was referring.

'Talking of unprofessional,' muttered Lestrade, 'fear not, gentlemen. Our dear Assistant Commissioner means me.'

'*You*, sir?' Dew was incredulous.

'It's not the first time, Walter. And I don't suppose it'll be the last. I've got two weeks unpaid leave and I'm going to enjoy myself. But first, I'm paying a call on the late Mr de Lacy. Lilley, you'll get over this morbid fear of blood, I promise you. And stop lolling, both of you. This is Scotland Yard,' and he went off, whistling, in search of a hansom.

De Lacy's man, Manfred, seemed as undeterred by the death of his master as he had been by the death of his mistress. The de Lacys had been childless and so it was at least on the cards that Manfred would be looking for another job before too long.

'I understood that the other police gentleman would be wishing to take charge of Mr de Lacy, sir,' he said, taking Lestrade's bowler.

'If you mean Mr Abberline, he isn't a gentleman, Manfred. No, I will be in charge . . .' He glanced through the netted curtains of the hall at Number Forty-three Mawson Gardens. 'At least for a while. Where is Mr de Lacy?'

'Walk this way, sir.'

Lestrade declined. If he walked *that* way people would talk about him. Manfred led the inspector upstairs into the master bedroom. On a single bed, propped up on pillows and grey of hue, lay all that was left of Howard Luneberg de Lacy, whose family had come over with the Conqueror.

'Your version of the story.' Lestrade glanced at Manfred, then raised the blinds to let the sunshine fall on the handsome features of the deceased.

'I was in the kitchen, sir, on Sunday last. Mrs Flanagan was preparing the breakfast. Flanagan was blacking Mr de Lacy's boots.'

'The Flanagans are husband and wife?'

'No, sir.' Manfred had the emotive delivery of a paperweight. 'Alan Flanagan is the cook's son. Mrs Flanagan is a widowed lady.'

'How many more staff, apart from Flanagan and Alan?'

'Beatrice, the downstairs maid and myself, sir.'

'Did the de Lacys have other property?'

'Mr de Lacy, no, sir. Mrs de Lacy had two villas. One in Cannes, the other in Ventnor.'

Lestrade turned the head of the corpse, as he had of the corpse's wife days earlier. There was dark brown blood over the pillows and on the sheets and nightshirt.

'You said Sunday,' Lestrade went on without looking at Manfred. 'Surely you mean Saturday?'

'With respect, sir,' Manfred stood firmly on his dignity, 'I mean Sunday – the day we found Mr de Lacy.'

'My constable called on *Sunday* morning?' Lestrade checked.

'Indeed, sir.'

Lestrade found this odd. Lilley had not mentioned skipping a day. They had gone to de Lacy to break the news of his wife's death on Friday, to find him too busy to attend the mortuary. Lilley had orders to go the next morning, Saturday. But he had not got there until the following day. What had happened to the lost weekend?

'Go on,' Lestrade said.

'Your Constable Lilley called at eight-thirty sir, to conduct Mr de Lacy to the mortuary.'

'And?'

'I told him Mr de Lacy had been up late the previous night, sir, and was not to be disturbed until nine. It was his custom on a Sunday to take his breakfast in bed.'

'What did Lilley say?' Lestrade paced the room, checking dressing table top, wardrobe and drawers mechanically.

'He insisted he be taken at once to Mr de Lacy. Reluctantly, I agreed.'

'You brought him here?'

'Yes, sir. I was about to announce the constable when he pushed past me and fell over.'

'Fainted!'

'I believe so, sir. I confess, even with Mr de Lacy thus,' he waved to the corpse, 'I was a little surprised.'

'Lilley hasn't been well,' Lestrade said. 'Tell me, Manfred, was Mr de Lacy in this position?'

'His eyes were open, sir. Other than that, yes.'

'You closed them.'

'Of course, sir. I couldn't leave him lying there like that.' The tone suggested that Manfred's motive was one of tidiness rather than humanity.

'Did Mr de Lacy sleep alone habitually?' Lestrade noted the single bed.

'Sir?' Manfred registered shock by raising an eyebrow.

'Dammit, man. It can't matter now and I have a murder or two to solve. Did Mr and Mrs de Lacy share a bed?'

'I believe not, sir, not for the last few months. Mrs de Lacy's bedroom is along the hall.'

'And of course as a fervent servant you wouldn't know why this should be?'

Manfred's other eyebrow joined the first and he shuddered. 'Absolutely not, sir. It was none of my business.'

Lestrade threw himself down in an armchair. 'Of course not. So, Mr de Lacy didn't go to the mortuary himself on the Saturday, even though he knew his wife was dead? Odd, wouldn't you say?'

'It's not for me to say, sir.' Manfred was guarded in death as he had been in life.

'Where had he been so late on Saturday night?'

'To the theatre, sir.'

'What did he see?'

'A play, sir.'

Lestrade stood up sharply. 'What play?'

'I believe it was *A Woman of No Importance* by some Irishman.'

'And do you know whether he went alone?'

Manfred hesitated and was immediately lost. 'I . . . er . . . believe he went with a lady, sir.'

Lestrade closed to his man like a shark suddenly tired of basking. 'And do you know who the lady was?' He placed his nose near to the manservant's.

Manfred coughed and wriggled a little, but there was no

escape from the jaws of the shark. 'I believe it was Lady Davinia Harcourt,' he said.

Lestrade whipped out his trusty notepad. 'Write the lady's address down there,' he said, and while Manfred was wrestling with the pencil stub, Lestrade checked the door. 'No key,' he said. 'Was Mr de Lacy in the habit of locking his bedroom door?'

'No, sir.'

'What time did he return from the theatre?'

'I don't know, sir. I retired about midnight. He had not returned by then.'

'If you had retired, who locked the house?'

'Mr de Lacy himself, sir.'

'And when you answered the door to my constable in the morning, was the front door locked?'

'No, sir, it was not.'

'Is that significant, Manfred?'

'Not unduly, sir. Mr de Lacy often forgot to lock the front door.'

'And yet there was no one to check for him?'

'It was his instruction, sir.'

'When he had been to the theatre or when he had been with a lady?'

Manfred's eyebrow lifted again. 'I don't understand, sir.'

The basking shark turned on him again. 'Yes, you do, Manfred. Did Lady Davinia return with Mr de Lacy on Saturday night?'

'I really do not know, sir. I was already abed.'

'"And Mr de Lacy had been a widower for only forty-eight hours, sir" would have been a better answer, Manfred,' Lestrade told him. He returned to the corpse. 'A sharp object, rammed with some force through the back of the neck. An ice pick, perhaps, a bodkin of some sort. Severed the spinal cord. Death would have been very quick. And between midnight and eight-thirty on Sunday morning, anyone could have crept in here through two unlocked doors and despatched him.' He was talking to himself. 'He would have had to have been lying on his side, probably facing away from the window. Manfred, was the room disturbed? Signs of a struggle?'

'None, sir.'

'So he was asleep at the time.' Lestrade checked the glass by the bedside, sniffing it carefully. 'Water,' he pronounced. A movement beyond the nets caught his eye. A hansom pulled up in the street below and a heavy, moustachioed man with a gardenia in his buttonhole got out, but not before an attractive redhead had hauled him back into the cab and kissed him passionately.

'So *that's* his auntie,' Lestrade murmured. 'What *is* her hand doing there? Manfred, the other police gentleman is on his way up. I would take it as a personal favour if you would delay mentioning my presence to Mr Abberline for at least ten minutes.'

'Of course, sir.' Manfred's middle name was discretion.

'But first, I'd be grateful if you could point me in the direction of the back door.'

Manfred did so and, on his way out, Lestrade patted something in the hall. It was a knobkerrie with a particularly large head.

It had to be admitted that Lestrade and Dew were looking in opposite directions when they collided. The crack of skulls and buckling of bowlers ricocheted through the lunchtime streets of Chiswick and the dazed coppers reeled apart.

'Sorry, sir, I was trying to catch your eye before Mr Abberline saw you.'

'An inch or so to the right, and you'd have succeeded, Dew.' Lestrade steadied himself against a wall. 'As it is, I think you've broken my nose.'

Gradually the two Constables Dew merged to be one and he dried his eyes.

'Well, what's your hurry?' Lestrade asked. 'I realized the Chief Inspector would not be far behind me.'

'Something else, sir. Arrived at the Yard shortly after you left. Hoped I'd catch you before you went on. Thought I'd better fly over to Chiswick.'

Lestrade took the proffered telegram marked 'Urgent'. Its contents came as a bolt from the blue.

'It's from Chief Inspector Blue,' he told Dew. 'Oh, of course, he was before your time. With me in "H" Division years ago. I think he got tired of quips about being the boy in blue and joined plainclothes, before he got tired of that too and went to Yorkshire.'

'If you're tired of London, you're tired of life, sir.' Dew was at his most philosophical on Tuesdays. Or perhaps it was the blow to his head.

'Quite, Walter, quite.' This was a side of Dew Lestrade had not seen before. He didn't really care for it. 'I've got to go to York, constable. If anybody asks, you haven't seen me. Got it?'

'Haven't seen your what, sir?' It was Walter Dew's contribution to levity. Lestrade ignored it and wandered away.

In those days the trains ran into a little station at Blenheim. And not to be outdone, Lestrade ran into a piece of topiary in the likeness of a huge man riding a huge horse and badly lacerated his face on the thorns that protruded from the animal's kneecaps.

'Are you all right?' a soft voice called with some concern.

Lestrade focused through the pain to see a beautiful woman with dark hair and eyes leaning over him as he struggled to free his trousers from the briar grip of the horse's raised forefoot.

'Puissant, isn't it?' The lady looked up admiringly at the giant hedge.

'Privet would have been more sensible, madam.' Lestrade touched his bowler with what dignity he could.

The lady was wondering just how a man apparently in possession of his faculties could have collided with a thirty-foot high statue in hedgery. 'The Great Duke,' she said.

Lestrade stood back to take in the flowing curls and leafy armour. It wasn't his place to say so, but it bore not the slightest resemblance to Wellington.

'I'm looking for Lady Randolph Churchill,' Lestrade said.

'You've found her.' The lady curtsied low, a fetching sight in her brown velvet riding habit.

'Ah. Inspector Lestrade, Lady Randolph, from Scotland Yard.'

'Inspector Lestrade.' She shook his hand warmly. 'Winston has spoken of you many times. I am delighted to meet you at last.'

'And I you, Lady Randolph.'

She linked her arm through his and walked to safer ground, down to the water terraces where the hedges were fewer. She produced a monogrammed handkerchief and dabbed the blood from his forehead. 'You poor dear. Blackthorn can be beastly, can't it? I'm rather afraid you've missed Winston. He's in India, you know. The Malakand Field Force with General Blood.'

Lestrade had always thought that an unfortunate name for a soldier.

'Of course,' Lady Randolph went on, 'there's talk of trouble with the Fuzzy Wuzzies. Winston will want to see action in the Sudan, I fear. I've written to the Sirdar.'

'Forceful man, the Sirdar, by all accounts,' said Lestrade.

'Really? I always found him rather woolly,' she said.

But it was not Winston Lestrade had come to see.

'It is not Winston I have come to see, Lady Randolph,' he said.

'My other son, Jack? I'm afraid he's in France.'

'Not your other son either, Lady Randolph, but your good Lady Randolph self.'

'I?' She stopped by the first of the fountains, cascading lazily in the afternoon air. Her head tilted a little to the right and she smiled at him in a way that caused a flutter to his heart. He mustn't miss lunch again, he thought to himself.

'I understand you knew the late Oscar Jones, the archaeologist.'

'Why, yes I did. We expatriates tend to stick together, Mr Lestrade.'

Lestrade had assumed Jones had been American, but he wasn't going to push the point.

'I am pursuing a murder enquiry, Lady Randolph.'

'Murder?' She instinctively clutched her throat. 'Good heavens.'

'The murder of one Richard Tetley, also an archaeologist. Did you know him?'

'I never met the man. But of course there was talk.'

'Talk, Lady Randolph?'

She gently broke away from him and wandered beside the lily leaves floating dead and dying on the dark water. A sudden gust of wind caught the fountain and Lestrade experienced a wet arm. He hastened after her; the wind changed again and the water caught him in the back of the head.

'Will you stay to dinner, Mr Lestrade? We're having a few friends. Nothing formal, you understand. Forty or so people.'

'I hardly think I am dressed for such a . . .'

'Nonsense. I doubt if Winston's things would fit you, but I expect I could dig out something of Randolph's. Good Lord, you poor man, you're soaking wet! Has it been raining?'

Lestrade held out his hand. 'Not recently,' he smiled.

And they walked towards the vast magnificence of Blenheim Palace.

'Nice place you've got here,' said Lestrade as the sweep of the North Front came into view.

Lady Randolph smiled. 'Like you, Mr Lestrade, I'm only visiting. I drift these days between here and London, waiting for news of Winnie. I live for him now,' she sighed. 'For him and through him.'

'When I met your son, Lady Randolph, he told me he couldn't decide whether he wanted to be a general or Home Secretary.'

Lady Randolph laughed, a warm, melodic sound that touched Lestrade's heart. He hadn't laughed in the company of a beautiful woman for a long time, it seemed to him.

'Tell me, Mr Lestrade.' She was suddenly serious, the eye-brows raised quizzically. 'Please forgive the imprudence, but I sense a sadness about you as there is about . . . Is there an emptiness in your life too?'

She stood before him, framed by the great grey stones that the first Churchill had watched rise from the ruins of medieval Woodstock. He found himself nodding, wet, tired and bleeding as he was. 'My wife died two years ago,' he said. 'Nearly three.'

She caught her breath. 'About the time I lost Randolph,' she said, looking deep into his eyes. Then she closed to him, clamping herself to his sodden sleeve. 'You shall be my escort tonight, Mr Lestrade. You shall sit by me and save me from being bored to death by the other guests. And I shall tell you all I can about poor Oscar Jones.'

When dinner was over and the ladies had retired, Lestrade sat back in his ill-fitting dinner jacket and enjoyed a well-earned cigar. True, Lady Randolph had been on his right hand and had been lovely and gracious in her cream mutton chop gown, but she had been cornered all evening by a doddery old admiral and she had been unable to escape in order to tell Lestrade what he wanted to know. And it had to be admitted that Lestrade's attention was rather elsewhere – to his left, to be precise, in the person of the gorgeous and golden Duchess of Marlborough. Her husband, Sunny, the Duke, was away on his interminable business trips and Consuelo, vivacious, curvaceous, voracious, was bored. Had it not been for her title, she would have been true to her Cuban ancestry and pressed her knee against Lestrade's, little knowing how recently it had been pressed by another. As it was, she made do by sending a note by one of the footmen. And unbeknownst to her, Lady Randolph was sending another footman with a similar message. They arrived at Lestrade's slouching form simultaneously and waited patiently while the inspector bestirred himself and read first one note, then the other. He looked up nervously at the flunkeys, whose smiles vanished, and they stared ahead in their silk livery and powdered wigs, as marble as the statues which guarded the crackling fireplace.

Consuelo's note had asked him to come at once, so he downed his brandy, bowed to the oblivious company who had decided that Lestrade must be an estate agent and ignored him accordingly, and left. He wandered through the vast empty rooms, heavy with velvet and ormolu, until he found the Red Drawing Room with its huge portrait of the First Duke. He was still staring at the flames that flickered below it when the door clicked behind him.

'Madam.' He stood to attention.

She flicked his tie with her fan. 'Mr Lestrade, you are a dull guest. I had expected you some little while ago.'

'I feel I should explain . . .' he began.

She held her gloved fingers to his lips. The sweet smell of her perfume filled his head with a warmth far lovelier than the brandy and the fire. 'There is no need,' she said. 'You think me forward, brash, even a little vulgar?'

'Lady Marlborough, I . . .'

'Well, you are probably right.' She looked up at the armoured, bewigged Duke towering over them both. 'Corporal John,' she sighed. 'You know, it is said that shortly before his death, he stood before this portrait and said, "This was once a man." That's rather sad, don't you think? Oh,' she took his hand, 'I asked you to join me, Mr Lestrade, because I saw in you a man unlike the others in there. A man unlike any of them. A man like him.' She swept her arm in an admiring gesture at the portrait.

'Your husband, madam . . .' Lestrade reminded her. At the corner of his eye he caught the Louis XVI clock. He had two minutes to meet Lady Randolph.

'. . . is away on business, Mr Lestrade, as I explained to you.'

'Indeed, madam, but that is precisely the point.'

She sighed. 'Oh dear, have I misjudged you, dear, dear Mr Lestrade?' She stood on tiptoe and planted a warm kiss on his lips. 'It's Jenny, isn't it?'

'No, it's Sholto,' he told her. 'Oh, I see. Jenny,' and he saw his escape. 'Yes, I'm afraid it is.'

'Of course. She is a dear, dear thing and she deserves happiness, God knows, but I think I should warn you that there is another. George Cornwallis-West . . .'

'I will take my chances, Lady Marlborough. Goodnight.' He bowed with what he hoped was the right angle for the aristocracy and fumbled through the doors behind him. Wiping the sweat from his brow, he adjusted his bow tie and fled through the vast emptinesses until he found the Long Library. The moon was filtering through on to the priceless carpets and the faded old leather of the spines.

From a darkened corner away from the fire a voice called, 'Randolph?'

He stiffened and turned to the darkness. 'Lestrade, madam,' he apologized, 'Lady Randolph.'

'How silly of me,' the voice came after a while. 'I was dozing for a moment.' She walked into the moonlight. 'Call me Jenny.'

'Would that be wise, Lady Randolph?'

'Wisdom, Mr Lestrade? What do I know of wisdom?' She offered him a seat. 'That's Chippendale,' she said.

'Perhaps I should sit somewhere else?' He hesitated.

'No.' She looked at him a little oddly. 'There will be fine. Tell me, was Consuelo's note the same as mine?'

Lestrade felt his lips bricky dry. 'It was more to the point, Lady Randolph,' he said.

She laughed, that tinkling musical sound he loved. 'Poor Consuelo. She means no harm, you know. She's deeply in love with Sunny but he's away so often.'

'Lady Randolph . . .'

'Randolph's mother thinks I don't miss my late husband, Mr Lestrade – Sholto, isn't it?'

He wasn't sure now.

'But I do. And now,' she snapped herself back from the distance of her dreams, 'I spend my time entertaining publishers in order to get my son noticed. Did you hear that old fool Longman earlier this evening?'

'About Oscar Jones, Lady Randolph.' Lestrade did not wish to be impolite but he had urgent business in the north.

'Of course.' She rang a little bell beside her on the table. 'The purpose of your visit. Our families were friends from way back,' she told him, leaning back in the snug chair, firelight dancing on her perfect face. 'Oscar was a bright boy. Fierce, ardent, intelligent. Not unlike dear Winston, but rather less piggy-looking. Randolph thought Oscar a genius. The poor boy died in Egypt, Sholto, six . . . no, seven years ago now. He was only twenty-four.'

A flunkey appeared at the library door, 'Scargill, brandies and coffee, please.'

The flunkey bowed and exited.

'How did he die?' Lestrade asked.

Her face became puzzled. 'I don't believe I know,' she said. 'But he died, I am sure, happy. He'd made his greatest discovery.'

'Had he? I thought he was working under Richard Tetley?'

'Oh, no, Sholto. Someone has been misinforming you. Look.' She produced from her sleeve a crumpled note. 'I found this while dressing for dinner and meant to give it to you earlier.'

He craned forward to read the faded words in the firelight. 'From Oscar?' he asked.

'Yes, a day or two before he died. In it, he says that he had found the tomb of a Pharaoh. He also says that he is anxious to complete his work before others can steal it from him.'

'Steal it from him?' Lestrade repeated.

'I believe they were his words. Ah, coffee and brandy, Sholto, one lump or two? Leave us, Scargill. As you see, the poor boy was rather low. He says he has even written to his dear old nanny to tell her of his fears. Could he have meant this Richard Tetley? They say he was devilish ambitious.'

Lestrade stood up. 'Lady Randolph, I fear I must be leaving too.'

She rose with him. 'Sholto, you can't. At this hour?'

'Is there a train?'

'I believe there is, at midnight, but . . .'

'Lady Randolph,' he took her hand, 'may I borrow Oscar's letter?'

'Of course, if it will help?'

'You have been generous and more helpful than you know.'

'Are you nearer to solving your case?' she asked.

'Inches nearer, madam, but inches nonetheless. Lady Marlborough . . .'

'. . . will be disappointed,' Jenny smiled. Her face lost its sparkle for a moment. 'But not as disappointed as I . . .' She held his hand for a long time and he slipped away into the dark.

'Give my regards to young Winston,' he said. 'I will leave the clothes with your man. Thank you, Lady Randolph.' He watched her for as long as he dared, her eyes bright in the moonlight.

'*A bientôt*,' she whispered, but he didn't speak Spanish, and was gone.

It was unfortunate that Mr and Mrs Blue had christened their only son Boyd. It was unfortunate that he had undertaken a career in the police force, for the colour of its uniform dogged him. It was also unfortunate that his height, at a little under five feet two inches, *ought* to have precluded his joining, but his zealousness forced him to cram newspaper into his boots and in the less than caring days of the seventies no one had measured too closely. So it was that Little Boyd Blue became a marked man. A man, appropriately enough for the police force, with a nickname.

He sat patiently in the tea rooms off the Shambles, watching the genteel of the city taking their morning refreshment. And among the well-to-do astrakhans and beavers and tweeds woven in the Dales, a rather shabby Donegal he thought he knew.

'They told me at the station I'd find you here.' Lestrade shook his hand, only to have Blue's bowler smacked smartly in front of his face.

'Not so loud, Sholto. If I'd wanted the world to know, we could have met at the gaol and shouted your arrival from the top of Clifford's Tower. How are you?'

'Confused, Boyd.'

'Ah, yes, railway repairs at Peterborough. Enough to confuse anybody.'

'No.' Lestrade sat down and began disrobing. 'Your telegram.'

Blue closed to him. 'I couldn't give much away.' He glanced to left and right and his jaw was poised to speak when the waitress arrived.

'Will there be owt else?' she asked.

'No, thank you,' Blue snapped. 'Don't dawdle, girl. Be about your business.'

'Er . . . I'll have a tea, please.' Lestrade stopped her.

She rolled her eyes heavenward. 'Very good, sir.'

'Don't encourage sulky floozies like her, Lestrade,' Blue hissed under his breath. 'Well, get on with it, girl.' He clapped his hands. 'You heard the lieutenant.'

Lestrade looked around him. Apart from the hum and the clatter of cups, he was unaware that anyone else had spoken. 'For a moment there,' he smiled, looking for somewhere to put his bowler, 'I thought you called me lieutenant.'

His laugh was cut dramatically short by a tug on his sleeve that brought his nose down sharply into the sugar bowl.

'This is an undercover operation, Lestrade,' Blue whispered. 'Didn't you *read* my telegram?'

Lestrade clicked his fingers in realization. '*That* was the word! Do you know, I wrestled with that all the way up. Undercover. Yes, of course, I see it now.'

'The question is, can the Yard spare you? I know it's a bloody cheek on my part, Sholto.'

'Well, life is of course frantic, Little . . . er . . . Boyd, but I couldn't let an old chum and colleague down.'

'Thank you my dear.' Blue was suddenly all smiles to the floozie. 'Just like the lieutenant likes it.'

The waitress gave Lestrade a look which implied that he had recently escaped from somewhere and answered a call from the far side of the room. "Ang about. I've only got t'one pair of 'ands.'

'Aren't you rather overdoing this?' Lestrade whispered. 'What is all this lieutenant business?'

'Just establishing your *alter persona*, Sholto,' Blue explained.

'Thank you.' Lestrade adjusted his tie. 'I'll establish my own. Now, what's going on?'

'You read of course about William Hellerslyke?'

'No.' Lestrade helped himself to one of Blue's chelseas. He was feeling homesick already.

'Don't you have papers in London, Lestrade?' Blue said and instantly regretted his volume. 'It was in all the dailies. Made front page of the *Yorkshire Post*.'

'*What* did?'

'The death of Sir William Hellerslyke, Bt.'

It was a new one on Lestrade. 'Go on,' he shrugged.

'He was found dead two weeks ago. In the saddle.'

'In the saddle?'

'Cadaveric spasm, the coroner reckoned. Looked for all the world as if he was on picquet duty.'

'A soldier, eh?'

Blue looked at his erstwhile colleague. Little doubts began to butterfly around in Boyd's brain. Had his choice been a sound one?

'The Yorkshire Hussars. They were – and still are – on manoeuvres nearby.'

'You think this Hellerslyke was murdered?'

'I'm sure of it. Rigid in the saddle, he was.'

'Cause of death?'

'Poisoning.'

'Type?'

'Now, there's the queer thing. Phosporus, the coroner said. Personally, I think he's bluffing. Leaves no trace you see.'

'Yes it does, Boyd. It glows in the dark.'

Blue looked at Lestrade and a snigger escaped in spite of himself. 'Get away!' he roared.

'I'm serious, Boyd.' It was Lestrade's turn to whisper. 'Twelve hours or so after death, the corpse gives off a very definite phosphorescent glow.'

'Well, I'm damned.' Blue sat back in his chair. 'Of course, I thought he'd choked at first.'

'Choked?'

'Yes, he had a locket in his teeth, wedged by the action of his jaws.'

Lestrade's chelsea landed squarely in his tea cup. 'Did you say a locket? In his mouth?'

'Yes. It's damned odd, isn't it?'

'Odder than you know, Boyd.' Lestrade fished the soggy cake out. 'What's your problem?'

'The county set,' said Blue. 'They're a close lot. To use the local vernacular, "See Nowt, Do Nowt, Say Nowt".'

'Which means they aren't very helpful?' Lestrade translated.

'Quite. I've visited the camp, of course. Made the usual enquiries. Went to Hellerslyke's home at Goathland. Nothing. Nobody knows a damned thing. But the poison isn't only in Hellerslyke, Sholto. It's in the air. I can smell it.'

'So you need a new face?'

'Exactly. I scratched around and thought of you.'

'Naturally,' Lestrade said. 'So what's your plan?'

'The Hussars have one more week of manoeuvres, including Hellerslyke's funeral tomorrow. Half Yorkshire will be there. Full regimental honours etcetera, etcetera.'

'How do I fit in?'

'Fit is the operative word,' Blue beamed, 'and I hope you will. How's your sabre drill?'

'My what?' Lestrade froze. He hadn't touched a sword in three years and then it had been an emergency. And the dark days of cutlass drill with the City of London force were long ago and far away.

'Here.' Blue slipped a key under the table to Lestrade. 'Room sixty-one, the White Swan Hotel. I've booked you in as Lieutenant Lister, Duke of Lancaster's Own Yeomanry. You're still using the old alias?'

Lestrade was annoyed. 'I'm annoyed, Boyd,' he confessed. 'Elephants and old policemen never forget, eh?'

'Less of the old, Lestrade. I'm forty-three, same as you.'

'Haven't done very well, have I? A lieutenant at forty-three?' Lestrade was checking his credentials.

'Doesn't work that way in the Yeomanry,' Blue told him. 'Who you are, not what, etcetera, etcetera. When you get to your room, you'll find a tin trunk under the bed. It contains all the uniforms you'll need.'

'Uniforms?' Lestrade panicked at the thought of more than one.

'Don't worry. In the trunk you'll also find a book of Dress Regulations. It'll tell you what to wear, when. There's also a Cavalry Drill Book for 1885.'

'Marvellous!' grunted Lestrade. 'Let's just hope they haven't changed the rules since then!'

'Come, come, Lestrade. Horses still have a leg at each corner, you know.'

'That's about all I do know about horses. Isn't there another way of doing this, Boyd?'

'Well, I thought of getting you in as a newspaperman, but they wouldn't tell a journalist any more than they told me. Less, perhaps. Whereas, a brother officer . . .'

'If my history serves me correctly,' Lestrade sneaked a sugar lump from the bowl, 'wasn't there a bit of a punch-up between Yorkshire and Lancashire?'

'You're talking about the Wars of the Roses, Lestrade,' Boyd reassured him. 'All rather a long time ago. I wouldn't worry. Here,' Blue handed him a large envelope.

'What's this?'

'It's a letter of introduction from your colonel to theirs. And a thoughtfully provided crape armband for tomorrow's service. The Minster, ten sharp. I'll be there, of course. Not that you'll be acknowledging me, Sholto, will you?'

'Oh ye of little faith.' Lestrade clicked his tongue.

'Report to the colonel tonight. Lord Bolton. He's staying at the Royal. And Sholto . . . wear your uniform. An officer of the Duke of Lancaster's Own wouldn't be seen dead in mufti like you're wearing.'

Lestrade bowed with a beam.

'All this,' he waved the envelope, 'and the uniform. How did you get it?'

'Let's just say the colonel of the Duke of Lancaster's Own owes me a favour.' Blue patted the side of his nose with his finger. 'I've been as thorough as I can, Sholto. But I need a face that's unknown and a mind that's sharp. I decided to settle for half that. Once you're at the camp, you're on your own. Don't expect any boys in blue . . . er . . .' He cursed himself for using the phrase. 'Any help from me or mine. The Yorkshire Constabulary have done their bit. It's up to you, now. Will you do it?'

Lestrade looked at the crape armband in the envelope, 'Tell me,' he said, 'do officers of the Duke of Lancaster's Own Yeomanry dress to the right or the left?'

6

A Horseman Riding By

There was no answer to Lestrade's knock at the door, but the giggling from within told him the room was occupied and he pushed it open. An elderly man with white hair and a military moustache struggled to his feet, stuffing yards of shirt into his trousers and throwing a comely lass off his lap.

'Er . . . that will be all for dictation tonight, Miss Hard . . . er . . . castle. Same time tomorrow, eh? And don't forget your pencil, what?'

The girl brushed past Lestrade, stuffing extraneous areas of bosom into her corselet.

'Er . . . memoirs.' The old man rummaged for his smoking jacket. 'Miss Hard . . . er . . . Parcel is taking dictation.'

'I see, sir.' Lestrade clicked his heels and saluted, the stab of his fingers on his gilt helmet forcing the chin-chain rather painfully into his lip.

'Er . . . as you were . . .' The old man waved at him in what passed among the aristocracy for a salute. 'Lieutenant . . . er . . . ?'

'Lister, sir.' Lestrade stood as straight as he knew how.

'Mister what?'

'No, sir. Lister. Lieutenant Lister, Duke of Lancaster's Own Yeomanry.'

The old man peered closer. 'Good God, yes. So you are. How's old Ellesmere?'

'Er . . . fine, thank you, sir. Nicest part of the canal, I always think.'

'Eh? No, no,' the old man chuckled until his apoplexy got the better of him and he subsided into an armchair. 'No, not the place. Your colonel, Frank Egerton.'

Blank.

'The Third Earl of Ellesmere,' the old man persisted.

'Ah, yes, sir. Of course.' Lestrade fumbled with the fastenings of his elaborate sabretache, only to get his fingers inextricably woven into his sword knot. In the end, he did the only thing left open to him and tripped headlong over his sword, lobbing his helmet into the waste-paper basket.

'Have a care, Hamster,' the old man said, steadying the officer.

'I have a letter from him, sir.' At last he pulled it out. 'Addressed to you, requesting that I may watch the manoeuvres of the Yorkshire Hussars for the remainder of their camp.'

'Really? Good God.' The old man rummaged on the dressing table for his pince-nez, stuffing various ladies' fol-de-rols into his pockets as he came across them, 'Tut, tut,' he said, in case Lestrade had noticed, 'I really must have a word with Lady Bolton. Very careless of her to leave her . . . er . . . things around. You married, Dempster?'

'Widowed, sir.'

'Ah, condolences etcetera, etcetera. How long with the Duke's Own?'

'Ooh, a little while now, sir.'

'How's young Rutherford? Not so young now, I suppose?'

'Not for me to say, sir.'

'Shrewd answer. Loyal to one's major, eh? I like that in a subaltern. Where are your estates?'

'Um . . . Lancashire, sir.' Lestrade thought it best to stay as vague as he could.

'Quite.' The colonel looked over his pince-nez. 'Well, this all seems in order.' He discarded the letter. 'So old Ellesmere's sent you to see some *real* soldiers in action, eh? When can you start?'

'Tomorrow, sir. If that's convenient.'

'Ah, problem there, Twister. Funeral. Willie Hellerslyke, B Troop. Camp suspended.'

'Of course,' said Lestrade. 'I heard about poor Captain Hellerslyke, sir. Perhaps I could pay my respects?'

'Of course, of course. The Minster. Ten sharp. Full regimentals of course. Look forward to having you on the camp.'

'Thank you, sir.' Lestrade saluted with a little more confidence now. 'Sorry to have interrupted your . . . er . . . memoirs.'

'What? Oh, all right, dear boy. All right. Hard to find at my age, y'see.'

'What is, sir?'

'Mmm? Er . . . good secretarial help, what else? Good night to you.'

It had been raining at the funeral of Captain Sir William Hellerslyke, Bt. Lestrade stood out like a sore thumb in his scarlet tunic and white plumed helmet. Everybody else appeared to be wearing greatcoats and forage caps. Unfortunately, the favour which the Third Earl of Ellesmere apparently owed to the Chief Inspector did not extend to overcoats, so Lestrade stood with the wet horsehair slapping round his face and the red dye from his sleeve running over his black crape armband.

The Yorkshire Hussars lined the route to the Minster, massive and grey in its medieval grandeur, and the Yorkshire Hussars bore the coffin, draped with the rose and crown emblem saved from looking like a pub sign by the majesty of the Princess of Wales's feathers. Behind, boots reversed in the stirrups, the dead officer's charger, shabraqued and throat-plumed, clattered over the cobbles.

Lestrade scanned the faces as he had countless times at other funerals. Grey anonymous eyes above grey anonymous moustaches. Blobby noses under dripping peaks. The officers clustered together like conspirators, but Lestrade's alien uniform was probably the cause of that. A bevy of bowlers entered at the South door and Lestrade recognized the one a foot below the others as belonging to Little Boyd Blue. Then it was caps off and a trumpet fanfare burst on to Lestrade's ear causing him to drop his helmet. Why did he have to be standing next to the Trumpet Major? And the Archbishop himself intoned 'For Man that is born of Woman hath but a short time to live . . .'

On the following day, which dawned deep and crisp and

even, everybody but Lestrade had a field day. He could have predicted it wouldn't go well when being introduced to the officers of the Yorkshire Hussars.

'I didn't know the Duke of Lancaster's wore their pouch belts over *that* shoulder,' one of them said.

'Er . . . a new field order,' Lestrade bluffed. 'Personally, I feel damned uncomfortable wearing it this way.'

He prayed everything else was in order. At least, glancing briefly down, each buttonhole of his patrols had a button in it. Conversely, the wind didn't half whistle around the upright side of his slouch hat.

'What do you think of the new Martini?' another asked.

'Um . . . well, I'm a brandy man, myself.'

There was an awful silence. 'Oh, very droll, Lister. I was referring to the new rifle.'

'Ah, *that* Martini.' Lestrade felt the ground shifting beneath him.

'Ah, Sar'n't Major,' the officer turned to the NCO, 'Lieutenant Lister's charger.'

The beast the sergeant major had brought was a glossy black animal, and from what Lestrade remembered of his mounted duty days, about forty-three hands high. Its eyes were those of a deadly snake and its teeth the size and colour of tombstones.

'No, really, I'll just observe.' Lestrade stood back, folding his arms to show his contentment.

'We couldn't allow it,' the officer insisted. 'Knew you'd like to ride. Put old Hellerslyke's troop through their paces, what?'

'Oh, I couldn't possibly . . .'

But Lestrade found himself being lifted bodily into the saddle. It was just as well. He couldn't possibly have got up there by himself.

'His name's Minstrel, sir,' the sergeant major told him. 'Answers to t'name of Minnie. 'Old 'is reins, sir. Steady. Steady. He's a bugger on t'turns. Oh, and watch it wi'sword. If you're a bit on t'late side wi' right protect, he'll 'ave yer 'and off. Goo on, Minnie. Goo on.'

The animal wheeled away from the knot of officers and Lestrade did his best to look comfortable. Thighs that pounded up and down the stairs of omnibuses were not used to gripping girths. He prayed and somehow he stayed.

An officer of Hussars cantered alongside him, thrusting out a hand. Lestrade grinned but kept both his hands firmly on the reins.

'Percival Daubney,' the officer shouted above the jingling bits. 'I'm the adjutant.'

'Sholto Lister,' Lestrade said, his teeth as clenched as his thighs.

'Ah, you're the chappie from the Duke of Lancaster's. Giving us the once over, eh?'

Once would certainly be enough, Lestrade thought.

'Care to ride with Hellerslyke's troop for the morning?'

'Well, I wouldn't want to spoil the show,' Lestrade said.

'My dear chap, not in the slightest. Come on,' and the adjutant lashed his animal's flanks and galloped across the open moorland, making green tracks in the frosted field. He wheeled into place in front of Hellerslyke's troop who came to attention in their saddles, sword blades erect.

Lestrade dithered. On mounted duty with the City of London constabulary he had only ever been one of the line, never leading it. Then, inspiration hit him and he tugged on the right rein. Astonishingly, the animal turned sharply about face.

'Men,' he shouted. Minnie's ears pricked up and the beast backed up a little. 'I know you have recently lost your commanding officer. I know too that Captain Hellerslyke would have thought it fitting that Lieutenant Daubney should lead the troop this morning. Lieutenant Daubney.' Lestrade threw out his arm in a wild gesture and instantly regretted it. Minnie swerved violently and snapped at Lestrade's right boot. Hardly surprising as it was up the animal's nostril at the time.

'Er . . . very well.' Daubney accepted and drew his sword.

Lestrade tried to do likewise but the sword knot twisted itself round his fingers and he dropped it.

'Corporal,' he shouted over his shoulder, for he could not turn the horse again, 'how's your tent-pegging?'

The astonished NCO urged his horse forward.

'Not bad, sir,' he saluted.

'There you go, then.' Lestrade pointed to the sword as quickly as he could before gripping the pommel again. His knuckles showed white even through the brown hogskin of his gloves,

'Just a little test we give them in the Duke of Lancaster's,' he muttered to Daubney.

'Ah, very good. Very good. Yes. Well, double up, corporal.'

The NCO wheeled his mount's head and cantered some yards from the troop. To the encouraging shouts of the men, he galloped forward, crouching low over the horse's neck, and then suddenly straightening as he thundered past Lestrade, threw the sword to him. With a dexterity which surprised him, the inspector-turned-lieutenant caught the thing, albeit by the blade, and he bit his tongue to avoid crying out.

'Smartly done, corporal,' he winced.

'B Troop,' shouted Daubney. 'Threes right,' and the bugle call ordered the turn.

'Guest of honour ahead,' Daubney called, 'on the rostrum with the colonel. Close order formation. The troop will advance. Walk. March. Trot.'

Lestrade was still trying to slope his sword as Daubney had when he felt the horses of the first rank crash into his rear. Minnie bucked and lashed out with his hind hoofs and there was a moment of panic. It was doubly unfortunate that the guest of honour on the rostrum with the colonel was Sir George Wombwell, Bt., very late of the Seventeeth Lancers, who had ridden down the Valley of Death with the Gallant Six Hundred. The old baronet's eyes narrowed in the frosty air as B Troop advanced with the rattle of sabres.

'Who's that on the black?' he asked Lord Bolton.

'Chap from the Duke of Lancaster's, George,' the colonel told him. 'Name of Spinster.'

'Damned curious name,' Wombwell observed.

'Damned curious rider,' Bolton commented.

'Rides like a bloody policeman,' Wombwell ventured.

'Well, that's the Duke of Lancaster's for you. Frank Ellesmere never was much of a judge of men.'

And Lestrade whirled past them, clinging on for dear life, the blunt side of the sword blade wearing a distinct groove in his shoulder.

Had anyone told Lestrade how good a bath under canvas could be, he would not have believed them. He smelt of horses, his legs wobbled, his backside felt like a hedgehog that had recently met a steamroller. Half of his right glove had gone, along with his leather sword knot, for Lestrade had not heeded the sergeant major's advice and his right protect had been a fraction late. Minnie would have swallowed his hand as well had not Lestrade dropped his sword entirely and, without being asked, the talented corporal of B Troop had raced to the rescue, leaned out over his saddle and flicked the weapon up from the ground.

Now, at last, Lestrade could soak his cares away and slowly the feeling in his body came back to him.

'Champagne, Lister?' the adjutant popped his head around the tent flap.

'Er . . . thank you.'

Lestrade had to confess to himself he had never drunk champagne in the bath before. Or perhaps this was the new Martini the other officers had been talking about. The adjutant popped his cork and Lestrade saw his chance to pop some questions.

'Tell me about Captain Hellerslyke,' he said.

'Willie?' Daubney pulled up a camp stool and straddled it. Lestrade couldn't see how the man's buttocks coped at all. 'Why do you ask?' He poured Lestrade a glass.

'I think I met him once. At Lady . . .' and he drowned the fictitious name in the bubbles as he sipped.

'Would that have been in Southport, I wonder?'

'Very possibly,' bluffed Lestrade, desperately trying to recreate the relevant atlas page in the curling steam.

'He had a villa at Southport. And another at Scarborough.'

'Did you know him well?'

'Not really. We shot together a few times, but essentially it was only at Camp we met. You know how things are in the Yeomanry . . .' and he guffawed, slapping his knee.

'Rather!' Lestrade guffawed too, but in trying to slap his knee soaked them both. 'Sorry.'

'You were at the funeral, weren't you?'

'Thought I ought. Joining a chap's unit for a few days and so on. Least I could do.' He was starting to enjoy the plum which was rolling around in his mouth. He almost sounded genteel in a proletarian sort of way.

'Fine show. Did you enjoy your ride today?'

'Marvellous,' Lestrade lied, 'marvellous. They're a fine body of men.'

'The best,' he said. 'You've nothing like them your side of the Pennines, eh?'

Lestrade guffawed again. His jaw was starting to feel like his arse.

'I hear Hellerslyke died rather oddly.'

'Damned oddly.' Daubney glanced around, then crouched over the soaking man. 'Foul play, of course.'

'No!' Lestrade did his best to look horrified.

'Police were called in.'

'Local chaps?'

'Some idiot called Blue. If you ask me, they should have sent for the Yard.'

'Yard?' Lestrade played the ignorant. He'd had years of experience.

'Scotland Yard.'

'Ah, yes, of course. Any good, are they?'

'Well, there is one chap I've heard of. Have you ever read any of those tales of that Sherlock Holmes chappie?'

'One or two,' Lestrade lied.

'Who wrote those, now? I'm no good on novelists.'

'Er . . . Conan Doyle, wasn't it?'

'That's right. Conan Doyle. Well, he uses this chappie I'm thinking of.'

'Oh?' Lestrade's ego began to soar.

'Of course, typical of damned novelists, he does the policeman down.'

'Really?'

'Yes. Makes him out to be a useless boundah, always getting the wrong man and so on. Ludicrous! Now, what was his name?'

'Er . . . Lestrade or something, wasn't it?'

'That's right. Well, I happen to know he's a really first-class chap.'

'Indeed?' Lestrade began to twirl his unwaxed moustache.

'And I happen to know something else. Lestrade is only a *nom de crime*, as it were.'

'Oh?'

'Yes. His real name's Abberline. He's the pride of the Yard!'

Lestrade choked on his champagne.

'Steady, Lister. Hate to see you go the way old Willie did!'

'How . . .' Lestrade's screech took a little while to find its level, 'how did he go, in fact?'

'Well.' Daubney topped up their glasses. 'It was Lady Day.'

'Lady Day?'

'Oh, sorry. A custom we have here in the Yorkshire Hussars. Twice during the month of manoeuvres we have a sort of open day – Lady Day because the ladies, wives, sweethearts and so on, are allowed to visit. We had a splendid luncheon in the marquee. Colonel was in fine form, pinching posteriors and so on. Well, that's the old man for you.'

'And Hellerslyke?'

'His usual self. At least he was until . . .'

'Yes?' Lestrade sat upright in the frothy water.

'Well, I'd just refilled our glasses. My guest was a Miss Barlow, a bit of all right, I can tell you . . .' He guffawed.

'Quite. Quite. What of Hellerslyke?'

'Well, he suddenly brushed past Henrietta . . . Miss Barlow, in a rather brusque manner. I said, "Steady old boy" and he had the grace to apologize, but his face was dark as thunder.'

'Do you know why?'

'Well, he kept glancing backwards over his shoulder. As though . . .'

'His pouch belt was slipping?' Lestrade was still playing the cavalry officer.

'As though he was afraid of something.'

'Did he talk about it?'

'He only said he couldn't believe it.'

'Couldn't believe what?'

'Well, that's just it. I don't know. He said it twice, "I don't believe it", just like that.'

'When did you see him last?'

'Not again until the picquets found him. He left the marquee there and then and strode off to his horse.'

'Was that usual? To leave a Lady Day luncheon?'

'No. *I* was the duty officer. Willie should have stayed there and entertained the ladies.'

'Did he have any guests?'

'Oh, yes.' Daubney guffawed. 'Three, in fact. Rather a one for the ladies, our Willie.'

'Was he now?'

'Look here.' The affable adjutant was beginning to see things more clearly through the steam. 'You're askin' an awful lot of questions. Not a peeler, are you?' He guffawed.

Lestrade guffawed even more heartily. 'Sorry,' he said. 'Know what my nickname is in the Duke of Lancaster's? Nosey. Nosey Lister.'

'Haw! Haw!' Daubney bellowed, flicking Lestrade across the face with his gloves. 'And you've barely got one, have you? Well, must fly. See you in the mess tent. Dinner's at eight. Got your mess kit?'

'Er . . . yes.' Lestrade thought he'd seen that listed in his trunk.

'By the way.' Daubney paused on his way out. 'You haven't a batman, have you? I'll get you Private Robbin. He'll lay things out for you. Toodlepip!' and he vanished in a cloud of horse liniment.

Lestrade learned nothing from Private Robbin about the sort of man Captain Hellerslyke had been. After all, Yeomanry Camp lasted for a month each year and apart from occasional Review Days, the men of the Yorkshire Hussars scattered to the corners of their large and very draughty county. At least, however, Private Robbin was more *au fait* than Lestrade in the manner of fastening mess dress and he laced up the blue vest accordingly and buffed the scarlet jacket with vigour. It might have been better, as Lestrade pointed out, if he had used a brush.

''Course, I found 'im, y'know.' Robbin huffed on Lestrade's shoulder cords.

'Captain Hellerslyke? '

'Aye.'

'What time was this?'

'Ee, it were near midnight.'

'Where, exactly?'

'In t'woods, back o't'camp.'

'Should Captain Hellerslyke have been there at that hour?'

''Appen,' the private nodded, ''e were on picquet duty.

Should have been relieved at eleven. Only no one could find 'im. We all searched in all t'directions of t'compass. Reckon 'e be off in York after t'Lady Day.'

'Why?' Lestrade tied the black armband on himself. 'Was that the custom for officers?'

Robbin adjusted his collar and closed to Lestrade. 'T'ain't for me to say, y'understand, but it were for 'im, aye. Proper ladies' man, they said.'

'They?'

'Folk, like. Nowt so queer as folk, tha knows.'

Lestrade had noticed that.

'So you expected him to be with a lady in York?'

'Aye. I know I shouldn't speak ill o't'dead, but there it is. No changin' it now. Any road up, I saw 'im, sittin' on 'is 'orse, 'e were. T'animal were munchin' t'grass as though nothin' 'ad 'appened.'

'But it had?'

"Appen,' Robbin confirmed. 'I said, "'Owdo, sir. Parky tonight, i'n't it?"'

'And what did he say?'

'Bugger all. 'E were dead.'

'But still in the saddle? Rigor mortis?'

'Well, that's as maybe, but 'e were bloody stiff an' all. And another thing, 'e 'ad this stuff down 'is jacket, all glowin' in the dark it were.'

'Phosphorus,' murmured Lestrade.

'Eh?' Robbin blinked.

'It was vomit, private,' Lestrade said, secretly admiring the cut of his jib in the mirror in the tent. 'Captain Hellerslyke had been poisoned with phosphorus. It glows in the dark.'

'Well, I never . . .' Robbin's voice trailed away.

'Probably not.' Lestrade tapped the man's shoulder. 'Or you'd be dead now. Time for dinner?'

He didn't learn much at dinner. Someone thought they ought to beg Sir George Wombwell for the umpteenth time to tell the story of the Light Brigade and Colonel Lord Bolton had to be nudged periodically during the telling of it as his snoring was making the silver rattle. At one point, Lestrade dropped the salt-cellar, only to have it scooped up in a deft movement by the tent-pegging corporal from B Troop.

The wine flowed and the cigar smoke curled and then, when the colonel and his guest were gone, the adjutant came up to Lestrade.

'You wanted to know about Willie Hellerslyke,' he said, stern-faced.

Lestrade searched the man's face. He had ridden headlong into traps before now. 'I was just idly curious,' he said. 'Nothing more.'

'Well, come with me. You might learn something.'

The adjutant led him through a maze of tent flaps and out into the chill night air. From the camp fires of the men, a fiddle had struck up a jaunty Yorkshire tune and the clap of hands and stamp of boots began to accompany it. From the horse-lines, the odd snort and stamp as the animals settled down to the autumn night with its promise of frost and stars. He led Lestrade up the hill on to the level and through the French windows of the great house that overlooked the park. From the city in the distance, the bell of the Minster chimed the hour. Dead midnight.

In the hall of the house, the furniture was arrayed as though for a trial. More spacious and comfortable than the Bailey, certainly, but essentially for the same purpose. Behind a large, leather-topped desk at one end sat three officers whom Lestrade recognized as the majors of the regiment.

Around the walls sat brother officers, still wearing their mess kits, still smoking their cigars.

A nod from the senior major, Alfred Myndup, and three more officers entered, two in mess dress flanking a third in levee order, the dim lights flaring on the silver lace of his jacket. He unhooked his busby and placed it on the desk beside a solitary chair. Then the sword which he unbuckled from its slings and placed out of the scabbard on the majors' desk.

'I spy strangers.' Another major pointed to Lestrade.

'Lieutenant Daubney,' Myndup barked, 'who is this gentleman?'

Daubney stood up. 'Lieutenant Lister, sir, Duke of Lancaster's Own Yeomanry. He believes he knew Captain Hellerslyke, sir, and as such I believed he ought to be present.'

Myndup ruminated. The quail was not being kind. 'Gentlemen,' he said, 'do we want to wash our dirty linen in public?'

The three majors' heads bent together and broke again. Myndup addressed the officer in full uniform. 'Lieutenant Hardinge, do you have any objection to Lieutenant Lister's presence?'

Hardinge looked at Lestrade. 'I have nothing to hide,' he said firmly.

'So be it. Lieutenant Lister, you may stay.'

'Thank you, sir,' Lestrade nodded.

'Lieutenant George Blisworth Hardinge,' Myndup faced the man in the dock, 'you have requested a hearing before your brother officers of the Princess Alexandra's Own Yorkshire Hussars in order to clear your name of the murder of Captain William Hellerslyke of this regiment on the fourth instant.'

Lestrade sat up.

'You are aware that, as a Yeomanry regiment, we are not empowered to hold courts martial of this kind and that no decision by this court can be regarded as binding.'

'I am aware,' Hardinge answered.

'And as such, we shall not be following the procedure as laid down regarding courts martial in Her Majesty's Regulations?'

'I am aware,' Hardinge repeated.

'Do you have a prisoner's friend, or do you intend to conduct your own defence?'

'I will defend myself,' Hardinge said.

'Captain Kilcommons,' Myndup sat back, 'you may proceed.'

A tall, sharp man emerged from the shadows at the far side of the room. He fitted a monocle into his left eye socket and stood looking at Lestrade for some time.

'Lieutenant Hardinge, what was your relationship with the deceased?' he asked.

'Brother officer,' Hardinge answered.

'He was a superior officer?' Kilcommons queried.

'Yes.'

'Was there any other relationship?'

'No.'

'How long had you known William Hellerslyke?'

'For about five years.'

'Before you joined the regiment, in fact?'

'Yes.'

'In what context did you meet him?'

'On a shooting weekend, near Scarborough, I believe.'

'What opinion did you form of the man?'

'I liked him,' said Hardinge, 'at first.'

'At first?'

Hardinge slammed his fist on to the table at his side. 'It is common knowledge, Captain, that William Hellerslyke seduced my sister. That seduction led to her death by suicide six months ago. For that, sir, I hated William Hellerslyke.'

'Hated him enough to kill him?' Kilcommons saw his opening, and pounced.

'Yes!' Hardinge was on his feet.

'Lieutenant!' Myndup pounded the desk with his gavel. 'May I remind you that we are all gentlemen here? You requested this hearing. Captain Kilcommons is merely playing devil's advocate. There is nothing personal in his remarks. Please remember that and conduct yourself accordingly.'

'Yes, sir.' Hardinge subsided. 'I apologize.'

'On the day Captain Hellerslyke died,' Kilcommons began to walk around, enjoying, it seemed to Lestrade, the limelight, 'were you in the luncheon party at midday?'

'I was.'

Kilcommons produced a sheaf of paper. 'I have here, Mr President,' he addressed Myndup, 'copies of the report of the County Coroner. May I submit them?'

Myndup nodded and accepted the papers, as did his fellow judges and Daubney. As adjutant, the lieutenant was frantically scratching down in note form all that proceeded. Lestrade took advantage of his busyness to glance at the report. Phosphorus poisoning. Probably ingested in wine. For Robbin to have found Hellerslyke dead and stiff at midnight, he must have drunk the deadly potion at about midday.

'Captain Hellerslyke died of phosphorus poisoning,' Kilcommons told the court, 'adminstered probably in his luncheon wine and probably by someone in the luncheon marquee.'

'How many people were there?'

All eyes in the court turned to the questioner. The adjutant looked askance at the man beside him.

'Lieutenant . . . er . . . Lister,' Major Myndup said, 'it is highly irregular for interruptions to come from the court. Especially, if I may make so bold, from a strange officer.'

'Forgive me, m'lud . . . er . . . Mr President. May I beg the court's indulgence and converse with Lieutenant Hardinge for a moment?'

Murmurs and rumblings ran the length of the room.

'Mr President, I must protest . . .' Kilcommons began, but Myndup's raised hand stopped him as the judges' heads nodded together again.

'Mr Hardinge,' he said, 'do you wish this gentleman to have converse with you?'

As nonplussed as anyone else, Hardinge agreed. Lestrade led him to the darkened end of the room, as far from the others as he could.

'Mr Hardinge, I am sticking my neck out as far as I dare. My name is not Lister, it's Lestrade. And I'm not a Yeomanry officer, I'm an inspector of Scotland Yard.'

'What?'

'I can't explain it all now, but I'm as anxious to find the murderer of Willie Hellerslyke as you are.'

'Why are you telling me this? Why the imposture?' Hardinge hissed.

Lestrade looked blanked.

'The cover,' Hardinge simplified it for him.

'The cover was the idea of the Yorkshire police.'

'So you're playing the spy, not quite in mufti?'

'You might say so. I'm telling you this because you need help.'

'I can clear myself.'

'Can you? This Kilcommons; what does he do for a living?'

'He's a barrister.'

Lestrade nodded grimly. 'I thought so. He has the look of the breed. Do you think this trumped-up schoolboy court is going to do you any good? Whatever evidence you give, they aren't going to forget it.'

'I've taken no oath,' Hardinge reminded him.

'That doesn't matter. By requesting this nonsense, you've laid yourself open. What's to stop Kilcommons or Myndup or anyone else from going to the police?'

'They wouldn't,' Hardinge insisted.

'Wouldn't they?'

'No. They are my brother officers. My peers. I've asked for this hearing.'

'Why?'

'To clear my name.'

'If these men are your brother officers they wouldn't expect you to clear your name. There'd be no point if they really trusted you. Would there?'

'Er . . . no . . . I suppose . . .'

Lestrade was in full flight, albeit in a whisper. 'And where do you suppose Kilcommons got those coroner's reports? This gentlemen's honour court of yours is turning a bit professional, Mr Hardinge, and if I'm any judge, a bit nasty.'

'What can I do?' Hardinge saw the point.

'Appoint me as . . . what do you people call it? Prisoner's friend? Let me defend you. Tell the court I am a barrister too. For god's sake, do it.'

'But you're not a lawyer.'

Lestrade fumed. 'And you're too honest, Mr Hardinge. Take my word for it, I've seen more cases of murder than you've had hot dinners.'

'Do you know enough about this one?' Hardinge asked.

It was a pertinent question, but Lestrade hadn't time to answer it. 'I'll have to think on my feet,' he said. It would be an unusual experience.

'Mr President.' Hardinge returned to the centre of the court. 'I should like to appoint Lieutenant . . . Lister . . . to prisoner's friend.'

Hubbub.

'Mr President, this cannot be . . .' Kilcommons protested. 'A strange officer.'

Myndup looked at his fellow judges then at Hardinge and Lestrade. 'Mr Lister, what are your qualifications to take up this appointment?'

'I am a barrister, sir,' Lestrade lied.

Kilcommons' monocle tumbled from his eye. Daubney hoped fervently that Lister was a better lawyer than he was rider.

'I am going to allow it,' said Myndup, much to Kilcommons' disgust, 'but, Mr Lister, I can give you no time to acquaint yourself with the details of the case.'

'Very well,' said Lestrade.

'Mr Kilcommons.' Myndup reconvened the court. Lestrade stripped off his jacket and sat there in shirt-sleeves and mess vest, doggedly watching his adversary's every move.

'Did you, on the day of Captain Hellerslyke's death, engage him in conversation?'

'I hadn't spoken to William Hellerslyke since the day after my sister died.'

'The day after?' Kilcommons scented blood and went for it.

Hardinge hesitated. 'I called on William Hellerslyke at his villa in Scarborough.'

'For what purpose?'

'I called him out.'

'Called him out?' Kilcommons worried him like a terrier. 'Do you mean challenged him to a duel?'

'Yes.'

'In other words you tried to kill him?'

'Objection!' Lestrade was on his feet.

'Mr Lister.' Myndup tapped with his gavel. 'I am not at all sure that objections raised in a criminal proceeding are applicable at this hearing.'

'Mr President,' Lestrade countered, 'my client's reputation is at stake. Mr Kilcommons is leading him. That is contrary to any law in the land.'

'How would you class a duel, Mr Lister,' Kilcommons snapped, 'if not attempted murder?'

'A duel, Mr Kilcommons, while being illegal under British law, is an affair of honour. The object is to satisfy that honour, not to kill.' Harry Bandicoot had taught Lestrade that a long time ago. He had not forgotten it. It was the only useful piece of knowledge Harry had ever imparted.

'Objection sustained, then.' Myndup was surprised that this scruffy-looking bad horseman could hold his own against Kilcommons. Things were getting serious.

The real barrister tried a new tack. 'What was the outcome of this affair of honour?'

'Nothing,' Hardinge told him. 'Hellerslyke refused.'

'What did you do?'

'What could I do? Under the law, my sister killed herself. Threw herself off Aysgarth Falls. The police couldn't touch him.

Under God, Hellerslyke was responsible. As if he had pushed her himself.'

'So your only recourse was to kill him yourself?'

'Objection!' Lestrade was on his feet again and into his stride by now. 'Counsel is badgering the accused.'

'No, I want to answer,' Hardinge interrupted. 'Yes, I wanted to kill him. I thought of it, many times. In the end, I . . . suppose I lost my nerve.'

'Until the luncheon on the day he died,' Kilcommons went on. 'I suggest, Lieutenant, that you had been waiting for your chance ever since your sister's demise. You seized your opportunity on that day to slip the poison into the captain's glass in the luncheon marquee.'

'No, I . . .'

'Lieutenant Hardinge,' Kilcommons shouted, 'I put it to you that in asking for this hearing, you have condemned yourself. Far from standing acquitted in the eyes of your brother officers you have openly admitted to a motive for killing the deceased. You also had the opportunity. And because you lost your nerve, as you put it, you carried out the act in the most cowardly way possible. You administered a poison that took long enough to kill so you were away from the scene of death. Captain Hellerslyke was out on picquet duty by the time it did its deadly work.'

Kilcommons swung away from the gaping Hardinge. 'Mr President, I submit to this court that Lieutenant Hardinge stands guilty of murder of Captain Hellerslyke and further submit that his name be struck from the roll of this illustrious regiment and civil matters be proceeded with.'

He sat down to a ripple of applause from some of those who lined the walls.

'The court recognizes Lieutenant Lister,' Myndup said, and Lestrade took Kilcommons' place in the centre.

'Mr Hardinge, how long have you been in this room?'

Everyone looked at each other. 'I don't know,' the lieutenant answered. 'Perhaps half an hour.'

'And in that time, have you had a chance to note the number of persons present?'

'Really, Mr President,' Kilcommons yawned, 'have we come here to listen to charades?'

'If the court will bear with me,' Lestrade countered, 'I wish to establish a point.'

'Very well,' said Myndup. 'Continue, Mr Hardinge.'

'About thirty, I suppose.'

'And how long were you in the luncheon marquee on the day of Captain Hellerslyke's death?'

'Over an hour,' he said.

'Long enough then to observe how many people were present?'

'I should say a hundred, perhaps two.'

'Who were these people?'

'Wives, ladies of the regiment. Some children.'

Lestrade faced the court. 'A hundred, perhaps two, any one of whom might have placed the poison into the captain's drink.'

'Oh, come, Lister,' Kilcommons intervened. 'Are you saying that a lady of the regiment killed him? Or a child perhaps?' Guffaws all round.

'You spoke of opportunity, Mr Kilcommons,' Lestrade rounded on him. 'The selfsame opportunity presented itself to anyone else in the luncheon marquee. Perhaps Major Myndup, Lieutenant Hardinge or even yourself, Captain.'

'How dare you!' Kilcommons was on his feet, fists clenched, monocle dangling ominously. A tap from Myndup's gavel defused the situation.

'Show me your hands, Lieutenant Hardinge,' Lestrade said.

'What?'

'Your hands, if you please.'

He pulled off the white, doeskin gloves and held his hands out in front of him.

'Let the record show,' he said to Daubney, 'that the accused's hands show no signs of burning.'

'Burning?' said Kilcommons. 'Why should they? What does that prove?'

'I fear you've lost us, Mr Lister,' Myndup said, seeing the confusion in the eyes of his fellow judges.

'How did you administer the phosphorus, Lieutenant?' Lestrade asked Hardinge.

'Dammit, man. I didn't.'

'Had you done, it could be done in one of two ways. The first way is to handle it in its waxen state. May it please the court, are there any pools or ponds nearby?'

Myndup consulted with the judges. 'No,' he said, 'other than the river that passes the abbey.'

'Have any horses died suddenly during camp?'

They consulted again. 'Dr Fyler, as veterinary officer to the regiment, are you aware . . . ?'

'One sore back, sir, since camp began. No other problems,' said the old officer from the corner. 'And certainly no deaths.'

'Have any explosions been reported?' Lestrade asked.

'Mr President,' Kilcommons howled, 'what is this nonsense?'

'With respect,' said Lestrade, 'one way in which phosphorus can be administered is by using it in its wax-like form . . .'

'So you said,' Kilcommons harangued him.

'In which case, it must be kept under water. If there are no ponds or pools nearby it cannot have been kept close at hand. The running water of a river would wash it away. And as no horses have died, it cannot have been kept in a horse trough.'

'Why under water?' Kilcommons demanded.

'Because phosphorus is highly comestible,' said Lestrade, deepening the confusion. 'Whoever handles it in that form would be risking an explosion on contact with air. At very least, his hands would be burned.'

Murmurs ran round the room.

'There is another way,' Lestrade told them. 'Mr President, may I indulge the court's patience still further and ask an orderly to get something?'

'Objection, Mr President,' Kilcommons interrupted. 'We cannot allow Other Ranks to be privy to any of this.'

'He's correct, Mr Lister. Protocol must serve – whatever the customs of your regiment, sir, here it will not do,' Myndup ruled. 'However, Mr Daubney, perhaps . . .'

'Certainly, sir.'

Lestrade whispered hurriedly to the adjutant who looked at him oddly and left the court.

Within a few frozen minutes he was back, clutching a tin.

'This', said Lestrade, 'is the other way phosphorus can be administered. It is a tin of Ratto rat poison, gentlemen. Your maidservants will be familiar with it. It costs twopence-halfpenny from any hardware shop or chemist and I daresay it lies among the dust of many of your outhouses; which is where, I would imagine, Lieutenant Daubney found this.'

The adjutant nodded.

'It contains several grains of phosphorus,' Lestrade told the court, 'enough to wipe out half of us in this room. Major,' Lestrade approached the bench, 'I notice you still have your brandy. May I ruin it for you?'

'Well, I . . . er . . .'

Lestrade flicked open the lid and tipped a tiny quantity into the balloon.

'Steady on!' echoed round the hall.

'I am not suggesting you drink it, Major,' Lestrade said, 'merely observe its colour.'

The judges did. 'It's cloudy,' said Myndup.

'And that's how it will stay,' said Lestrtade. 'A smaller quantity would cloud less, but might not be lethal.'

'What's your point, Lister?' Kilcommons examined the drink too.

'Would you drink wine that was cloudy?' Lestrade asked him.

'Well, I . . . how do we know Hellerslyke noticed?'

'We don't,' Lestrade admitted. 'Just as we don't know that Lieutenant Hardinge placed anything in his wine. Gentlemen,' Lestrade turned to the court, 'why did Mr Hardinge wait for six months to kill his man? Why not shoot him out of hand, on the road? Smash his skull with a poker in his study? Run him down in a four-in-hand? I'll tell you why, because unlike some members of this regiment,' he scowled at Kilcommons, 'Lieutenant Hardinge is a man of honour. Hellerslyke seduced his sister, jilted her and refused to take the consequences. When Mr Hardinge was unable to avenge her death honourably, he could not avenge it at all. There is as much evidence that any one of you poisoned William Hellerslyke as that Lieutenant Hardinge did it.'

He sat down to general applause. Kilcommons approached the bench. 'Mr President . . .'

But Myndup held up his hand. 'This court is dismissed,' he said. 'Lieutenant Hardinge, pick up your sword. And welcome back to the regiment.'

There was a cheering and back-slapping and hand-shaking

all round, but Lestrade noticed Kilcommons slip out of a side door and engage an Other Rank in conversation. He didn't like the look of it.

'Lister.' Hardinge stopped him as he made for the French windows. 'I owe you my honour,' he said. 'How can I thank you?'

'See me to the edge of the camp,' he said.

'Of course, but why?'

'Er . . . I'm afraid of the dark,' Lestrade said.

'How did you know all that about phosphorus?' Hardinge asked as they walked, hooking up his sword again.

'Years of experience,' Lestrade said, watching the blackness ahead.

'Mind how you go,' Hardinge said. 'The ground is a little treacherous around here. You know, you missed your way as a policeman. You'd have made a superb advocate.'

Lestrade laughed. 'I look so awful in a wig.'

'So who *did* put phosphorus in Hellerslyke's wine?' Hardinge asked. 'I'd like to shake him by the hand.'

'In his wine, nobody. As I showed in court, it would have been too visible. It was in his food, but how *his* food and no one else's is the problem. And then there's the timing. I'm not happy about it.'

'Why?'

'Well, phosphorus can kill in less than twelve hours. But it can take three or fours days. No one mentioned Hellerslyke feeling unwell before the day he died, so he must have taken it on the morning of his death.'

'Ah, you mean, not necessarily in the luncheon marquee at all?'

'Quite.'

'But how does that help us?'

'I'm not sure it does, yet.'

A commotion to their left stopped both men in their tracks. 'Mr Hardinge, sir, horse down in the lines.' A corporal came hurrying out of the darkness.

'That's the way to your tent, Lister.' Hardinge pointed ahead. 'You can't miss it. I'll join you later,' and he ran off with the corporal.

This was what Lestrade had been expecting. He even

expected what followed, but he wasn't prepared for the numbers. First one, then three, then five full dress jackets emerged from the blackness, their white frogging and silver buttons glowing in the flitting moonlight.

Lestrade took stock of the situation. The odds were five to one. His sword was in his tent. Besides, he wasn't much of a swordsman. His skill with a blade was best confined to tackling a Coburg prior to toasting it over the fire. His trusty brass knuckles, his four companions for twenty years, were in his Donegal in his hotel room. Two fists against ten. Assuming, that is, they weren't armed. Ten fingers against fifty. Or more precisely, eight fingers and two thumbs against forty and . . . He was still doing the mental arithmetic when the first blow hit him – one of the items he hadn't had time to count: a boot hit him high in the ribs and he went down. Another crashed into his kidneys and he arched his back.

'Captain Kilcommons' compliments,' snarled one of the attackers. Lestrade rolled sideways hard and brought the man down. He grabbed the barrelled sash around his waist and wrenched it off. He remembered something that old George Wombwell had been saying inside during his interminable recollections of the Charge of the Light Brigade: how a fellow officer, Captain Morris, had kept a dozen Cossacks at bay by the moulinet, a constant whirling of his sword. Lestrade did the same now with the heavy end of the sash, twirling round in a widening circle, roaring and shouting. The man whose sash he had hit him from the blind side and Lestrade swung him over his shoulder and wrapped the sash round his throat. The soldier knelt in the frost, gasping and gurgling.

'One more step, gentlemen, and I'll break his neck.' It was pure bravado, of course. Lestrade had no clue how to break a neck, but he hoped it sounded impressive. It didn't and the four of them closed on them.

'You men there!' A voice stopped and scattered them. The crouching Yeoman struggled upright, snatched back his sash and was gone.

Lieutenant Daubney arrived at the trot. 'Lister, my dear fellow, are you all right? What's going on? I'll see those men . . .'

'No,' Lestrade gasped, 'it's all right. What you could do for me is help me to your tent. I'm not sure mine's going to be very safe tonight.'

'My dear fellow, of course. You're hurt.'

Lestrade did his best to stand. 'Only a few splints' worth.' He held his ribs. 'But I'd kill for a brandy.'

7

The Wheel of Misfortune

'But apart from the broken rib, Mr Lestrade, how did you enjoy your stay with the Yorkshire Hussars?'

The inspector woke up sharply and jarred his side anew. A lovely girl with dark red hair was smiling down at him.

'I'm sorry,' he said, 'I must have dozed. Miss Hardinge?'

'Elsie,' she said, 'and don't apologize. George told me what happened. You were very brave to defend him. He's feeling particularly guilty, being called to that horse at the very moment you were attacked.'

Lestrade smiled, subsiding gratefully on to the ottoman again. 'He needn't,' he told her. 'It wasn't exactly chance, you know.'

She sat down beside him and rang the bell for tea. 'I don't understand.'

'The horse was a blind,' he said. 'A ruse to get your brother away while a few gentlemen of the Hussars used me for punching practice.'

'How dreadful,' she said. 'Will you arrest them all?'

He chuckled. 'I'm after bigger fish,' he said. 'Miss Hardinge . . .'

'Elsie,' she reminded him.

'Elsie. You were at Lady Day when William Hellerslyke died?'

'Yes, I was.'

'Did you notice anything unusual? In the morning? In the luncheon marquee?'

'I don't think so.' She frowned to remember. 'I'm pretty good at remembering details. Or so Monsieur Lamartine says.'

'Monsieur Lamartine?'

'My tutor. I attend a finishing school at Geneva, Mr Lestrade.

I have my coming out soon, you know. Oh, will you come? Say you will.'

He looked into her earnest, pleading eyes.

'Of course,' he said. 'I'd love to.'

'Good!' She clapped her hands together. 'Would this help you?'

'What?'

She bounced away from him and rummaged in one of the decks of her brother's bureau. 'This.' She held up a triumphant piece of paper. 'It's a guest list for Lady Day.'

Lestrade took it and ran his eye down the names. Half of Yorkshire seemed to have been there. Still, it began to narrow fields.

'Ah, tea. Nanny, where's Chepstow?'

'On the River Severn, missy,' the tray-carrying crone trilled, 'as you well know.'

'Oh, Nanny!' She swiped the air, narrowly missing the old girl's bombazine-encrusted shoulder. 'Nanny's little joke, Mr Lestrade. Chepstow is the name of our butler.'

'It's the way I tell 'em, missy,' the old girl croaked, her single tooth wobbling with mirth. She clattered the tray down. 'Who might you be, young man?' she asked.

Lestrade resisted the temptation to tell her.

'This is Inspector Lestrade, Nanny,' Elsie said. 'He's a friend of George's.'

'Inspector? Well, have you found my umbrella?'

'Er . . .' Lestrade wasn't following much of the conversation.

'When I was in York last, I left my umbrella on the tram. I reported it and the inspector told me he'd make it his life's work to find it. Are you one of his men?'

'Different department,' Lestrade thought it simplest to say.

Nanny grunted. 'Well, I'd better get my knitting then.'

Elsie looked alarmed. 'Why, Nanny?'

'Chepstow's handling the coal delivery,' she said. 'That's why I brought the tea. I didn't realize you was alone with a gentleman, missy. I'll get my knitting and sit with you.'

'No, Nanny.' Elsie shepherded the crone towards the door. 'Mr Lestrade is a policeman. It's all right to leave me alone with him.'

Nanny looked up, at once frightened and aghast. 'Like I left Miss Vicky alone, with that Hellerslyke?'

'Wait!' Lestrade's voice stopped them both. 'Miss . . . er . . .'

'Nanny,' said the old girl.

'Nanny.' Lestrade was gentler. He took her arm and led her to the ottoman. 'Nanny, did you know Mr Hellerslyke?'

Nanny spat contemptuously, to be answered by the metallic pinging of the firedogs.

'I see. Would you tell me what happened – between Miss Vicky and Mr Hellerslyke?'

Nanny looked up at Elsie. 'This is not for your ears, my girl. Off with you.'

Elsie's eyes flashed indignantly. 'Nanny, I'm seventeen.'

'Elsie,' Lestrade said, 'please?' and something in the iron of his voice made her go.

'I'm eighty-three,' Nanny said. 'I was Nanny to old Mr Hardinge in his day and now to his three babies. Two babies it is now.' She blew her nose on her apron so that the Sèvres on the dresser rattled. 'It's my fault, you see,' she sobbed, 'that Miss Vicky died. I shouldn't have left them alone.'

'Why?' Lestrade asked.

She looked at him hard. 'You've got kindly eyes, Mr Inspector,' she nodded, patting his hand, 'not like him. Not like Willie Hellerslyke. He only ever wanted one thing from Miss Vicky.'

'One thing?'

She nodded, swallowing back the tears. 'The One Thing that is a fate worse than death.'

'Ah,' Lestrade realized; 'that Thing.'

Nanny nodded.

'It was me she told,' she said, drying her tired old eyes. 'Elsie was away. And anyway, she's only a gel. Georgie would have been furious. She was afraid he'd have gone out after Hellerslyke with his gun. Anyway, I think she loved him. Really loved him. That's why she . . . killed herself.'

'What happened?'

Nanny sighed, wringing her gnarled old hands in her apron. 'She went out for a walk,' she said. 'I offered to go with her. She'd been strange ever since she knew she was . . . with child. I told her we'd manage. Worse things have happened, I told her. We all loved her.'

'What did she say?'

'She sat on her bed, in her bonnet and shawl, and said that was the point. *He* didn't love her. She couldn't bear that. Then she went. I watched her going out across the lawns as I'd watched her all her life. That funny little way she had, that swaying of her dress.' She breathed in deeply, fighting with the memory of it. 'It was Chepstow who found her. At the bottom of the Falls. They brought her back, her hair all wet, her dress ruined. I tried to dry it . . . to make it better. I always used to make it better,' and she fell sideways, sobbing silently.

Lestrade cradled the old woman's head for a moment, then called for Elsie, who held Nanny's head and smoothed the silver hair, whispering softly. The inspector collected his bowler and crept away.

'But I made it better in the end,' Nanny whispered in between gulps to Elsie. 'I told Coquette.'

Chepstow had loaded Lestrade's uniform trunk into the landau and George Hardinge had driven him into York. Back in the Shambles, Lestrade arrived at the supper rooms at the appointed hour. A hearty fire roared and crackled in the grate and the Barnsley chop was followed by a treacly parkin that tied itself round Lestrade's tonsils.

'So,' Blue leaned forward, 'I've fed you royally. What have you got for me?'

'I won't embarrass you, Boyd, by opening my waistcoat and shirt here in full view of Yorkshire's finest.'

'Eh?'

'A handful of Yorkshire Hussars decided to take turns to see who could kick me to death first. Must've been trying out new issue boots.'

'Good God,' Blue said, wiping the froth of his nut-brown ale from his moustache. 'Rumbled you, did they?'

'I don't think so. Let's just say I rather upset one of the officers of the regiment by siding with the scapegoat they'd got lined up for Hellerslyke's death.'

'When we talked to them, the buggers clammed up. One of them actually said, "William Who?" So we're no further forward.'

'There's this.' Lestrade produced the paper. 'A guest list of visitors on the day Hellerslyke died.'

'Good God. There's half Yorkshire on this list.'

'I thought so. Well, that's your problem, Boyd. Your boys haven't anything better to do. They can look up all those. But they won't find anything.'

'How do you know?'

'It's my guess – and it's only a guess, mind you – that whoever poisoned the late captain either used an alias or sneaked into the tent uninvited.'

'Was that possible?'

'There are nearly three hundred names on that list. They wouldn't all have fitted in the tent itself. Anyone could have mingled with the crowd, slipped in and doctored his lunch.'

'Lestrade!' a voice called across the room. It was George Hardinge.

'Mr Hardinge,' Lestrade rose with difficulty. 'Do you know Chief Inspector Blue?'

'Ah, yes. We met briefly at camp.'

'Mr Hardinge is the scapegoat I was telling you about,' Lestrade said.

'I see. You'd better join us, Mr Hardinge. Lestrade here was telling me his cover hadn't been blown and here you are. Curious.'

'Mr Hardinge was the exception,' Lestrade confessed. 'And if you receive a clandestine visit from a Mr Kilcommons with a cock-and-bull story which tries to implicate Mr Hardinge, just ignore it.'

'Sholto, I'm not sure I can.'

'Take my word for it, Boyd. This is not the man you want.'

'No, but I know a man who might be,' Hardinge said.

'Yes?' A raucous, bored voice shattered the conversation. The waitress stood over them, idly chewing her pencil stub.

'Old Peculiar,' Hardinge ordered. Lestrade assumed it was a justified insult and waited until the sulky floozie had gone.

'You interest us strangely, Mr Hardinge,' he said, blowing the froth away from his glass.

'I've just come from the old man, Lord Bolton. I tendered my resignation from the Yorkshire Hussars. Sorry, Lestrade, after all your hard work to clear me. Not to mention the pasting you took.'

Lestrade shrugged. It didn't surprise him at all.

'I realized that you were right. They were no brother officers of mine. Besides, I like the cut of the Yorkshire Dragoons better. I'll probably join them next season.'

'Are you saying Lord Bolton did it?' Boyd tried to follow the conversation's drift.

'No,' Hardinge chuckled. 'He's had his hands full with a Miss Hardmuscle for some weeks. He can't cope with much more than that. As I was leaving, Daubney, the adjutant, met me. He's about the only decent chap in the regiment, apart from the old man.'

'And?' Lestrade looked with horror as a deep bowl of brown arrived.

'Old Peculiar,' Hardinge explained. 'Try some?'

'No, thank you,' Lestrade said, a little too quickly. 'I'll stick to my parkin.' It was no more than the truth.

'Seems Hellerslyke's batman had a word with him.'

'Private Robbin?'

'Yes, that's right. He'd remembered something about the day Hellerslyke died.'

'Oh?' Lestrade and Blue leaned forward, but the aroma of the Old Peculiar drove them back.

'Hellerslyke received a present. In his tent shortly before luncheon.'

'What was it?' Lestrade asked.

'A box of chocolates. Made by Rowntree.'

'Rowntree?' Lestrade looked from one to the other.

'A local firm. I buy their Caramel Nutties. Can't leave them alone,' Blue admitted.

'Did Robbin know who'd delivered them?' Lestrade asked.

'No. But he does remember a card. On the one side it said "Because the Captain loves . . ." and on the other side "Coquette".'

'Coquette? Is that a make of chocolate?'

'I always thought it was a French tart,' Blue said. Lestrade hadn't been far wrong.

'Did Robbins know if Hellerslyke ate any?' Lestrade asked Hardinge.

'Yes, he had two or three. Robbin was a bit miffed because he didn't offer him one. And that's not all.'

'Ah?' The policemen risked the casserole to lean forward again.

'Hellerslyke said he didn't care for them. That they had a rather bitter taste.'

'Phosphorus,' the policemen chorused and looked around quickly to make sure the ruminating room had not overheard.

'These chocolates,' said Lestrade, 'can they be bought anywhere?'

'Anyone who is anyone buys them direct,' Hardinge told him. Blue had not known that, but then he wasn't anyone. 'The Rowntrees have a bijou little emporium in Walmgate.'

'Mr Hardinge, you've been of great help,' said Blue. 'Leave it to us now, please,' and he rose to go.

'Lestrade.' Hardinge took the inspector's hand. 'Though I may have given you the clue to Willie Hellerslyke's murderer, I hope you'll understand when I say I almost hope you don't catch him.'

It was bright and early on a frosty morning that Lestrade walked under the great city gateway bound for the premises of Messrs Rowntree. The smell of chocolate hit him like a sickly wall as he entered the lavish, glass-fronted door.

'Good morning, sir.' A bespectacled young man hove into view, in apron and white gloves. 'What will it be, sir? My Little Nuggets? Hazelnut Surprises? And would you care for a cup of cocoa while you ponder? A fruit gum, perhaps?'

'I'm not quite sure. A friend of mine serves with the Yorkshire Hussars, currently on manoeuvres nearby. A secret admirer sent him some of your chocolates and he said they were perfection.'

'Ah, that'll be our Perfection Confection Selection, sir,' the young man said. 'Each centre hand-crafted by our loving care, enrobed with succulent chocolate and with just a hint of brandy essence.'

'My problem . . .' Lestrade leaned on the counter confidentially and placed his elbow squarely in a tray of Mint Imperials that flew in all directions, as befitted the Empire. 'Sorry.' He helped the young man pick them up and watched amazed as he polished each one and put it back in its wrapper. 'My problem is that I didn't actually see or taste the chocolates myself. How can I be sure they are the same?'

'Perhaps your friend could spare the time to accompany you to the shop?' the young man suggested.

'Ah, I fear not. He's been called away,' Lestrade said. He did not elaborate.

'That's no problem, sir,' the young man beamed. 'We keep a careful record of personal deliveries. And of special orders.' He opened a chocolate-coloured ledger. 'When did your friend receive his chocolates?'

'Er . . . let me see. It would have been the fourth inst, I believe.'

'Very well, let me see.' He adjusted his pince-nez. 'Old Mrs Hallett bought her usual bon-bons. There was an order from the School of Dancing – hazelnut whirls. Ah, here's one – Perameles.'

'Perameles?' Lestrade repeated. 'A regular customer?'

'No. I've never heard the name before. It sounds rather Greek, don't you think?'

Lestrade spun the ledger to him. 'Perameles,' he said again. 'No Christian name. What's this?'

The young man spun the ledger back to him. 'Praline Cluster. Oh, yes, a very sound choice. Is that, I wonder, what your friend received?'

'Very possibly,' muttered Lestrade, 'but with a few additions. Is there another unusual name on that date?' They probably didn't come any more unusual than Perameles.

'No. The only other order was from Twelvetrees, a stately home not far from here. It's a monthly regular. Would you care for a box of Pralines then, Mr . . . er . . . ?'

'Lister,' said Lestrade and the young man wrote it down. He disappeared behind a velvet curtain and emerged moments later with a box wrapped in ribbon.

'Fascinating,' said Lestrade. 'How do you make them?'

'Haha,' the young man laughed, 'trade secret, I'm afraid.'

'Perhaps I could see the manager,' the inspector persisted. 'I really would like to know the ingredients and perhaps see over your premises.'

'I am Benjamin Seebohm Rowntree.' The young man straightened. 'And I'm afraid my father's answer would be the same as mine. Impossible. That will be one and sixpence please.'

Lestrade rummaged in his pockets, wondering how he could charge this to expenses. He paid up and unwrapped the ribbon. 'If I wanted to add something to these chocolates,' he said, 'how could I go about it?'

'Add something?' Rowntree's suspicions were growing. 'What do you mean?'

'Well, a liqueur, perhaps. Rather more of the brandy essence.'

'We don't make those as such, but it could be done by . . . Wait a minute. Who are you?' Realization dawned. 'Why are you asking all these questions? You're a spy, aren't you?'

'A spy?' Lestrade had long ago perfected his look of innocence. It fooled no one.

'You can't fool me with that look of innocence,' Rowntree told him. 'I've been working among the poor of York for years. I know the disingenuous when I see it. You're a spy for Terry's, aren't you? I never thought they'd stoop so low. Are you going to leave? Or do I call a policeman?'

Lestrade raised his hand. 'Thank you, Mr Rowntree. I'll see myself out,' and he leaned towards his man, 'but I'd be very careful what you call policemen.' And he grabbed his chocolates and ran.

Winter was coming on as Lestrade travelled south. There were delays at Peterborough due to railworks, but they gave him time to think. Captain William Hellerslyke, late of the Yorkshire Hussars, had a reputation as a womanizer. There was probably a trail of broken hearts and broken promises all over the Ridings. But one of them had gone astray. Victoria Hardinge had fallen pregnant – what a silly phrase, he thought again, as he had every time it crossed his mind – and when the balance of her mind was disturbed, through unrequited love, she had thrown herself into the foaming waters of Aysgarth Falls. Revenge, then, as the motive? But who was this Coquette who left him the poisoned chocolates? And were Coquette and Perameles the same person? Or two? He was still pondering this as the train pulled in, snorting and squealing, to Euston. And the last person he expected to see was Walter Dew.

'Dew.' Lestrade threw his Gladstone to the constable as he alighted on Platform Four. 'You're the last person I expected to see. As the late Mr Holmes used to say, apparently ad mausoleum, "What's afoot?"'

'It's funny you should say that, guv'nor. There's a gentleman here who's anxious to meet you.'

'How did you know when to expect me?' Lestrade asked.

'I didn't. Skinner, Lilley and I have been waiting for every train in our rest time for the past two days.'

'Nobly done, Walter.' Lestrade approved enterprise. When it came from Dew, he was rather unnerved by it, but he approved nonetheless.

'Across the road, sir.' The Yard men emerged into the raw fog of a November London. 'In the café.'

Lestrade saw behind the ornate plate glass a face he thought he knew. He sat down at the table in front of it. 'Dr Watson.' He shook the man's hand. 'It's been a long time.'

'I hate to say it, Lestrade, but it's good to see you.'

'Two teas, miss,' Lestrade ordered, observing that Watson still had his. 'This man's paying.' He pointed to Dew, who began to thrust his arm into his trousers. 'Not now, Walter,' Lestrade reminded him, 'there are ladies present. Now, doctor, what can I do for you?'

John Watson was a solid, respectable man, the wrong side of forty-seven. He had been the confidant of the late and legendary Sherlock Holmes, whose exploits were, as Lestrade and Watson spoke, being embroidered and indeed invented by Watson's co-author, another quack by the name of Conan Doyle – Conan the Barbarian as one reviewer had called him. Watson was worried.

'It is not generally known,' he confided to Lestrade, 'that I belong to a club of bicyclists. We call ourselves the Wheel of Fortune.'

'Very colourful, doctor.' Lestrade tapped Dew's wrist. The man was slurping his tea again.

'Well, to cut short a long story . . .' Watson must have been worried. This was not his usual style at all. 'One of our number has died in rather mysterious circumstances.'

'Go on,' said Lestrade.

'It was last Sunday. My Poor Law practice was very slack, so I left Dr Wyatt in charge. Bunions, smallpox, you know, the trivial things. He can handle those.'

Lestrade nodded.

'I went out with the club. We met as usual at the Tottenham Court Road and pedalled north into Hertfordshire. We stopped for luncheon at the Rose at Tewin, prior to our return. It was on the way back that it happened.'

Lestrade and Dew waited.

'One of our number, Hughie Ralph, forged ahead. He usually did.'

'A scorcher, eh?' Like all policemen, Lestrade disapproved of racers.

'An *aficionado* of the road, Inspector,' Watson corrected him. 'Hughie was an advanced rider. You've doubtless read Crawley's *Art of Bicycle Riding*.'

'Old Creepy? My constant companion,' Lestrade lied.

'Quite. Hughie was an expert – sidesaddle, mounting in motion and so on. Marvellous stuff. A joy to behold.'

'What happened on the return ride?' Lestrade asked.

'He came a cropper.'

'Fell off,' Lestrade translated for the benefit of Dew whose pencil stub raced feverishly over the pages of his notepad.

'Quite,' Watson went on. 'Unheard of. None of us had ever seen Hughie Ralph come off before. He lay motionless on the road. When I examined him, he was dead.'

'Broken neck?' Lestrade asked.

Watson shook his head. 'Mild contusions,' he said. 'But I couldn't find a pulse.'

'What did you do?'

'All I could. A couple of the ladies became hysterical, of course. Ladies will. I attempted artificial respiration, but they objected. As for poor Hughie, no avail. He was gone.'

'Heart attack?' Lestrade tried again.

'The damnedest thing.' Watson's voice fell to a whisper. 'We carried him to The Long Arm And The Short Arm at Lemsford, the nearest inn, and laid him out in the back room. I rang his doctor from Welwyn Police Station. They'd just had a telephone machine installed.'

'Why his doctor?'

'I didn't want to take responsibility. I thought there was something odd about it and I was right.'

'In what way, odd?' Lestrade asked.

'The others went ahead. I stayed with the body. It was evening before Hughie's doctor arrived, together with the local constabulary. And by that time it was dark.'

'And?'

'And Hughie's body was glowing, Lestrade. Like a glow-worm. Uncanny, it was. I've seen some sights in my time, but nothing like that. I could have read my Bicycle Union Code of Conduct by him were it not for the oil lamp's rendering that unnecessary.'

Lestrade's extra sugar lump had plummeted into his tea. Dew was wiping his sleeve and notebook down accordingly. 'Phosphorus,' the inspector said.

'What?' the doctor and the constable chorused.

'Answer me this riddle, doctor,' Lestrade said. 'What glows in the dark?'

'Phosphorus?' Watson was no fool.

'And Hughie Ralph and Willie Hellerslyke,' he said.

'Willie who?'

'Someone I almost met recently in Yorkshire,' Lestrade said. 'Tell me, doctor, you're a man of the world; where is the easiest obtained source of phosphorus?'

'Er . . . Bryant and May matchgirls?' Watson suggested. He had long been suspicious of Annie Besant.

'Rat poison,' Lestrade corrected him, 'and some beetle powders. Let me ask you another. What are the odds on two men, probably unknown to each other, being despatched by the same method within two weeks of each other, a hundred and fifty miles apart?'

'Good God!' It was a common enough rejoinder from Watson. 'What does this mean, Lestrade?'

'It means, doctor, that I appear to have stumbled on a little conspiracy. What do you know about this Ralph?'

'Not much, really,' Watson said. 'We've ridden together, spoke by spoke, for a few months. He's something or other in the City. Well off, one gathers.'

'Well enough off to be murdered?'

Watson shrugged.
'Married?'
'I think not. But, Lestrade, you know what this means, don't you?'
'Tell me, doctor.'
'If Hughie Ralph was poisoned, it must have been by someone in the club.'
'Not necessarily, doctor, although of course I shall have to make enquiries. What did the Hertfordshire police do?'
'Had several pints in The Long Arm. That was about it.'
'They didn't find the glow peculiar?'
'I'm not sure they noticed it.'
'Probably just as well. Will your fellow Spokesmen be meeting again?'
'One last jaunt before the weather sets in. We'd planned to do the same route in honour of poor Hughie. Next Sunday, I believe.'
'Can you get me a machine?'
'I may have an old Kangaroo available.' Watson rubbed his chin.
'I was hoping for a bicycle, doctor,' Lestrade said, straight-faced.
'I see no need for levity here, Lestrade. A man is dead.'
'Indeed,' said Lestrade, his face unchanging. 'Let me know when and where to meet, doctor. Pass me off as . . . what . . . a friend, cousin, something. I'll accompany you and find out what I can. Probably get further that way than in an official capacity. Besides, I'm rather off hooks at the Yard at the moment.'
'Ah, Nimrod Frost at his surly best, eh?' Watson recognized a suspended policeman when he saw one. 'All right. Sunday, at dawn. Corner of Tottenham Court Road and Oxford Street. I'll bring the machine. Have you a Norfolk jacket and plus fours?'
'I expect young Dew here can lift me those articles from Police Lost Property, Islington. In the meantime, doctor, I'd like from you a detailed list of club members and Constable Skinner can start earning his keep by making some enquiries at the Stock Exchange. Two more teas, Dew.'

* * *

Lestrade came off suspension that Saturday. A cursory nod from Assistant Commissioner Frost was all he got in recognition of the fact. Skinner had been prised out of Lestrade's office, on the desk of which he had left 'Lestrade's' specs, still occasionally finding time to search for his own, and had gone to the City. Lilley had been despatched to the rooms of the late Hugh Ralph in Bloomsbury. He was still visibly shaken when he returned, and not a little stirred.

'Why is it, constable,' Lestrade peered over the steaming tea, 'that whenever you return from a routine enquiry you look like death?'

'Sergeant Dixon is on the desk, sir.' Lilley sat down heavily. 'He got his finger caught in a ledger. It's all turned blue . . .' his eyes rolled upwards.

'Yes, well, it will match his uniform, lad. Now, concentrate. Bloomsbury. Ralph's rooms.'

'Ransacked, sir.' Lilley shook himself free of the spectacle of abject horror he had witnessed.

'Ralph's rooms ransacked?' Lestrade put his cup down. 'You'd better tell me about it, constable.'

Lilley consulted his notebook. 'I entered the premises at Number One hundred and forty-eight, Gower Street at eight o'clock this morning, sir. I was let in by the housekeeper, a Mrs Beeton . . .'

The Yard men looked at each other. 'Good,' said Lestrade.

'The place was in . . .' Lilley strained to read his own writing.

'Gower Street?' suggested Lestrade.

'Turmoil,' said Lilley. 'Furniture upside-down, drawers scattered about. Cushions ripped.'

'What did the housekeeper make of it?'

'Rather more of a mess, sir, or she would have if I hadn't stopped her and told her it was evidence.'

'Quite right. When had she seen Ralph last?'

'On the Friday previous, sir. He had given her the week off on account of her ailing sister in Macclesfield.'

Lestrade had been there. He knew there wasn't much else to do but ail in Macclesfield.

'And when had she returned?'

'The previous evening, sir.'

'Did she enter Ralph's rooms?'

'No, sir. The first time was when I knocked her up, so to speak. Proper shocked, she was. First by all the mess, then by the news of the master's death, as she put it. She was quite taken queer, had to sit down.'

'Really?'

'Yes. Well, I must admit I had to sit down with her. Quite turned us both up.'

'Did she have any idea why the rooms had been turned over?'

'None,' Lilley shrugged. 'Nor could she tell me what was missing. I tried to pump her.'

Lestrade looked askance. 'Really?' he said again.

'I suggested it might be students from the University.'

'What did she say?'

'She didn't think they'd bother to come all the way down from Oxford.'

'Forced entry?'

'No sign of it, sir.'

'Pass key, then?'

'Probably.'

'Valuables taken?'

'Some nice antique vase things still there, one smashed. Quite a bit of silver. Loose cash. A few bonds.'

'Bonds?'

'That's what Mrs Beeton said they were. Is it a clue, do you think?'

'I leave clues to Drs Watson and Conan Doyle, Lilley.' Lestrade leaned back with his hands behind his head. 'I deal in evidence. Ah.' He turned at the click of the door. 'Constable Skinner. What news of Change Alley?'

'The bottom's gone out of South African gold, sir,' Skinner told him.

The inspector shook his head. 'It had to come,' he said ruefully.

'It's the cyanide process, of course.'

'You're a mine of information today, Skinner. What's all this got to do with Hughie Ralph?'

'Is that how he died, sir?' Lilley asked. 'The cynanide process?'

Lestrade and Skinner looked at each other. 'May I, sir?'

Skinner asked. 'In the cyanide process of mining, the ore is crushed and treated with a three per cent solution of . . .'

'Yes, thank you, constable,' Lestrade interrupted him, 'we'll leave the percentage solutions to others, shall we? I've got enough on my plate at the moment without a blow by blow account of the mysteries of Witwatersrand.'

He cocked a smug eyebrow at Skinner. Only that morning he had read that word in the *Sun*. His timing was perfect. 'Hughie Ralph,' he repeated.

'Would appear to have been a rather shady gentleman.' Skinner sat down and opened a capacious Gladstone bulging with papers. 'I've only had a few minutes to compile a few notes, sir, on my way back from the Exchange.'

'And?'

'Railways, sir. A major fraud as far as I can ascertain from the figures, running to several thousand pounds.'

'Where?'

'The Belgian Congo.'

'Convenient,' Lestrade mused.

'Ah, but that's the beauty of it, sir. Railway frauds have been impossible in this country since George Hudson.'

'Before my time, constable,' Lestrade shrugged.

'And mine, sir, but in Africa, well, corruption is rife. He sold shares in six fictitious companies.'

'Ruined hundreds, I suppose?'

'No doubt, but one in particular.'

'Ah?'

'This is only gossip, of course, Inspector.'

'Of course, constable, but where would we be without it?'

'A little jobber I know on the floor told me of an unfortunate named Elliott. From riches to rags overnight apparently.'

'Do we know the whereabouts of this Elliott?'

'The workhouse, perhaps in Poplar. I couldn't glean more than that.'

Lestrade nodded. 'Any other specific names in this swindle?'

'None I could find. Most of them were Dutchmen or Germans in the Congo.'

'No Belgians?'

'Too mean, apparently,' Skinner observed.

'Right. Lilley, get over to Poplar. Find this Elliott and get what you can from him. You've done well, Skinner. Ask Constable Dew for one of his excellent cups of tea and then write up all this paperwork. I've got to get on my bicycle.'

Sunday dawned chilly and crisp. Lestrade had donned a borrowed Norfolk jacket and plus fours, courtesy of the Police Lost Property Department, and met Dr Watson at the end of Tottenham Court Road.

'Morning, Lestrade,' he greeted him.

'I think so.' Lestrade peered through bloodshot eyes and tightened the tweed cap-flaps under his chin. 'But I wouldn't put money on it.'

'Couldn't get you a Kangaroo,' Watson told him. Lestrade breathed a sigh of relief. 'But I thought this Facile was rather appropriate for you.'

Lestrade looked at the dwarf ordinary resting against the wall. It suddenly looked infinitely more dangerous than the horse he had borrowed from the Yorkshire Hussars. It had a large wheel at the front and a smaller one at the back and a saddle like the business end of a harpoon. He looked with envy at Watson's bamboo-framed Whippet and snarled inwardly.

'Heigh-ho for the open road,' called Watson, suddenly a changed man as the ground sped beneath him and he swung a leg over his saddle bags and was gone. Not so Lestrade. He had never been a scorcher. Not for him the running start and the flying wheel. He squared his back against the wall and gingerly stepped on to the pedals. His groin was thrust upwards somewhere below his cravat and he crouched, as he saw Watson doing ahead of him in the mist.

'Come on, Lestrade,' the doctor called.

'There's an east wind blowing, Watson,' Lestrade said by way of explanation that he was veering sideways. He could have managed a safety bicycle, but the Facile was a sportsman's machine and at dawn on that Sunday, Lestrade felt anything but a sportsman.

The still-sleeping city fell behind and, one by one, waving figures fell in behind the pair. Watson, at the head, sounded a bugle as each newcomer arrived and they made for the country. The sun was high and the ground mist had all but cleared as the little troupe wheeled into the village of Lemsford. They had decided not to go on to Tewin because their latest recruit was already lagging far behind. They had been riding for hours and Lestrade was not ready for the sudden camber by the bridge. Watson blasted his bugle to slacken speed, but Lestrade was not attuned to the notes and the Facile sailed serenely onwards as the others took the bend. Lestrade gestured frantically, emitting a silent scream as man and machine parted company in mid-air, only to meet again in the great equalizer of the River Lea.

There was a scramble down the bank and members of the Wheel of Fortune Club hurried to the inspector's rescue. Facile and fallen were lifted bodily out of the murky waters, both dangling with weeds.

'Are you all right . . . er . . . Lister?' Watson remembered the agreed alias.

'Yes,' Lestrade trilled, a little too brittly to be truly convincing. 'Faulty chain, I think.'

'Better get him into The Long Arm,' said Watson. 'He's delirious.'

Mine host was less than genial, but after much arguing and the crossing of palms with silver, he allowed Lestrade to bath and lent him a rustic dressing gown on which his senile pet mastiff was prone to sleep. The smell would have dropped a weaker man, but Lestrade sat in the snug while the club members toasted themselves by the fire and talked of this and that. Watson stood up after the beef sandwiches and held his tankard aloft. 'Ladies and gentlemen,' he said, 'members of the Wheel of Fortune, I give you absent friends.'

'Absent friends,' they chorused. Lestrade watched them intently. Two did not drink. He would talk to them later. First, he must rescue his socks from the flames.

It was a little after two o'clock that the troupe set off, Watson blowing his bugle with the sort of hot air that had made him famous in his own little way. Lestrade's jacket had shrunk and his cuffs barely reached to his elbows. What with the smell of the incontinent mastiff and the Lea about him, he was not pleasant company. Besides, the fall at the bridge had knocked his saddle askew and his left knee protruded at an odd angle to maintain his foot's contact with the pedal. He slid his machine into line along the Great North Road beside the lady who had not drunk the toast.

'A lovely day, Miss . . .'

'Trelawney,' she said. 'I haven't seen you before, Mr . . .'

'Lister,' Lestrade said. 'I fear the good doctor didn't introduce me.'

'Have you recovered from your cropper, Mr Lister?' she asked, beginning to scent something about Lestrade.

'Oh, yes, quite, quite,' he laughed. 'Confoundedly silly, really. Faulty chain.'

'I see.'

His knee brushed her voluminous skirts and she veered away. Unsure of himself or the Facile, he veered with her and furthered his cause. 'I understand one of your club passed away on the last ride.'

'Why, yes.' She looked at him through her veil, an attractive girl of uncertain years, though pale and weak-looking. 'Hughie Ralph. This ride was in his honour, really.'

'I couldn't help noticing, Miss Trelawney, that when we drank a health to absent friends, you didn't drink.'

She turned away.

'I assume absent friends did refer to Mr Ralph?' he persisted, his knee prodding her upper thigh.

'I assumed so too, Mr Lister,' she said.

'Didn't you like him?' Lestrade asked, keeping his banter as light as he could and his eyes on the road.

She turned to him sharply. 'No, Mr Lister, though I can't imagine what business it is of yours, I did not like Mr Ralph. He was a boor. Insulting. He spoke incessantly of his money, of his prowess in the world of business. And he made revolting remarks.'

'Remarks?' Lestrade wobbled closer.

'Yes,' she hissed, 'but even he was not so revolting as you!' Miss Trelawney brought her brass Cyclorne sharply down on Lestrade's offending knee and he swerved away, howling instinctively. She pedalled furiously and wedged herself between two other ladies as Lestrade left the road. To the astonished surprise of the other members of the club, he hurtled across a ditch and ascended a slope before coming to a halt in a hawthorn bush.

'What's he doing?' one member asked another.

'Gone for a pedal, I suppose,' came the reply.

'Rides like a policeman,' said a third.

'You go on,' called Lestrade. 'Call of nature,' and he disappeared behind a tree as though to relieve himself. He did so by banging his head on the rough bark to try to alleviate the pain in his leg. Then he dragged the Facile back to the road to tackle his next target.

'Good run,' he called gaily to the man who had not drunk the toast at The Long Arm.

'Care to make it better?' he asked.

'I don't follow,' Lestrade told him.

'Neither do I. I lead,' he said. 'Cecil.' He shook Lestrade's hand and their front wheels nuzzled together.

'Lister. Do you mean a race?' Lestrade hoped he hadn't heard right.

'Exactly. Five pounds says I'll make it to the Tottenham Court Road before you. Are you game?'

'Why not?' Lestrade beamed through clenched teeth, noting the gathering gloom of dusk.

'You've got a lamp?' Cecil asked.

'Oh, yes. Tell me, before we start – shocking about old Ralph.'

'Wasn't it?' Cecil said without feeling. 'Did you know him?'

'Vaguely,' said Lestrade, 'via the City. Colleague of a colleague. That sort of thing. You didn't like him either?'

Cecil looked at him. 'Not particularly. I'll be frank, Lister. Hughie Ralph was an exhibitionist. All this standing on the handlebars, circling on one wheel. Rank showing off.'

'He was a scorcher, then?'

'Of the inferior type, yes.'

'So you weren't sorry when he died?'

Cecil looked sharply at Lestrade. 'I wouldn't put it as strongly as that,' he said and crouched over the handlebars. 'Now then, doctor,' he called to Watson, 'there's a wager afoot. Lister and I to the Tottenham Court Road. Anybody else?'

'I'm game,' Watson called, amazed at Lestrade's bravery. 'Are you sure about this, Lister?'

Lestrade smiled, weakly.

'Lamps on, gentlemen.' Watson stood on his pedals and

sounded the bugle. Like a bat out of hell, Cecil sped forward, spraying Lestrade with the contents of a puddle. Watson hunched crablike over the handlebars. 'Come on Lestrade,' he whispered, 'can't let the side down now. If you don't put up a good show, the others may smell a rat. I told them you were something of a scorcher yourself.'

'Oh, good,' said Lestrade and his left foot slipped off the pedal. Arguably, the rat was preferable to the mastiff, but there it was.

'Tally ho!' shouted Watson and he shot away into the country.

By the time they rattled through the suburbs, it was well and truly dark. Watson and Lestrade vied with each other for last place, skirmishing with little boys with sticks, haycarts and yapping dogs as they rode. Of Cecil, there was no sign, until Lestrade caught sight of him, pedalling like a maniac along Oxford Street at the end of their run. By now, the inspector's cap had gone, his legs felt like lead and the Facile was heavy with mud. Who was to say whether it was the clutch of constables on duty or the tramlines or both that ended the race, at least for Lestrade? Certainly, his wheels became inexorably linked with the metal grooves in the road and so his path was more or less mapped out for him. Struggling to turn his wheels, he found them locked. Struggling to use his brakes, he found them jammed. Struggling to avoid the front of the oncoming tram, he fell off and bowled over the three constables who were minding their own business on the corner.

''Ello,' said one.

''Ello,' said the second.

''Ello,' said the third. ''Aven't we seen you somewhere before?'

'Perhaps.' Lestrade was trying to disentangle his foot from the mangled spokes of his front wheel.

'I don't like scorchers,' one of the constables said, hauling the battered inspector upright. 'You're under arrest, laddie.'

'What for?' Lestrade asked him.

'Disturbing the peace,' the constable answered.

'Damaging a tramline,' said the second.

'Riding a vehicle in a manner likely to cause an accident,' said the third.

Lestrade beckoned the constables to him. 'Gentlemen, I am Inspector Lestrade of Scotland Yard, working under cover.'

At that moment Watson arrived. 'Lister, are you all right?'

The three constables stepped back. 'And impersonating a police officer,' they chorused.

8

Up, Up and Away

The night in the cells had done nothing for Lestrade's disposition. His backside ached, his shins were barked, his pride was dented beyond recognition. He was just glad it was the long-suffering Constable Dew who came to collect him in the morning and no one of higher rank. He ignored the fumbling apologies of the desk sergeant and made his way out to the light.

A grey face hailed him from the parked hansom. 'Lestrade, there you are.'

'Hello, Watson.'

'Can I give you a lift, old man?' The doctor was trying his best at bonhomie, but Lestrade took it personally. When he had narrowly missed the tram last night, he had been forty-three. This morning he felt a hundred and eight. He sat gingerly on the seat opposite Watson and Dew squeezed in beside him. A glance from his guv'nor sent him across to the other side. Dew was unmoved by a similar scowl from Watson.

'I am prepared to forego the cost of the Facile, Lestrade,' Watson said, 'under the circumstances.'

'Good of you, doctor.' Lestrade's look would have decimated a less impervious man.

'Did you discover anything?' Watson asked.

'Scotland Yard, driver,' called Lestrade and the cab moved off. 'I discovered anew why I never took seriously to the cycling craze,' he said, 'and that Facile wheels and tramlines do not go together.'

'I thought they did,' grinned Watson, but realized the insensitivity of the remark and changed tack. 'About Hugh Ralph, I mean.'

'Well, I questioned mine host at The Short Arm in Lemsford while my clothes were drying – put that notebook away, Dew; this is not for public consumption.'

'Very good, sir.' Dew knew a raw nerve when he trod on one.

'He could tell me very little about the day Ralph died that I did not know already. Perhaps mine host at the Rose, Tewin would be more helpful. Can you remember anything about that lunch?'

'Good Lord.' Watson leaned backwards. 'Now you're asking. I believe we had ham. Some of us partook of the pâté, but I've been in Afghanistan, Lestrade. I've seen what pâté did to some of our chaps on the frontier. Not a pretty sight, I assure you.'

'I thought they were Pathans, doctor,' Dew said and then retired into his corner.

'I'm sure it wasn't, doctor,' Lestrade nodded, hoping to avoid the full blast of Watson's war memoirs. 'No one else in the club complained of feeling unwell?'

'No, I don't believe so.'

'Did you notice your fellow guests at the Rose? Those who were not of your party?'

'Scarcely at all, I'm afraid. I'm sorry, Lestrade. Not exactly being an expert witness, am I?'

Lestrade looked at him. 'Don't blame yourself, doctor, you've had no training. Anyway, it scarcely matters. Hugh Ralph is one of two victims.'

'One of two? Ah, your Willielyke chappie.'

'Hellerslyke,' Lestrade corrected him. 'What we have to establish is a link. Two men, of an age, both well-to-do; one titled, one not. Both died by the same means – phosphorus poisoning.'

'Do we know any more than that?'

'Not for the moment,' said Lestrade. 'And you realize that I am only confiding in you, doctor, because of your medical training.'

'And because of my association with Sherlock Holmes,' Watson beamed proudly.

Lestrade made no comment, but removed pieces from Dew's tie knot. 'Does a capital kedgeree, Walter, your wife?'

'Very fair, sir. Very fair,' and Dew joined in the search.

The cab lurched to a halt on that wet Monday outside the Yard's side entrance. Lestrade and Watson went inside, but Dew was still paying the fare when they emerged again and leapt inside the hansom.

'Come on, Dew.' Lestrade poked his head out at the bewildered constable. 'Down in Epping Forest, something has stirred.'

Beyond the village of Theydon Bois, out across the levels of gorse and broom, near the hamlet of Bowells, a little hollow lay in those days sloping towards the south-east. It was lunchtime before the trio found it. Sergeant Dixon's directions had been less than Ordnance Survey. By then, a stretcher covered in a blanket was being lifted on to the waiting hearse.

Lestrade was first out of the hansom and he identified himself to the officer in the centre of the thicket.

'Not just now,' the officer called. 'I won't be a moment,' and he finished what he was doing and emerged from the bushes. 'Thanks for coming. I'm Inspector Failsworth.' He wiped his hand before extending it. 'Hold on a minute, sergeant.' The officer crossed to the stretcher party and pulled back the blanket. There lay a man of thirty-five or so with a shock of dark hair, a drooping walrus moustache and a thin trickle of dark blood over his collar.

'Have you had a doctor look at this?' Lestrade asked.

'Er . . . no. I thought I'd better move him before we had too many crowds.'

'Doctor Watson,' Lestrade shouted to the hansom.

Failsworth was impressed. These Yard men carried their own medical teams with them. Watson arrived at the double with his little black bag and set to work. 'You'd better put him down, gentlemen,' he said to the stretcher-bearers. 'Can't risk elongation of the *brachialis anticus*, you know.'

That went without saying and the policemen complied. The pay didn't run to risks like that.

'He's been dead some time, Lestrade,' Watson said. 'Last night, probably.'

Lestrade turned to follow Failsworth. 'Where exactly was the body found?'

'Over here,' and he ducked into the bush. 'No, no. The sergeant will show you. I . . . er . . .' He closed briefly to Lestrade. 'I've got a bit of a problem, you see. Shan't be a moment,' and he vanished again. Lestrade followed the sergeant to a depression in the grass. The mark of the body was clear in the flattened hollow but the milling, stamping plates of many policemen had ruined all other clues.

'Who found the body, sergeant?' Lestrade asked the man.

'I did, sir, on my way off duty this morning.'

'What time was this?'

'It would be about eight-thirty, sir.'

'Do you usually walk this way?'

The sergeant straightened, as though his deportment were in question. 'Always, sir,' he said.

'Had you seen the deceased before?'

'No, sir.'

'Show him, sergeant.' Failsworth had arrived again.

'But the grass is wet, sir,' the sergeant complained.

'You've got your cape on, man,' Failsworth observed. 'Down you go.'

The long-suffering sergeant removed his helmet and assumed the position of the corpse.

'On his back, then, one leg tucked beneath him?' Lestrade checked. 'All right, sergeant. Thank you.'

'Lestrade!' Watson's startled cry brought both inspectors hurrying over, except that Failsworth had to duck behind a bush on the way.

'What have you found, doctor?' Lestrade rummaged through the blanket folds to get a better view.

'Cause of death, a blow to the base of the skull, done with a sharp pointed implement like a stiletto. Look.' Watson turned the head to show Lestrade the neck, blood matted into the hair. 'Entered between the first and second vertebrae and severed the spinal cord. The *coup de grâce*.'

Lestrade could see the grass Watson was referring to. The man must have been struck from behind. He would have fallen face down if the blow had been hard enough. But if it hadn't, he might have had time to turn, which would have accounted for the sergeant's finding him on his back.

'But that's not all, Inspector.' Had Watson turned a shade greyer? Probably a trick of the light. He forced open the dead man's cold lips with his gloved hands. 'I've heard of men so tough they chew iron and spit nails, but I've never seen anything like this.'

There was a small, thin square of metal lodged between the dead man's teeth. In his death agony, his lips must have closed over it.

Lestrade gripped Watson's sleeve. He vaguely heard Failsworth arrive, offer his apologies and disappear again.

'Good God, Lestrade, what's the matter?' Watson whispered. 'You look as though you've seen a ghost.'

'As a matter of fact, I've seen six.'

'Eh?'

'Be good enough to accompany Inspector Failsworth here . . . er . . . there,' he saw the man was waving from his bush, 'to the station, doctor. There'll have to be a coroner's report, of course, but I'd find *your* report enlightening.'

'My dear fellow.' Watson shook him heartily by the hand. 'I can't tell you how touched I am.'

'I know, doctor,' Lestrade nodded, straightfaced, 'but we must do what we can.'

'It's just like the old days,' Watson shouted gleefully as they bundled the deceased into the glass-sided hearse, 'with Holmes. Shall I bring my service revolver?'

'I don't think so,' Lestrade said. 'I'm not sure Epping is really ready for it, are you?'

'Ah, but what of Romford, I hear you ask.'

Lestrade had heard no such thing. He turned to Failsworth, who was adjusting his dress. 'Shan't be two shakes of a . . .' he began, but thought better of it.

'Inspector, I'd like your report on this as soon as possible. I have reason to believe it is one of a series of murders I have been too blind to connect until now. Do we know who this man was?'

'No, but I'll leave no stone unturned. I'll send a runner to the Yard as soon as I have anything for you.'

'Excellent,' said Lestrade, convinced as he was that Failsworth was an expert when it came to running, and as he crossed to the hansom he heard Watson urging on the hearse driver by cracking his whip and shouting, 'The game's afoot!'

The windows of New Scotland Yard blazed late that night. Inspector Sholto Lestrade sat on the radiator in his office trying to keep the circulation in his nether regions going. November was bitter. Christmas was coming and the goose was getting no fatter. Walter Dew arrived with Lestrade's umpteenth cup of tea in time to see his guv'nor pinch the last Osborne.

'Right, gentlemen.' He scanned the three men in the same boat as he. 'Let's go through it again. Skinner, Murder Number One.'

The constable used his pencil to point to the notes pinned on the wall to his left. 'Captain Archibald Fellowes, late of the Second Life Guards. Coroner's report says cause of death, drowning . . .'

'What do you say?'

'In the absence of my own observations, sir, I'd have to say the same.'

'Would you, laddie?' Lestrade sucked in his breath and nearly choked on the last Osborne. 'Remind me not to recommend you for promotion. Go on.'

'He had been in the water for about two days and the body was bloated and battered, probably by floating debris and embankment buttresses.'

'Are you all right, Lilley?' Lestrade asked as the constable's eyes rolled upwards.

'Fine, sir,' the constable managed.

'Go on, Skinner.'

'There were two rather curious things about the corpse. One was a number of seeds found on his clothing, which on closer inspection turned out to come from Kew Gardens. And the second was the presence of an Ashanti war medal between his teeth.'

'There's more than pride being swallowed in this case,' Lestrade said, rubbing his moustache ruefully. 'What do we know about this Fellowes?'

'Charterhouse. Sandhurst. Commissioned Second Life Guards

1889. Went to the Ashanti campaign on a rather hush-hush mission. Decorated and mentioned in despatches. But . . .'

'But?' Lestrade opened his eyes. *Any* chink in the armour would be welcome now.

'Well, I'm still not happy with his diary, sir. May I?'

Lestrade gestured with his hand and Skinner took the floor, pacing it as he had seen his guv'nor do.

'I haven't a shred of real evidence,' he said, looking at them all, 'but I think the real hero at Coomassie was Captain Hely, Fellowes' brother officer.'

'Why?'

'As I explained, sir, the handwriting alters at that point in the diary. Something perhaps like this. Hely got himself cut off by King Prempeh's spearmen. Fellowes could have gone to his rescue – should have gone – but he didn't. Not one of that twelve-man platoon came back from that mission, whatever it was, except . . .'

'Fellowes,' the others chorused.

'Where does that leave us?' Lestrade asked.

'With a motive of revenge,' said Skinner. 'Hely and his men were dead. But those men must have had families, friends. What if one of them somehow knew the truth? That Fellowes' heroism was a lie. He was in a private nursing home for over a month on his return to England. Er . . . "nervous exhaustion" was given as a reason to the Army Medical Board.'

'And the Ashanti medal?' Lestrade asked.

'A final gesture of contempt,' Skinner said, finding his chair again. 'A symbol that the debt had been repaid, the wrong righted.'

'And all you have is a change of handwriting?' Lestrade asked.

'Yes, sir.' Skinner was no fool. He realized the weakness of it.

'Have you followed through on Hely's family or those of the other members of the platoon?'

'I've started, sir, but frankly, it's a vast job. The War Office aren't exactly helpful. When one is a mere constable . . .'

'It's the same when one is a mere inspector, Skinner,' Lestrade told him. 'The same stiff upper lips and military moustaches. A fortress of scarlet tape. I know. I've been that way myself. Dew, Murder Number Two.'

The constable took Skinner's pencil and prowled as Skinner had done. 'Sit down, Walter. You look as though it's feeding time at the zoo.'

'Sorry, guv'nor. Richard Tetley, archaeologist. Found in the second chamber at Wookey Hole cave, Somerset. Cause of death: unknown.'

'Ah . . .' Lestrade had not had time to follow that one up.

'Couldn't the Somerset Constabulary help us there, sir?' Skinner asked.

'They could, but if I know Chief Inspector Guthrie, they won't. Harry Bandicoot said he'd put pressure on their Chief Constable to get me the coroner's report . . . odd that. Still, I'll hazard a guess, gentlemen, that the cause of death was phosphorus poisoning. Go on, Dew.'

'The body was found by an Arthur Bulleid, also an archaeologist, at about midday on the day in question. The deceased had a carved animal in his mouth, sir. A beetle.'

'Right, gentlemen, let me stop you there.' Lestrade continued to perch himself on the radiator by the window. Across the river, the lights of Southwark twinkled beyond the silent, black barges. 'What do we have in common so far? Who haven't I asked? Lilley?'

'Things in the mouths of the deceased, sir.'

'Quite. And apart from that?'

'Er . . .'

'Two *men*, sir.' Skinner looked earnest.

'From which you deduce?'

'Er . . .'

'In your various enquiries,' Lestrade said to them, 'have you established any link at all, other than the manner of their deaths, between Fellowes and Tetley?'

Silence.

'All right, Dew. Have we a motive for Number Two?'

'Perhaps something to do with Egypt, sir – with the Curse of the Pharaohs.'

'Rubbish,' scoffed Skinner. 'In terms of the arcane . . .'

'Let's not go off at a tandem,' Lestrade stopped him. 'What are you saying, Walter?'

'It may have something to do with Oscar Jones, the American archaeologist working with this Tetley in Egypt.'

'Rather like Captain Hely, who worked with Fellowes in Africa.'

'Sir?' Dew was lost.

'Ah, I see.' Skinner was off and running. 'So they are both crimes of revenge, perpetrated by the same person?'

Lestrade nodded grimly. 'But who? We have assorted members of the public at Wookey Hole on the morning of Tetley's death. Unless he was in the habit of walking around and chewing marble beetles, the murderer placed the scarab in his mouth immediately after death. He would, therefore, have had to have been present at the time. For Fellowes, we know he had been in Kew Gardens shortly before his death, but when, why and with whom, we haven't the faintest idea. And talking of fainting, Lilley, you'd better give us Murder Number Three.'

The young constable fussed over his notes. 'Howard Luneberg de Lacy and his wife Marigold.'

'Forget Marigold,' said Lestrade. 'At least for the moment.'

The trio of constables looked at him for an explanation.

'First, she was battered to death, not at all consistent with our man's methods. Second, she was a woman. All the others have been men. And third, the husband did it.'

'De Lacy himself?' Dew asked.

'With the heavy-topped stick I saw in his hall stand. Oh, he'd have wiped it clean of blood, of course, but it's a safe bet. And the lady who's known as Liz, who frequents the Crystal Palace Park, heard Marigold refer to her companion as Looney. Howard Looneberg de Lacy.'

'Why would he kill his own wife, sir?' Dew asked.

'They're not all as pleasant as Mrs Dew, Walter,' Lestrade smiled, lighting up a cigar. 'Besides – Skinner, what did you discover about Mrs de Lacy?'

'She was a very wealthy woman, sir, in her own right, I mean. Mr de Lacy had run up some pretty enormous gambling debts and a maidservant told me she had heard them arguing about it. Mrs de Lacy refused to give him a penny more unless . . .'

'Unless she was dead,' said Lestrade. 'In which case, all her worldly goods would become her husband's. Which brings me to a central question, Lilley. Why did you delay for a day before taking de Lacy to the mortuary to identify his wife?'

Lilley turned pale. 'I'm sorry, sir,' he said. 'I couldn't get over the sight of . . . Mrs de Lacy. I just couldn't face her again the next day.'

'And by the next day, you had another sight on your hands. Tell us about it.'

'Mr de Lacy had been stabbed to death by a sharp object in the base of the skull . . .' The constable wavered for a moment. 'By person or persons unknown at some time between midnight when he came home and morning when I found him.'

'And what is the connection with the other murders?'

'There was a wedding ring in his mouth, sir . . . Would you excuse me for a moment?' and he hurried to the door.

'Well, Skinner,' Lestrade said. 'In Lilley's absence, what is the significance of the ring?'

'If you're right about the death of Mrs de Lacy, then this is a revenge slaying too.'

'Exactly,' nodded Lestrade. 'That's our pattern.'

'Wasn't Mrs de Lacy due at the Bandicoots'?' Dew suddenly asked.

'She was, according to her husband. Why do you ask, Walter?'

'Oh, I don't know,' said the constable. 'Just seems a big coincidence, that's all.'

'Skinner, you'd better check on Lilley,' said Lestrade. 'I won't have the Yard knee-deep in fainting constables. Dew – the death of Willie Hellerslyke – Murder Number Four.'

'Captain Sir William Hellerslyke, Bt., died on picquet duty with the Yorkshire Hussars, while on manoeuvres. Cause of death, phosphorus poisoning.'

'Suspects?'

'A very long list of people who attended a luncheon with the regiment on the day he died. But especially a Lieutenant Hardinge, whose cruelly jilted sister threw herself off a waterfall while the balance of her mind – and clearly her body – was disturbed.'

'What a marvellous way with words you have, Walter. You should really write a book one day.'

Dew beamed, broadly.

'Motive, then?'

Dew scowled deeply. 'Revenge?' he postulated.

'The pattern again,' nodded Lestrade. 'And for the first time, some evidence – two names. One, the writing on the card that accompanied the poisoned chocolates – "Coquette". The other in the ledger in Mr Rowntree's shop – "Perameles". What does that name suggest to you?'

'Coquette Perameles?' Dew stroked what passed for a chin. 'A French Greek?'

'The worst sort of foreigner,' Lestrade muttered, half to himself. There was a knock at the door and a sergeant of the Essex Constabulary stood there, shivering in his cape.

'A message from Inspector Failsworth, sir,' he said.

'Ah, Dew, get this man a cup of tea. He looks frozen.'

'That's kind, sir. I can't stay long.' Clearly the sergeant had his inspector's problem.

'Sit down, sergeant.'

Skinner returned with a pallid-looking Lilley and they resumed their positions.

'Murder Number Five, gentlemen,' said Lestrade, reading the essence of Failsworth's note. 'The corpse in Epping Forest was one Gerald Mander, aged thirty-two. Of private means. Clubs – Reform, Athenaeum, Montgolfier. Single. Address, Sixty-three, Cadwallader Street, SW4. Anything else from Inspector Failsworth?' he asked the sergeant.

'No, sir.' The man hugged the warming cup to his numb cheeks. 'He was in and out, you might say. He was on his way to Cadwallader Street as I came here.'

'Right. Dew, the inspector will remember you from this morning. Go with the sergeant here. My compliments to Inspector Failsworth. Any information he has from the dead man's address, I want it.'

He sensed a hesitation in Dew's stride. 'What is it, constable?'

'I went off duty an hour ago, sir,' Dew reminded him.

'So did I, Dew,' his guv'nor told him. 'It's a bastard, isn't it?' And he watched the policemen go.

'Excuse me, sir,' Skinner broke in. 'I couldn't help noticing that.'

Lestrade looked down, hurriedly. Was something amiss? Had Messrs Inkester, Bespoke Tailors to the Metropolitans, somehow let him down?

'That piece of metal, sir.'

Lestrade threw it on to the desk. He had been playing with it, unaware, for the last half an hour. 'What of it, Skinner?' he asked.

'May I see it, sir?'

Lestrade handed it to him.

'I thought so,' Skinner smiled. 'Aluminium.'

'What?'

'Aluminium, sir; the name of the metal. Note the bluish tinge.'

'What do you know about it?'

'A great deal, sir. It is found naturally in the form of bauxite, though it does occur in other silicates.'

'What is it used for?' Lestrade asked.

'Dozens of things, sir. Since the electrolytic process of Hall in America and Héroult in France . . .'

'And where do you suppose I found this piece?'

'I've no idea,' Skinner confessed.

Lestrade leaned towards him. 'Wedged between the molars of the late Gerald Mander', and the constable and the inspector glanced down as Lilley hit the floor.

The station wagon rattled past Napoleon III's mausoleum and on up the hill. Soldiers saluted at the main gates and Dew gave them the wave of a Field Marshal. Inspector Failsworth had discovered that the late Gerald Mander spent every waking hour messing about in balloons and since the papers in his desk made many allusions to the Balloon Section of the Royal Engineers based at South Farnborough, it was here that Lestrade and his constable found themselves the next day.

The inspector was shown into an office, not unlike his own but four times bigger, and asked to wait. His heart leapt in surprise as an eager young officer with thick pince-nez and a central parting walked into the desk.

'Morning,' he called cheerily, 'Charles Davenport, the Honourable,' and he held his hand vaguely in Lestrade's direction.

Now this posed a problem for Lestrade, for he had met this man before. A quick glance downwards told him his memory served him aright. Rather than the dark blue trousers of the

Royal Engineers, the crimson and yellow of the 11th Hussars hove into view. As though to confirm Lestrade's worst suspicions, an enormous Irish wolfhound padded silently in, saw Lestrade and snarled.

'Quiet, Paddy,' ordered Davenport, and fumbled for his chair. 'Mr . . . er . . .'

Now this posed another problem for Lestrade, for when he and Davenport had met, what was it, three years ago, he, Lestrade, had been calling himself Athelney Jones. It had been one of those other occasions when he had been 'off hooks' with the Yard and he had felt obliged to use the rather dubious alias of the Inspector of River Police.

'Lestrade,' he came clean this time, 'Inspector of Scotland Yard.'

'Ah, yes.' Davenport picked up a bundle of three pencils. 'Cigar?'

'Er . . . not just now. I find the lead doesn't agree with me.'

'Got your telegram,' Davenport went on. 'Shame about poor old Gerry. Was it an accident?'

'No.' Lestrade read the man's shoulder chains. He had been promoted since they last met. '. . . Major. Mr Mander was murdered.'

'Good God!' The news made Davenport pause in mid-strike as he was about to light the pencils.

'Do have one of mine.' Lestrade thrust a cigar into the major's mouth.

'Oh, thank you. Damned decent. Does "Sally" know?'

'Sally? I understood Mr Mander to be unmarried.'

'Unmarried?' Davenport looked confused. 'Oh, I see. No, Sally is Gerry's brother. His name is actually Cuthbert, but it's a sort of family joke you see – Sally Mander. Good, eh?'

Lestrade remained unmoved. 'We have not been able to locate any members of Mr Mander's family so far, sir,' he said. 'Identification of the body was made by his manservant. Was Mr Mander in the army?'

'Good Lord, no. Civilian through and through. As a matter of fact, we're all on the periphery here. I, of course, am in the Prince Albert's Own, doing a spot of liaison with the Engineers.' He leaned forward secretively. 'Not really my cup of tea, actually. I say . . .' He adjusted his bottle-bottoms and peered quizzically at Lestrade. 'Haven't we met before?'

'I think not,' Lestrade said, a shade too quickly.

'Surely,' Davenport persisted. 'Weren't you the chappie who ran into Oswald Ames in the Jubilee procession? It was in the papers.'

'Was it?' Lestrade had been lucky to escape that.

'Yes. The journalist chappie had you off to a tee. I remember being struck by the poetry of the phrase – "A fellow with parchment skin and eyes weary of the world".'

'No, I think you must be confusing me with someone else.'

'I remember.' Davenport suddenly clicked his fingers. 'You were the chappie who investigated that business of the regimental goat of the Welch. Tell me, did it die?'

'I'm afraid I cannot discuss cases, Major Davenport.'

'Oh, quite. Quite. Walls have ears. I do understand. How can I help in this tragic business of Gerry Mander?'

'I'd like to know first how well you knew him?'

'Ah.' Davenport threw his feet up on the desk, knocking over a bronze statuette which Lestrade caught deftly if rather painfully on his kneecap. It immediately raised a thin red line on his trousers. 'Three or four years now.'

'What kind of man was he?'

'Nice enough chap. Obsessed with ballooning, of course. In the blood, apparently. He and Sally won prizes all over the place – Paris, Berlin. Sorry, Lestrade. I haven't offered you a drink. Now where does the adjutant keep the stuff?' And he began to ferret in a broom cupboard.

'If Mr Mander was a civilian, why was he here at all? An army base?' Lestrade asked.

'Ah.' Davenport produced a bottle of Cleen-O For Linoleum. 'That I can't divulge, I'm afraid. Like your cases, you see. Rather hush-hush.' He found some glasses. 'Water?'

'I don't drink on duty, sir,' Lestrade thought it expedient to say and was relieved when Davenport put the bleach away.

'Quite right,' he said. 'Damned unprofessional. Let's just say we have some rather important work going on at the moment.' Davenport leaned towards him. 'Of National Strategic Importance,' and he tapped the side of his nose. 'Do you know,' he said, squinting again at Lestrade, 'you bear an uncanny resemblance to a colleague of yours – Inspector Jones, do you know him?'

'Er . . . vaguely,' bluffed Lestrade.

'Ah,' beamed Davenport triumphantly, 'I never forget a face. Shall we talk to Sally? I'm sure he can be of more help than I,' and he reached on to the side table and carefully placed a tea cosy on his head. He adjusted it in the mirror, then tutted to himself. 'Silly me,' he said. 'Here I am in undress fiddling about with a pillbox when I really need my torrin. Feels a bit floppy, though. Must have a word with my batman,' and he replaced the cosy on the dummy head and snatched up the folding cap instead. 'Follow me,' he said and collided with the door frame. 'Tsk, these Engineer chappies,' he said. 'What a place for a broom cupboard.'

Davenport and Lestrade and Paddy the wolfhound crossed the open fields where the gas wagons of the Royal Engineers were drawn up and men stood idly round in groups, patting horses that stamped and whinnied. At a barked command, they formed a huge circle around the deflated sheets and the gas began to pump from the huge pipes. Slowly, as Lestrade and Davenport watched, the thing rose before them like a giant mushroom, until it left the ground and hovered above them, dangling with ropes and baskets and weights.

A man in a heavy overcoat emerged from the scarlet uniforms and inspected the rigging.

'Ah, Sally.' Davenport led Lestrade forward. 'This is Inspector Lestrade from Scotland Yard.'

'Hmphh,' Mander grunted and continued his inspection.

'I'm afraid I have some bad news for you, Mr Mander,' Lestrade said. 'Your brother is dead.'

As Mander turned, Lestrade stepped backwards. The shock hit him like a slap. It was like looking again at the corpse in Epping Forest. 'Mr Mander and yourself are twins?' Lestrade said at last.

'It appears we were,' grunted Mander. 'How did he die?'

'He was stabbed, sir. His body was found yesterday morning in Epping Forest, near the village of Bowells.'

Mander looked at Davenport, at Lestrade, at the distant figure of Dew waiting with the black police station wagon.

'It's a fine day for a flight, Mr Lestrade. Care to join us?'

'Well, I . . .' and he found himself being bundled into the basket by the capable hands of the Royal Engineers, rather as those of the Yorkshire Hussars had bundled him recently into the saddle of Minstrel, the black charger.

'Watch out, Davenport,' Mander called as the major was hauled aboard. 'Get a whiff of that sulphuric acid and granulated zinc and I'll guarantee it'll bring tears to your eyes.'

'Here, Paddy.' Davenport slapped his thigh and the wolfhound leapt bodily into the basket, knocking Lestrade to one side.

'Cast off,' roared Mander and the little army of Engineers scurried in all directions, loosening ropes, untying knots and otherwise letting go. Lestrade gripped the sides of the basket as the thing swayed and creaked.

'Let go ballast!' ordered Mander and he and Davenport began throwing the roped weights over the side. 'Look out below!' The Engineers scattered and let out a cheer as the balloon began to rise. Lestrade's stomach lay with the wolfhound at his feet. The dog was snoring loudly, but the noise was lost as the wind began to take the balloon and it drifted lazily to the south.

'Compass bearing?' Mander asked Davenport.

The major crouched over a control panel in one corner of the basket. 'Er . . . thirty . . . no, wait a minute, thirty-five . . .'

Mander pushed him gently out of the way and looked for himself. 'All right,' he said, 'we'll be clear of the trees in a moment.'

Lestrade didn't know whether to look up, where the great grey balloon with its ropes sailed like a stately globe overhead, or down, where the figures of the Engineers began to look like red and white ants and the gas pumps on the wagons like tiny coffins. To all sides of him, the horizon was yawing crazily, trees and houses now far below.

'It's a grand day for it,' Davenport shouted over the wind and he and Mander proceeded to arm themselves with layers of scarves and gloves. The cold whipped through Lestrade's Donegal and in a sudden snatch of wind, his bowler was gone, to tumble and fly like a dust speck over the South Downs. He thought he'd better focus on something and do his job before he saw his breakfast again. 'When did you see your brother last?' he asked Mander.

'Three days ago,' came the reply. 'Here at Farnborough.'

Lestrade glanced down briefly. Farnborough had gone. In its place a mad patchwork of winter fields, the uplands still grey with frost.

'Can you think of anyone who would want to see him dead?'

Mander looked grimly at Davenport who squinted meaningfully back at him.

'No one,' Mander said.

'You don't seem very upset by the news of your brother's death, Mr Mander,' Lestrade thought it was time to observe.

The balloonist looked at him. 'My brother and I were not close, Inspector. We shared the same face and the same passion for aerial ascent but of recent years we'd drifted apart.'

Lestrade thought it sounded like him and his stomach.

'You see, it's not true that identical twins feel things simultaneously, although . . .'

'Although?' Lestrade sensed an oddness of mood.

'You say my brother was stabbed?'

'Through the neck. The weapon was not a knife, at least, not a conventional one. Why?'

'I'm not feeling myself this morning,' Mander told him.

Lestrade was not at all surprised by that. He felt as though his feet were floating round his ears.

'Exhilarating, isn't it?' shouted Davenport, impervious to the increasing greyness of Mander.

'Davenport, keep your hand on that tiller,' Mander snapped, 'Lestrade, pass me that water bottle, will you?'

Lestrade found it lying near the prone wolfhound who raised its shaggy head and growled at him. It was the story of Lestrade's life. Mander swallowed greedily, as though his life depended on it.

'Can you tell me what you and your brother were engaged upon here, Mr Mander?'

'I cannot discuss that, Lestrade,' he said. 'You must look elsewhere for your murderer.'

'Was there a lady in his life?' Lestrade asked.

Mander began to twist his neck and tug at his cravat beneath the furs. 'No, not particularly. But as I said, we were not close.

It's funny though, I did have a lady visitor apparently, yesterday evening . . .' and he attempted a smile but it turned to a scowl and he vomited loudly over the side. Lestrade turned away from the spectacle, to come face to face with the wolfhound who had risen on his haunches and was resting his paws on the ropes. He drew his warm, wet tongue the length of the inspector's face.

'He likes you!' laughed Davenport, wrestling quietly with a pair of binoculars. 'Something wrong with these damn things.' He shook them.

Mander rejoined the group. 'Davenport, we'd better get down.' His voice was a croak. 'I'm not well. I haven't felt sick in a balloon in twenty years. Lestrade, I had a visitor . . .' and he turned again to retch over the side. Suddenly, he slumped to his knees. Lestrade caught him and hauled him into a sitting position.

'Is he all right?' Davenport asked. 'Good God, what's that disgusting smell? Paddy?'

The wolfhound looked outraged, but Lestrade knew the animal was innocent.

'That smell is phosphorus, Major Davenport,' he said, tugging at Mander's scarf and cravat. 'This man has been poisoned. Get this contraption down.'

But even as he spoke, Mander's head flopped to one side and he stared with sightless eyes at the wolfhound who whimpered and curled tightly into a corner.

Davenport began hauling at ropes and weights and pulleys and the gas began to rush out of the vast globe. 'Don't breathe it in,' he shouted, 'cover your face,' and Lestrade threw himself against the shaggy flank of the hound who snarled anew.

Davenport had donned a pair of impenetrable goggles over his already impenetrable spectacles and the balloon began to lurch violently to the left. 'Damn these westerlies,' he shouted. 'Lestrade, you can't stay down there. Give me a hand,' and he and the inspector struggled with the inflatable as it raced across the Downs.

'Where are we?' Lestrade shouted, his voice brittle with wind and panic. He thanked God he was wearing brown trousers. Davenport peered myopically over the side. 'The South of England somewhere,' he said. That was good enough for

Lestrade, at least for the moment. 'No, wait a minute,' the major corrected himself, 'that looks like Normandy down there.'

For a moment, Lestrade experienced hysteria. Surely, Normandy was in France. They had crossed the Channel. Who knew what terrors awaited them on the ground? Perhaps even now the guns of the French artillery were trained on them. As he gripped the lurching, buffeted basket, the tops of the trees began to rattle and scrape on the wickerwork.

'I can't hold her!' Davenport was screaming. 'I can't hold her! Bale out!'

'What?' Lestrade looked at him in disbelief. They must have been sixty feet above the ground.

'Jump!' and the officer of the Eleventh Hussars leapt over the side, his crimson legs racing through the air until he disappeared into the middle of a flock of sheep grazing on the hillside. Lestrade was alone. Alone that is save for an Irish wolfhound and a poisoned corpse. He knew then that he had never been so alone before. His only thought was to get down in as few pieces as possible and he began fumbling with the balloon's neck. The gas rushed out, searing his hands and arms, but he held on and turned his face away.

Two men, wandering the lanes below, saw him struggling with the inflatable. They stopped and one said to the other, 'Look at that chap. He balloons like a policeman.'

Lestrade saw the solid grey tower of a church hurtle past on his left and, with a crunch and sickening jolt, the basket hit the ground and ropes and weights cascaded on to his head as he rolled gracefully among the gravestones. It was some time before he came to himself, being licked around the frozen ears by the wolfhound. His head was resting on an angel, crouched in stone over a veiled urn. He remembered thinking how odd that there should be an English gravestone in Normandy.

'What the bloody 'ell's 'appened 'ere?' a voice behind him boomed, though to Lestrade the words were indistinct.

He sat upright, to be confronted by a sexton with a mean-looking scythe.

'*Bonjour*.' He mustered his only French and patted his chest. 'English,' he said, and then again, more loudly, 'English.'

'Well, I'm bloody 'appy for yer,' the sexton said.

'You speak remarkably good English,' said Lestrade.

'Thanks,' grunted the sexton, helping him up. 'I've only bin practisin' for these sixty year.'

'Wait a minute.' Lestrade clutched the man's sleeve to steady himself. 'Isn't this Normandy?'

'Normandy be buggered.' The sexton spat in the grass. 'Normandy be five mile that way. This be Church Crookham.'

'Church Crookham? Where's Farnborough?'

'Over that bloody 'ill,' said the sexton. 'Where do you blokes come from, that's what I'd like to know?'

'It's a long story,' Lestrade told him, grateful for the feel of terra firma below his feet. He walked shakily to the basket to where the body of Sally Mander lay among ropes and canvas. The terror was there still.

It was carpet time again that night. Lestrade, patched up where he had collided with the undergrowth by the regimental surgeon at Farnborough, stood squarely on the mat in Nimrod Frost's office. He had borrowed Dew's bowler in lieu of his own, which for all he knew still circled in the eddying air currents over the South Downs.

'An unauthorized flight, Lestrade,' Frost was saying, his cheeks quivering in the lamplight. 'You might have killed someone.'

'It might have been me, sir.' Lestrade was in no mood for kid gloves.

'Well, it's out of my hands now.' Frost struggled to his feet. 'You are to wait here,' and he waddled to the door.

For a while Lestrade stood stock still. He had never liked this room. It had been unbearable under Melville McNaghten. It was unbearable under Nimrod Frost. His ribs ached, his hands and arms smarted from the flaying effect of the gas. He was about to turn and leave when a small, silver-haired man entered and sat down in Frost's chair.

'Do you know who I am, Inspector?' he asked.

Lestrade took in the moon cheeks, the small, clear, grey eyes and the weak chin. He didn't need to see the scarlet tunic under the astrakhan coat. 'You are Field Marshal Viscount Wolseley,' he said.

'Sir Garnet will do. What's my job?'

Was this a test? Or did the man have a genuine problem?

'You are Commander-in-Chief of the British Army, sir,' Lestrade told him.

Sir Garnet leaned forward. 'And as such it is my duty to have a word in your ear, Inspector. Have a seat.'

A seat offered in this office was unheard of. Lestrade had to look for one. The leather of the chesterfield was cold comfort.

'What do you know about the brothers Mander?' Wolseley asked.

'With respect, Sir Garnet, this is not a court martial. I ask the questions here.'

'Lestrade!' The door crashed open and Assistant Commissioner Frost stood there, quaking. But Wolseley held up his hand.

'Leave us, Mr Frost, would you. Totally, I mean.' His voice was firm.

Frost shook some more but controlled himself. 'Will that be all, my lord?' he asked.

The Field Marshal smiled. 'For now, yes, but could we have some tea?'

Frost screamed silently and spun on his heel, as neatly as a man of sixteen stone could, and vanished.

'Mr Lestrade, I know I have no jurisdiction here. But two men are dead. I think we need to work together.'

'Together then,' said Lestrade, passing a cigar to Wolseley. 'Question for question. First, how is Major Davenport?'

'Davenport? Oh, that myopic idiot in the Depot Troop of the Eleventh Hussars. He landed, apparently, on a flock of sheep and the wool broke his fall. He however broke his leg. Damned bad form, that.'

'Breaking his leg?'

'Baling out of a bally balloon. You and Mander were civilians. It was his duty, as the only soldier present, to see that you were safe.'

'Mander was already dead.'

'What? I thought he was killed in the fall.'

'He died of phosphoric poisoning, unless I miss my guess.'

Wolseley sagged back in Frost's chair. The man's weight over the years had caused chronic indentation and he almost disappeared, but struggled upright again. 'So much for military intelligence,' he said.

There was a knock at the door and a uniformed constable brought in a tray with Bath Olivers and real china cups, with handles. Lestrade basked in the unaccustomed luxury and he was mother while the tea-bobby left and Wolseley marshalled his thoughts.

'I thought Sally Mander died accidentally, I must admit. I really came to see you about Gerald.'

'He was stabbed,' Lestrade told him. 'In Epping Forest, by person or persons unknown,' he picked up Frost's ornate letter-opener and weighted it, 'by a sharp, semi-blunt object. Sir Garnet, my second question – what was the hush-hush something or other the Mander brothers were working on?'

Wolseley fought his way out of the leather armchair and paced to the window. 'I'm sorry,' he said, 'I cannot divulge . . .'

Lestrade stopped him. 'I should tell you that the murders of the Mander brothers are only part of a larger conspiracy.'

'What?'

'Five others, to date. There's no telling how many more we may yet find.'

'That's extraordinary,' Wolseley shook his head.

'You fought the First Ashanti War, Sir Garnet,' Lestrade joined the old soldier by the window.

'I did,' he answered.

'So did two officers called Fellowes and Hely – the Second War. Hely died there. Fellowes died recently.'

'Archibald,' Wolseley realized. 'In the Life Guards.'

'He was another,' Lestrade told him. 'Like the Manders. Do you know why?'

Wolseley shook his head, not once, but several times. He crossed the floor, looked at Lestrade and crossed back. 'I want your word, Lestrade.' Wolseley looked his man in the eye, as he had done at the head of the Twenty-fifth Foot in Burma, as he had against the Mutineers in India and facing the Fuzzy Wuzzies at Tel-el-Kebir. 'Your word, mind.'

Lestrade looked back, as he had looked back at Sir Charles Warren, Commissioner of Police, as he had looked on the ghastly corpses of the Ripper, as he had looked Death in the face as often as Sir Garnet. 'You have it,' he said.

Wolseley relaxed and turned to the twinkling river-lights through the window. 'The Austrians have built a rigid airship,

Lestrade. Not a balloon of the type you flew today and in which the Manders made their name. It has a metal frame, was built by a Kraut named Schwartz and is not unlike your cigar in shape.'

'I see.'

'I wonder if you do, Lestrade,' Wolseley said. 'Imagine not one of those, but hundreds. We know the Germans and the French have been experimenting with petrol-driven airships for the past eight years. They're still at the experimental stage but it's vital that we catch them up.'

Lestrade's eyes narrowed. 'You're talking about an army in the sky,' he said.

'Cayley, Stringfellow and most recently Ader – they worked or are working on other types of aircraft. I don't mind telling you, Lestrade, if there's ever another European war, I hope I'm long dead. I wouldn't want to see that. Imagine, bombs thrown from balloons. It's monstrous.'

'Like bolts of lightning,' Lestrade mused.

'Exactly,' said Wolseley grimly, 'lightning war. I'm just too old.' He sighed. 'The Manders, foremost among our civilian balloonists, were working on a pioneer airship. Like Schwartz's, it is to be made of aluminium.'

'What?' Lestrade's heart jumped.

'Aluminium. It's a light metal, stretches like a skin over the framework.'

'Who knew about the Manders' work, Sir Garnet?'

'Well, half the bally Royal Engineers saw them at work at Farnborough, but only a tiny handful know about the airship.'

'Have you questioned them?'

'At length. As far as I know, they are all sound. The problem is the Manders themselves. Not long ago, they had a reputation for recklessness. A man was killed. All blown over now, of course.'

'So you think the Manders were killed by a foreign power, to slow up our progress in this field or to protect a strategic secret?' Lestrade asked.

'I did think so, but you say others have died in a similar way.'

'They have,' Lestrade nodded. 'But I have known murderers kill a number of unconnected people, just to confuse, whereas in reality there is only one actual target – or two, in the case of the Manders.'

'That's fiendishly clever,' marvelled Wolseley. 'Where does it get us?'

'I'm not sure, Sir Garnet. May I question those privy to the secret work on the airship?'

'Yes, but proceed warily, Lestrade. If this got out, it would blow an enormous hole in our national security. The safety of England is in your hands.'

'Thank you, Sir Garnet. I'll do my best,' and he shook the Field Marshal's hand.

'Oh, Lestrade.' Wolseley stopped him at the door. 'What I've just told you is of the utmost secrecy, of course, but what I am about to tell you is downright unprofessional. I don't mind admitting I feel a cad to mention it.'

'Go on,' said Lestrade, sniffing a revelation.

Wolseley looked uncomfortable. 'It's about Archie Fellowes – in the Ashanti business.'

'Oh?'

'Well, it's only a rumour, of course. Nothing in the official files.'

'I know. One of my best men checked, as far as he was allowed.'

'Quite. But there is a rumour that Fellowes lost his nerve at Coomassie. It *is* an eerie place, I can testify to that from my time there in '73. But they say he ran out on Hely and his men, just left them there and skedaddled. Played the coward.'

'Really?' Things were beginning to fit into place for Lestrade.

'Now it's only a rumour, Inspector,' Wolseley wagged a warning finger at him. 'Apparently he spent some time in a nursing home. Bit namby pamby, what?'

'A rumour is better than nothing,' Lestrade said, 'and at the moment, it may be all, Sir Garnet.'

Lestrade spent a dogged four days interviewing members of the Royal Engineers Balloon Section. They may all have been foreign agents as far as he was concerned, but he could link none of them with phosphorus, Epping or, specifically, either Mander. He eyed their bayonets suspiciously and when no one was looking, lunged at the office wall at Farnborough, now that Davenport had vacated it, to see what sort of hole one made. The trouble was that plaster did not have the same consistency as neck and the experiment was not a total success. For an hour or so he contemplated sacrificing Paddy the wolfhound in the cause of forensic science by skewering him to the floor, but the sensitive beast got wind of it somehow and scurried out.

One corporal of Engineers did prove useful, however. He told Lestrade that Sally Mander had had a visitor the night before he died, which confirmed what Mander had begun to say before the irresistible urges of phosphorus poisoning called him over the side of the balloon basket. No, the visitor in question had not seen Mr Mander, but had left him a box of chocolates. Where were they now? Presumably, in Mr Mander. The corporal had no precise knowledge of the workings of the human alimentary canal and would be drawn no further on that point. The box? Gone. Had there been a calling card? He couldn't remember one. What did this person look like? The corporal was very definite on this point. Tallish, perhaps five feet four, with a very large hat and muffler wrapped over the face.

'Man?' Lestrade asked. 'Woman?'

A moment's pause. 'Yes, sir. I'd say so.'

Lestrade narrowed his eyes. It was the end of an imperfect day. 'Which?'

The corporal looked helpless. 'If my stripes depended on it, sir, I couldn't tell you. Do you ever meet people – and you're not really sure?'

Lestrade found himself nodding. It was the way of the world.

9

'Bus Stop

It was in the middle of that December that William Terriss, the actor, was hacked to death in the darkness of a doorway at the Adelphi. But the weapon was a carving knife, not the stiletto for which Lestrade was searching, and in any case his assailant, Prince, had been caught red-handed.

The London press buzzed with the Terriss case and the Manders passed into history. But at Scotland Yard there was a little knot of men who did not, could not, forget. They sat over their mugs of tea as the snow fluttered against the window panes and the river outside lay dark and grim in its white banks.

'So what did you learn at the Crystal Palace, Dew?' Lestrade asked.

'The Mander brothers were regular exhibitionists there, sir. "Aerial Presti . . . Presti . . . sleight of hand By Appointment" – that's what the handbill says.'

'By appointment to whom?' Lestrade asked.

'The Duke of Connaught, apparently.'

'And what of the accident?'

'Ah, yes, that's quite interesting. It was three years ago. A bloke named Parmenter teamed up with them for a while. Seems he was a brilliant balloonist in his own right. They were making an ascent over the Crystal Palace Park for the benefit of the May Day crowds – and Parmenter fell out.'

'Dead?'

'As a dormouse.'

'How did it happen?'

'Well, that's the peculiar thing. There were just the three of them in the basket. A fourth bloke who carried the flask of tea, or whatever, didn't go.'

'Why not?'

'I hoped you'd ask that, sir,' Dew beamed. 'Because the Manders told him not to. Gave him some guff about ballast the bloke didn't believe.'

'You talked to this bloke?'

'Yes, eventually. He does trapeze acts in the circus now.'

'What did he make of the Manders?'

'Well.' Dew leaned forward, conspiratorially. Lilley and Skinner did likewise. 'He reckons the Manders did Parmenter in.'

'I see.' Lestrade was the first to move back from the circle. 'So it's a matter of "Did he fall, or was he pushed?"'

'Exactly, guv'nor,' said Dew.

'If he was pushed,' ruminated Lestrade, 'what was the motive?'

'Yes, I was about to ask that, sir,' said Skinner.

'Oh, good.' Lestrade delivered his most withering look.

'This bloke I talked to said this Parmenter was drawing bigger crowds than the Manders.'

'Professional jealousy, then?' Lestrade said.

'They'd had flaming rows before,' Dew told them. 'Lots of witnesses to that.'

'And on the day of the fateful flight?'

'Apart from this bloke, I couldn't find anybody who was there.'

'Right,' said Lestrade, 'what do we know about Parmenter?'

Dew flicked through his notepad. 'Third son of Ezekiel and Roberta Parmenter of London and New York. Educated at Eton and Harvard.'

'Where?' Lestrade asked.

'Eton, sir.' Dew was a little surprised. 'It's a public school.'

'No, I mean Harvard,' Lestrade corrected him.

'Ah, that's another public school,' Dew was less assertive this time.

'Actually, it's an American university,' Skinner told them.

'Go on, Dew,' ordered Lestrade.

'He seems to have become involved in ballooning in the United States and spent half of each year there.'

'That's all?'

'He was something of a daredevil by all accounts. High-wire stuff as well as ballooning. He crossed the Niagara Falls on a rope several times, like that Blondel bloke.'

'Did he carry a lute?' Skinner asked.

They all looked at him.

'All right, Walter,' Lestrade said, 'you've done well. Lilley, Poplar Workhouse. The victim in the fraud perpetuated by Hughie Ralph.'

'Ah.' Lilley rummaged for his notepad. 'It was Bethnal Green, sir.'

'Bethnal Green?'

'George Hypericum Elliott was very difficult to find. He kept getting a pass to find work and then disappeared. In the end, he'd turn up under an assumed name at a different workhouse. When I finally tracked him down he was called Lawrenson.'

'Lawrenson?'

Lilley nodded. 'George Hypericum Lawrenson.'

That name rang a bell for Lestrade but he couldn't place it. 'What did he say?'

'He's dying, sir,' Lilley had turned his usual colour of the snow beyond the window. 'TB, he told me. I felt very sorry for him, sir.'

Lestrade nodded. 'It's that sort of job, laddie,' he said. 'You've just got to keep a sense of prospective.'

'There's something about this case, sir,' Lilley said.

'Elliott?' asked Lestrade.

'Elliott, Ralph, the Manders, all of them.'

'What's that?' Lestrade was prepared to turn any stone by this stage.

'Why don't we just let him go, sir – the murderer, I mean?'

Dew sprayed tea all over Skinner's tweed.

'Why should we do that, constable?' Lestrade asked quietly.

'Well, sir, I mean . . .' He resorted to his fingers. 'If we're right . . .'

Lestrade assumed that wasn't the royal 'we'.

'. . . then all these victims have deserved all they got. One, Captain Fellowes ran out on his men. In effect, he murdered them. Two, Mr Tetley may or may not have stolen the archaeological credit from Mr Jones. He may even or may not have killed him. Three, Mr de Lacy bludgeoned . . .' The word shook him once he had said it. '. . . caused the death of Mrs de Lacy – you said so yourself. Four,' he was running dangerously low on fingers, 'Captain Hellerslyke was responsible for the death of Miss Hardinge . . .'

'Even so, Lilley,' Skinner broke in, 'the whole fabric of society is at stake. As J. S. Mill was the first to point out . . .'

'What Constable Skinner is trying to say,' said Dew, 'is that we can't take the law into our own hands. We're not judges and juries.'

'Precisely so, Dew,' said Skinner and Dew scowled at the junior man.

'But this . . .' Lilley was unusually persistent. 'This is not justice.'

Lestrade's pencil stub rapped out an insistent refrain on the desk and the hubbub died down. 'What else did Elliott tell you?'

'He'd had it cushy all his life – servants, nannies and so on. Only kid. Spoiled to death . . .' He suddenly didn't care for the analogy. 'Hughie Ralph ruined him, all right. He invested thousands in his African railway schemes, believing they were genuine. When he found out they weren't, it was too late. He lost his friends, his family. Blokes ignored him in the club. He went to pieces and they found him lying blind drunk in an alley somewhere, coughing blood.'

'Let that be a lesson to us all, gentlemen,' Lestrade said.

'I don't think I'll ever be able to afford railway shares, sir,' chuckled Dew.

'Indeed not, Walter.' Lestrade reached across and rattled a tin on the filing cabinet. 'I was referring to the tea kitty. Somebody hasn't put in his tanner.'

Dew blushed crimson and dug deep into his pockets.

'I'm off for luncheon,' Lestrade said. 'They've let me out today,' and he made for the lift.

Across the slushy yard below his office the inspector trudged, wrapping his muffler round his battered face. The snow crystallized on his new bowler, then melted on the felt. He caught the extended hand from the hansom door.

'Sholto,' a voice greeted him.

'Harry.' Lestrade felt his hand pumped heartily as Squire Bandicoot hauled him in.

'Sholto.' Letitia, radiant as ever in the crisp air, reached over and kissed him. 'You got my telegram.'

'I did,' he said, tipping his hat. 'You both look well.'

'Mr Lestrade.' A frail figure unwrapped itself from a pack of furs.

'Miss Balsam.' Lestrade tipped his hat again. 'How are you?'

'Very well,' she smiled. 'Letitia and Harry have brought me up to do some Christmas shopping in town. Aren't they kind?'

'They are,' said Lestrade. He knew that of old. Harry Bandicoot had saved his life and got him out of more scrapes than he cared to remember. 'When did you get here?'

'Yesterday,' Harry told him. 'We're staying at the Grand. Luncheon is on me. Sholto, can you join us for dinner?'

Lestrade looked a little awkward, not an unusual pose for him. 'I'm not sure I have the dress for it,' he said.

'Nonsense.' Letitia took his arm. 'Come as you are. Look.' She rummaged in her portmanteau and produced a sepia photograph of a little girl. Lestrade's little girl. He looked at it and smiled. Then he turned quickly away to look at the red brick of the Yard.

'The Grand, driver,' called Harry and the hansom lurched forward.

Lestrade hadn't had a lunch like that in a long time. And it was good to talk to Harry and Letitia again. Miss Balsam spent most of the meal asleep, snoring demurely until Letitia nudged her awake. She was tired. All the excitement of the trip to London and the years had taken their toll. Letitia tucked her up in her room while Lestrade and Harry went to the hotel's billiards room.

'Call,' Harry tossed the coin.

'Heads,' said Lestrade.

'You break.' Harry hung up his jacket and rolled up his sleeves. 'I heard no more about Richard Tetley, Sholto. Has the trail gone cold?'

Lestrade's white ball came back to him without colliding with any of the others. 'In a manner of speaking, Harry,' he said. 'You know of course I shouldn't divulge anything about the cases I'm working on.'

Bandicoot held up his hand. 'I know,' he said, racking up the points on the brass scorer. 'I was on the Force once, remember.'

'I remember,' nodded Lestrade. 'You never got me that coroner's report, by the way.'

'The Chief Constable wouldn't budge, Sholto.' Bandicoot chalked his cue. 'I did try, but he was adamant. Just wouldn't call in the Yard officially.'

'Guthrie got to him first.' Lestrade crouched for his shot. 'Never mind. By the way, did you know a chap called Parmenter?'

'Parmenter?' Bandicoot paused to think. He couldn't do anything else while he did that. '"Armpits" Parmenter? Captain of Fives at Eton?'

'I thought his name was Henry, at least according to Walter Dew's report.'

'Henry, yes.' Bandicoot played his shot, a crafty one that caught Lestrade's knuckle resting idly on the cush. 'We called him "Armpits" because he was always sweating. Captain of Fives, Athletics, Sculls.'

'You were no slouch in your day, Harry. Was Parmenter a rival?'

'Not really. He was four or five years my senior. We only boxed once.'

'What happened?'

'I knocked him out.'

'Somebody knocked him out of a balloon.'

'I remember that. About three years ago, wasn't it? I never really knew the chap, but it was a terrible accident.'

'Yes, only it wasn't an accident, Harry. Two men, brothers by the name of Mander, pushed him.'

'Good God!'

'Did you know the Manders?'

'Mander?' Bandicoot paused. Lestrade was certainly taxing the man's mental capacity today. 'Weren't they in the paper recently? Aren't they dead too?'

Lestrade nodded. 'There are times in this job when I think I know more dead people than live ones. Set 'em up again, Harry. It's my shout,' and he went off in search of the bar.

Bandicoot did not meet Lestrade on a daily basis. He had no idea how rare an event that was.

Lestrade managed to borrow an evening suit from the Islington Lost Property Department and it didn't fit him at all badly. In fact, on second thoughts, as he passed a mirror, it didn't fit him at all. He even managed to get back to the Grand in time for dinner. Nanny Balsam would not join them. Let the young folks have fun, she said and she retired early with her knitting. She had retired already in fact, from nannying, but there was always someone to knit and sew for. Rupert and Ivo, the Bandicoot boys, were four now and growing fast and Nanny Balsam loved making frothy dresses for little Emma.

Harry ordered and Lestrade managed to identify the soup before devouring it. Conversation was easy and pleasant as it always was when he was with Harry and Letitia. He hadn't realized how much he needed a rest like that and was tackling the trout when a worried-looking Constable Dew hurtled through the dining-room and whispered in Lestrade's ear. The inspector straightened and his face turned grey.

'Where?' he asked.

'The Highway,' Dew told him.

'Letitia, Harry.' He tugged the napkin from his neck. 'I have to go.'

'Trouble, Sholto?' she asked.

'I'm afraid so. It's a gang war and a bad one.'

'I'm coming too, Sholto.' Bandicoot was on his feet.

Lestrade looked at him. 'Out of the question,' he said.

'Sholto.' Harry looked back at him through steady blue eyes. 'Remember Hengler's Circus?'

Lestrade remembered. He had been staring death in the face. He had been curled up, bound hand and foot, bundled into a cannon and was about to be launched into eternity when Harry Bandicoot had happened by. The murderer had fired, but Harry had fired faster and Lestrade was still here because of it. Yes, Lestrade remembered.

'Letitia,' Lestrade said, 'this could be dangerous.'

She hesitated for less than a second, then smiled, squeezed the inspector's hand and said, 'Then you'll need Harry.'

Both men bent to kiss the radiant lady, one on each cheek, and they left. Walter Dew stood there, grinning inanely at Mrs Bandicoot. He had a loving wife too.

'Dew!' Lestrade bellowed and the constable scurried after them.

Dockland was off Lestrade's usual beat. In fact it was out of the Metropolitan area altogether, but when trouble on this scale brewed, it was all hands to the pumps. It was a strangely silent scene into which Lestrade's cab whirred, the horse padding through the new snow, lit by the isolated green gaslamps of the East End.

A large crowd of policemen from the City and Metropolitan forces stood at one end of the Ratcliffe Highway, stamping their feet and blowing on their hands in the cold. Beyond that, and to one side of them, an even larger force of roughs in caps and mufflers muttered darkly. Two hundred yards away a solitary omnibus stood at an odd angle in the centre of the Highway, its horses unharnessed and waiting nearby, snorting periodically to break the silence. Now and then, a head would peer over the top rail of the open-topped 'bus and vanish again. Only one head remained there in the lurid snow-light, framed by the halo of the nearest gaslamp.

The crowd of policemen parted to let Lestrade, Dew and Bandicoot through. In the centre sat a quaking figure, crouched on three orange boxes that audibly groaned beneath him. He was clutching a head wound.

'Lestrade,' the figure hissed, 'where have you been?'

'I was off duty, sir,' Lestrade explained.

Assistant Commissioner Frost was less than impressed. 'Well, now you're here, do something.'

'Certainly sir.' Lestrade was calm. 'But first, may I know the situation?'

'The situation is this. In those doorways is one of the worst gangs in London – Rupasobly's. See that man on the 'bus – the one on the top deck? Well, he's one of Rupasobly's people. And he's dead. The rest of them on the 'bus are Maguire's. Except for the driver, the conductor and a woman passenger. Maguire is holding them hostage.'

'What for?'

'He says he'll kill them unless we guarantee him and his men safe conduct out of the city.'

'His men killed Rupasobly's man?'

'He says not.' Frost nursed his head. 'But you know these Irish. They'd kill anybody for the price of a pint.'

'Have you talked to Rupasobly?'

'I tried.' Frost held up his bloody handkerchief. 'One of his thugs threw a snowball at me. It had half a brick in it. Talk to him, Lestrade. Make him see sense.'

'What's to say I won't get the other half of the brick?' Lestrade asked.

'He knows you, Lestrade. You've got a knack of dealing with the riff-raff. If this gets out of hand, it'll get ugly.'

'I'm afraid it will,' nodded Lestrade as another cab arrived on the scene. 'Here's Chief Inspector Abberline. Bandicoot, Dew, with me,' and he crossed to the far wall. 'Dew, get your truncheon out,' he ordered.

'Sir?'

'Your truncheon, man. Get it out. Hold it up in the air. Harry, are you armed?'

Bandicoot looked askance. 'Good Lord, no.'

'Right. Put both hands in the air. Gentlemen, we're going to walk across the street that way.' He jerked his head behind him. To Bandicoot, it seemed an odd way to walk, but his ex-guv'nor knew best. This was alien territory to the Somerset squire. He'd only once entered the East End when he was a copper and he'd narrowly escaped a beating then. Toffs were particularly likely prey for men without scruple, without money and without hope. 'We will walk slowly, spread out and there will be no sudden moves. Understood?'

Bandicoot and Dew nodded. The body of policemen shifted to watch as the three of them padded softly through the snow, churned now by cab wheels and stamping, shifting size twelves. They made an odd sight – two men in regulation bowlers and Donegals, the inspector's rather better made than the constable's, both of them with the condensation freezing on their regulation moustaches. The third, a head taller, in topper and astrakhan, cut in altogether a different style. All three men had their hands in the air.

'Chubb!' Lestrade shattered the silence. 'Chubb Rupasobly. Come out, come out, wherever you are.'

A single snowball crashed and broke on Lestrade's shoulder. It contained nothing but snow.

'Who wants him?' a voice shouted.

'Inspector Lestrade,' he answered.

'What's that in your hand?' the voice shouted back.

Lestrade raised his brass knuckles higher and threw them ostentatiously into the snow. Dew did the same with his truncheon.

'What about the swell?' the voice called.

'That's you, Harry,' whispered Lestrade. 'Show them your hands are empty.'

Bandicoot turned them in the air. Lestrade walked on.

'That's far enough!' the voice shouted.

'I want the organ grinder,' said Lestrade loudly, 'not his monkey.'

There was a ripple of whistles and applause from the distant omnibus. A tiny figure broke silently from the darkness of the buildings and stood before Lestrade in wide-awake and cigar, his fingers dazzling with rings.

'Hello, Chubb,' said Lestrade.

'Mr Lestrade,' trilled the midget, 'this is a pleasant surprise.'

Lestrade nodded. 'Mrs Rupasobly?' he asked.

'Very well,' the midget said, the grin fixed on his evil face.

'And all the little Rupasoblies?'

More guffaws from the 'bus.

'This isn't a social call, Mr Lestrade. Who's the fancy dan?'

'This is Harry Bandicoot, Chubb. He's a friend of mine. And this . . .' He turned to Dew.

'We know 'im,' Chubb said, clenching his teeth. 'So what's to do?'

'I want to talk, Chubb. This is a bit public, isn't it?'

'Come this way, then.'

'Sholto.' Harry half turned and dropped his hands. Rupasobly backed like a cornered rat into the shadows. There was a flash in the darkness that Lestrade recognized as a knife blade.

'No!' he shouted. 'It's all right, Chubb. Bandicoot here is new at this. He doesn't know the rules.'

There was a silence.

'It's your move, copper,' Chubb hissed.

'Lestrade!' a voice roared from behind the trio. Lestrade recognized it as Abberline's. 'Come away. You're not achieving anything by talking to that deformed animal.'

There was an inrush of air. Another single snowball hurtled across the street, missing Lestrade by inches and crunching into the centre of the police circle. There was a squeal.

'I expect that smarts, Mr Abberline,' called Rupasobly. 'There was half a brick in it.'

'Chubb.' Lestrade took two paces forward. 'We can reason this out. What do you want?'

'The head of Cosh Maguire,' hissed the dwarf. 'Oh, and his balls too. I may as well have the set. I can make a pawnbroker's sign out of them.'

Lestrade closed to the edge of the darkness. A dozen more chivs gleamed in the frosty starlight. 'Chubb,' Lestrade said quietly, 'the whole area is ringed with coppers. You can't get out!'

'We'll take a few of you bastards with us!' another voice said.

'That you may,' said Lestrade, 'but if Commissioner Frost sends for the army, that's it. It'll make Bloody Sunday look like a chapel outing.'

'Is that likely?' Not even Chubb Rupasobly wanted to take on the British Army. He had a reputation for winning fights and he wasn't sure he would win that one.

'Frost's got a headache, Chubb,' Lestrade said. 'Now Abberline's got one too. Neither of them's got a very long fuse as it is.'

'So what do you suggest?'

'Let's you and me take a little walk to that 'bus; have a little chat with Maguire. See if we can't talk this thing out.'

There was another silence.

'Lestrade, you know my boy Turk, don't you?'

An ugly head with stubble and broken teeth emerged briefly from the shadow of a doorway and grinned.

'The Annie Oakley of Shoreditch? Intimately.'

'Well, then, you'll know he's as good with a chiv as he is with a snowball. He'll be watching us all the way to the 'bus. Any nonsense from your boys in blue or that Irish scum and there'll be three blades in your back – your two and his. Savvy?'

'Savvy,' said Lestrade.

The dwarf stepped into the gaslight, took off his rings and diamond tiepin and passed them to a confederate. 'No point in antagonizing that Irish filth,' he said. 'If they see gold they go berserk. Comes of eating spuds all your life. And Lestrade . . .' He reached up and caught the inspector's lapels, 'I do mean your life. You!' Rupasobly jabbed Bandicoot in the navel. 'You come with us. If that Irish trash try anything, you're big enough to cover me. Savvy?'

'Er . . .'

'He savvies,' Lestrade spoke for him.

The odd trio began their walk. Again, all three of them had their hands in the air. The bowler was dull under the gaslight, the topper shining and, at waist-level, the wide-awake floating outsize on the tiny head.

'Lestrade, what's going on?' Abberline called, the body of policemen shifting sideways as he began to walk in echelon with the trio.

'Stay where you are, Chief Inspector!' Lestrade shouted. 'Leave this to me now, please.' He half turned to see Turk take up his place on the edge of the shadows, a whole kitchen-range of knives in his fist. The policemen stopped. 'Whatever happens now, keep your men back,' he said.

The omnibus seemed miles away. The gas and moonlight shone on the gleaming brassware and the oil lamps flickered at front and back. One by one they were blown out.

'Far enough!' an Irish voice grated.

''Evening, Cosh,' called Lestrade cheerily.

'Mr Lestrade, sor,' another voice came back, 'where's dat handy little brass knuckle you've got?'

'Back there in the snow,' Lestrade said. The man was well informed, for a navvy.

'Who's the toff?' Maguire asked.

'Harry Bandicoot. He's a friend of mine.'

'Move away, Mr Bandicoot. There's a funny little bug at your feet.'

'Thank you,' said Bandicoot. 'I'm comfortable where I am.'

Rupasobly looked up at him. 'When I can get my hands down,' he whispered, 'I'll give you my card. If you ever need a job, look me up.'

'Mr Lestrade,' Maguire shouted, 'tell that poison dwarf I want him in front.'

'I'll stand in front,' said Lestrade.

'No, you won't!' Turk shouted from the far end of the street.

'All right,' shouted Lestrade, his hands still in the air. 'Harry, you stand in front of Chubb. Chubb, you stay where you are. I'll stand behind you.'

'Ah,' said Bandicoot, 'changing from line to column, eh? This reminds me of the Corps at Eton.'

Lestrade and Rupasobly looked at him.

'Before you do that, Mr Lestrade,' the Irishman called, 'tell that misfit midget I want to see all his weapons. *All* of them.'

Rupasobly snarled.

'Chubb,' said Lestrade quietly, 'do it for my sake. By the way, Turk *is* a cool type, isn't he?'

Rupasobly chuckled and slowly produced a knife from his pocket. He held it up to the light and dropped it in the snow. Then he clawed out an iron jemmy and dropped that. Then a pocket pistol. Then a lead and leather life preserver.

'*All* of them!' growled the Irishman.

Rupasobly produced a steel Sikh throwing quoit with its murderous circular blade and tossed it aside.

'Now you make your move,' said Maguire.

The three of them manoeuvred before the parked 'bus. There was consternation from the policemen. 'What the bloody hell is Lestrade doing?' Frost asked.

Abberline shook his head. 'Looks like a gentlemen's excuse me,' he muttered.

'All right,' called Maguire, 'so what's the deal, Mr Lestrade?'

'Mr Rupasobly wants his man back, Cosh.'

The Irishman popped his head over the rail and spat volubly.

'I want something else,' said Lestrade.

'What's that?' Maguire asked.

'First of all, I'd like to put my hands down if it's all right with you.'

'You know my boy, Seamus?' Maguire asked.

A tousle-haired figure swung out from the stairs of the 'bus and waved.

'The Annie Oakley of Ballybrophy? Of course.'

'For the benefit of that fancy dan in front of the insect,

Seamus is a legend in his own lifetime with the throwing-shillelagh. Any funny business and he'll part your hair for you, mister.'

'We understand that, Cosh,' Lestrade called from the back. Rupasobly was no problem, but Bandicoot obscured his view of the 'bus. He couldn't count the number of the opposition, but he guessed a dozen. In the shadows behind him, perhaps thirty of Rupasobly's people. There must have been as many coppers clustered around Frost and Abberline, like an infantry square facing Fuzzy-Wuzzies. God alone knew how many more of all three sides were closing in on the scene from all the streets around. It must have been nearly midnight, early by East End standards. The pubs weren't closed yet.

'Well, Cosh,' Lestrade did his best to smile. 'How's Mrs Maguire?'

'She's fine, Mr Lestrade.'

'And the sixteen little Maguires?'

'Padraig's got a touch of the tuberculosis – and of course there's the ringworm and the smallpox – but apart from that, fine.'

'Good, good. Now, Cosh, about this little problem of ours . . .'

'Don't play around with the Irish bastard, Lestrade,' hissed Rupasobly.

'I'm sorry, Mr Lestrade,' the Irishman shouted, 'I thought I heard somebody break wind.'

'Nothing,' Lestrade said quickly, 'just nerves. Now, Cosh, what happened?'

'Nothin',' said Maguire, 'nothin' at all.'

'Tell that Irish sod he's lying,' snarled Rupasobly.

'Tell that Polish dwarf . . .'

'Gentlemen!' Lestrade raised his hand again. 'This is getting us nowhere. Chubb, what do you say happened?'

'This bog-trotter knifed my boy.'

'Bollocks. We found 'im like this.' Maguire fetched the corpse at his elbow a smart one round the head.

Rupasobly moved as though to rush the 'bus. Lestrade heard movement from behind and Bandicoot heard it from in front. Knife and shillelagh were raised in the air. Both men were seconds from death.

'You'd better tell me about it, Cosh,' Lestrade shouted, hoping that his voice sounded less hysterical than he was.

'Like I said, Mr Lestrade,' the Irishman answered, 'two of my boyos were on the 'bus. They knew this son-of-a-bitch but left him alone. I didn't want trouble with Rupasobly. It's Christmas. I was going to have my sainted mother over from Wicklow.'

'You *are* a whitlow!' snarled Rupasobly.

'Chubb,' Lestrade hissed, prodding him in the back with his toe. 'So how did we all end up here?' Lestrade asked Maguire.

'Another of the dwarf's idiots got on and started talking to this one.' He tapped the corpse again. 'He realized he was a goner and started picking on my lads. There was a punch-up on the top deck. There's teeth all over the place up here to prove it.'

'And then?'

'Word gets round, Mr Lestrade, you know that. Me and my lads got here first. The driver stopped the 'bus and the passengers got off, except for one, I believe. The driver said he wasn't goin' a step further, so we unhitched the bastard's horses and pushed a life preserver up 'is throat. Then Rupasobly's boys arrived. It's his little legs, you see. Can't get anywhere fast enough.'

'You . . .'

'Chubb!' Lestrade hissed again. 'Let me talk to the driver and conductor,' he called to Maguire.

There was activity on the 'bus and a figure rose head and shoulders above the others. 'I'm the driver,' a Cockney voice called, the first one Lestrade had heard, apart from Dew's, all night.

'Inspector Lestrade, Scotland Yard,' he called. 'Did you hear what Mr Maguire said?'

'Yes.'

'Is it true?'

'I dunno 'ow it started, guv. But 'e's right about 'ow it finished.'

'Where's your conductor?'

Another head popped up and the driver's popped down.

'Did you see how it started?' Lestrade asked him.

'I saw this bloke get on and talk to the dead 'un,' came the tremulous reply. 'He fell against the wall and then all 'Ell broke loose. Look, I've lost a tooth, guv'nor. I've got a wife and kids. Get us out of 'ere.'

He was yanked sharply down by somebody. Lestrade heard the driver say, 'Blakey, stop that bleatin'. Remember you are an hemployee of the Walthamstow and District Homnibus Company. You do your sobbin' on your own time.'

'Spoken like a true idiot,' purred Maguire.

'Cosh, I'm coming aboard,' said Lestrade.

'Why?' the Irishman shouted.

'Think of me as a referee,' Lestrade said. 'I want to see fair play, that's all. I want to examine the corpse.'

'All right. Seamus, watch him. Any tricks, Lestrade and you're a dead man.'

'Turk!' Rupasobly trilled. 'Watch Lestrade. He's going on the 'bus. Any tricks and he's a dead man.'

Doubly reassured, Lestrade circled the dwarf and the giant and as he passed Bandicoot he heard him whisper, 'May you always have the last shot, Sholto.'

The rail felt icy cold under his hand. A number of Irish roughs made way for him to take the stairs. He stumbled over a pair of feet and realized he was momentarily out of sight of the Annie Oakley of Shoreditch. But Harry was not, his broad, unassailable back blocking out the light, and in his shadow hid Rupasobly. Besides, the Annie Oakley of Ballybrophy was grinning up at him, cradling the smooth knob of his shillelagh and longing to practise his deadly art.

'Let him through, there!' barked Maguire. ''Tis himself coming up the stairs.'

Lestrade emerged on the top deck, the only figure walking upright. He was already the target for knife and club. He only hoped that no copper had got hold of a gun and that his silhouette under the green moon was unmistakable enough. He looked at the doubled-up driver and the quaking conductor and the assorted roughs in mufflers and titfers draped about the floor and seats. He looked at the corpse. The dead man was about twenty-five with a shock of black hair and a heavy moustache. His face was criss-crossed with old scars and his eyes stared straight ahead. Lestrade felt in his pockets. A tram ticket, a switchblade knife which Maguire lifted from him and a gold watch, which the Irishman also confiscated.

Lestrade straightened. 'This is Tom "The Sheep" le Mouton,' he called down to the little figure obscured beyond Bandicoot.

'That's right,' said Rupasobly.

'We can all go home, then,' said Lestrade.

'What do you mean?' shouted Rupasobly.

'Chubb, you and the Maguire gang have been at each other's throats for years. What do they carry?'

A moment's pause. 'Shillelaghs,' he said.

'And?' Lestrade's breath spread out on the night air.

'Chivs.'

'What sort?'

'Eh?'

'I'll tell you,' said Lestrade. 'Broad blades, mostly single-edged. Am I right?'

'What of it?' snapped Rupasobly.

'This man has been skewered through the neck,' Lestrade told him, 'by something no wider than a pencil. It's your boys who use stilettos.'

'And those Wop bastards,' roared Rupasobly.

Realizing the scenario might move up the road to the Italian quarter, Lestrade grabbed the conductor and hauled him upright. 'Who was sitting behind this man?' He pointed to the corpse.

'Er . . . I don't know.'

'*Think*, man,' Lestrade pressed his tipless nose against the conductor's. 'Your life, all our lives, may depend on it.'

'Er . . . um . . . a woman. It was a woman.'

'On her own?'

'Yeah. Got on at the Tower, I think.'

'Old? Young? Colour of coat? Hair?'

''Ow the 'ell should I know? I see thousands of passengers, guv'nor. Wait a minute . . .'

'Yes?' Lestrade gripped the man's lapels.

'She definitely 'ad 'air.'

'Thanks,' said Lestrade. 'Chubb, any of your men in the habit of dressing up as a woman?'

There were shouts of anger from the shadows and whistles and hoots from the 'bus.

'I should be very careful, Mr Lestrade,' Rupasobly said quietly.

'What about yours, Cosh?'

This time the cheers and cat-calls burst from Rupasobly's corner and the Irishmen fell silent. Maguire closed to Lestrade.

'I'd keep your distance, Cosh,' the inspector whispered, 'there's a knife on me out there somewhere and I don't know how good Rupasobly's man is.'

The Irishman relented.

'Gentlemen,' Lestrade said, 'this has nothing to do with either of you. The Sheep was murdered by person or persons unknown. By a woman, in fact.'

'That's right,' shouted Maguire. 'We'd no need to creep up on the bastard from behind. If any of my boys done it, it'd be face to face.'

'Chubb?' Lestrade called quietly.

'A misunderstanding then, Mr Maguire,' he trilled.

'Precisely so, Mr Rupasobly.'

'We'll say goodnight, then.' Rupasobly clicked his fingers and a lackey leapt from the shadows to pick up his discarded armoury.

'Top o' the evening to you,' Maguire called.

'We'll just take The Sheep home,' said Rupasobly, as his men warily closed in.

'No, you won't,' Lestrade said firmly. Abberline and the knot of policemen, now grown to nearly a hundred, advanced on the 'bus. 'He's mine for a while, Chubb. You can have him later. Leman Street Mortuary.'

A silence. Nobody moved.

'Merry Christmas, Mr Lestrade.' Rupasobly smiled and disappeared through the throng of his boys.

From the 'bus, a fiddle struck up 'The Wearing o' the Green' and Maguire's lads tumbled out and skipped away across the snow.

'Merry Christmas, Mr Lestrade, sor,' said Maguire and shook him warmly by the hand. 'Here,' he slipped him a bottle, 'one of Mrs Maguire's specials. It'll put hair on your caubeen.'

Lestrade had had one of Mrs Maguire's specials before. He was in no doubt of it. The inspector looked at the driver and conductor cowering on the floor. 'Gentlemen, I suggest you catch your horses. This 'bus is running late.'

He leaned over the side. 'You men,' he called to the nearest constables, 'up here on the double. I want this body delivered to Leman Street. Harry,' he called to the squire, 'you can put your hands down now, I think.'

As he reached the bottom stair, there was a whisper from inside. He frowned into the darkness. A middle-aged lady slumped in a seat in a corner. Lestrade crouched beside her, wondering what unspeakable outrage Maguire's mob had perpetrated on her person. Then he smelt her breath. 'One of Mrs Maguire's specials,' he said to himself.

The lady woke. 'Marble Arch?' she asked.

'Not yet, love,' Lestrade patted her hand. 'I'll give you a shout when we get there.'

When Lestrade arrived at the Grand, it was breakfast time. He was shown into the room with its stiff white tablecloths and clutter of silver.

'Ah, Mr Lestrade.' He heard an elderly voice he thought he knew.

'Miss Balsam. Good morning. I was hoping to catch Harry to thank him for last night.'

'I believe the lambs are lying in this morning, Inspector. Won't you join me? There's toast and the marmalade is quite delicious.'

'Well, I . . .'

'Now,' she wagged a matronly finger at him, 'I'll wager you haven't eaten since last night. I must insist.'

Lestrade smiled and sat beside her. He was not of the class to have had a nanny himself, but he could imagine how all Miss Balsam's charges must once have jumped.

'Waiter,' she called, 'another cup, if you please. You will take coffee, Mr Lestrade?'

'Thank you,' he said and helped himself to the toast. She noticed he had used the wrong knife, but said nothing.

'Now,' she closed to him, 'do tell me what happened last night.'

'I'm afraid I'm not at liberty to . . .'

'Stuff and nonsense!' She slapped his wrist with her napkin. 'If you were smaller, I'd smack your legs. Harry will tell me anyway . . .' She looked at him engagingly.

He laughed. 'Yes, I suppose he will. Very well, but you must understand, Miss Balsam, that this is strictly between the two of us.'

'Of course,' she frowned, horrified that he should imply it was not.

'A man was found dead on an omnibus.'

Her cup hit the saucer. 'Good heavens! How awful. I should hate to go on public transport. One never knows against whom one would fall.'

'He appeared to have been sitting alone,' Lestrade told her.

'What was it? Heart?'

Nice of the old girl to be familiar, Lestrade thought. 'Murder,' he said.

She bit heavily on her toast and for a second her dentures remained clamped to it as her lips came away. With a deft after-bite she regained them. 'What is the world coming to?' she said, shaking her head.

'The man was a petty crook.'

'Oh, but even so.' She was still aghast when Letitia joined them. Lestrade rose and she kissed him.

'Sholto, this is a lovely surprise. I didn't think we'd see you again this time. Good morning, Nanny,' and she kissed the old girl on her tousled forehead.

'Hello, dear. Mr Lestrade is telling me about the events of last night. A fellow has been foully murdered.'

'I know, Nanny,' said Letitia as the waiter hovered. 'No, just coffee, thank you. Harry was full of it.'

'I came to thank him,' said Lestrade.

'No need to.' She held his arm. 'He was glad to be of service.'

'All the same,' Lestrade said, 'he could have been killed.'

'He was pretty dead when I left him just now!' Letitia laughed. 'Who was this man on the 'bus, Sholto, the one who'd been stabbed?'

'Stabbed?' Nanny Balsam repeated. 'Oh dear me. Oh dear, dear me.'

'His name was le Mouton,' Lestrade told her, 'known as The Sheep in the circles in which he moved.'

'Of course,' said Miss Balsam.

They looked at her.

'Letitia,' she scolded, 'I taught you the rudiments of French. *Le mouton* means the sheep.'

'Yes, Nanny.' She patted the old girl's hand. 'Do you know who killed him, Sholto? Can none of us ride on an omnibus again?'

'I think the odds against the same thing happening to you or to Miss Balsam are very long,' Lestrade reassured her. 'Le Mouton was on borrowed time anyway.'

'In what way, Mr Lestrade?'

'He was a flimp . . .'

Nanny Balsam fanned herself with her napkin.

'Sorry,' he smiled. 'Force of habit. I mean he was a snatch pickpocket, operating all over London, usually in crowds. He was on the edge of a gang led by one Chubb Rupasobly.'

'Good Lord!' Letitia suddenly straightened.

'What's the matter, dear?' Miss Balsam asked.

'I knew I'd heard the name le Mouton before,' she said. 'Nanny, you remember, last year. Roger Lytton. He was walking in Hyde Park when this rough tried to pick his pocket.'

'No, dear, I'm afraid I don't.'

'Yes, yes, you must. Sholto, I am right, aren't I? Roger was a distant cousin. We were all deeply shocked.'

'What happened, dear?' Miss Balsam was confused.

'Roger grappled with the man and the man pushed him. He fell and hit his head on a park bench. He died in hospital.'

'And le Mouton was charged with murder,' Lestrade said, 'only there was confusion among the witnesses.'

'Confusion?' Miss Balsam repeated.

'One of the things which makes my job difficult, Miss Balsam, is the unreliability of witnesses. There are, what . . .' He glanced around the breakfasters, '. . . thirty or so people in this room. If a man were to burst in now and attack you . . .'

She inhaled violently and a toast crumb nearly did for her. Steadied by Letitia and Lestrade and soothed by a timely gulp of coffee, she recovered.

'Very well, then . . .' Lestrade thought it best to correct himself. 'If he attacked me.'

Miss Balsam felt a little safer.

'I guarantee we'd have thirty or so different descriptions of the man in question.'

'So this sheep went unpunished?' Miss Balsam asked.

'So it would seem,' said Letitia. 'Roger's family felt most awfully about it.'

'I'm not so sure he did go unpunished,' Lestrade told them. 'Letitia, where do the family live?'

'The Lyttons? Cheltenham. Parabola Road, I think. Isn't it, Nanny?'

'I'm sorry, my dear, I must be getting old. The Lyttons, you say? They only seem to impinge on the periphery of my consciousness. I do seem to remember being introduced to Bulwer Lytton, the novelist. I told him my favourite was *What Will He Do With It?*'

Letitia patted her arm. 'No, Nanny. Not the same family. Do you need to visit them, Sholto?'

'I may learn something,' he said.

Letitia sighed. 'Very well, I'll give you their address. But . . .'

'But?'

She whispered in his ear. 'They are a little . . . odd, Sholto.'

'Odd?' he whispered back.

'Well, no, not odd.' She smiled. 'More . . . peculiar.'

'Peculiar?' He was none the wiser.

'Perhaps . . . unusual is the right word.'

'Oh, good.' Lestrade's smile was more fixed than usual.

'Sholto!' It was a grotesquely robust Harry Bandicoot who crossed the dining-room in three bounds. 'Kidneys and mushrooms, waiter. I could eat a horse.'

10

Number Thirteen, Parabola Road

Lestrade took the midday train from Euston. He also took Dew and Lilley. They followed the meandering Chelt for a while, alighted as dusk gathered and booked in at the Fleece Hotel, apt considering they were here in connection with The Sheep, le Mouton. Dew spent the night doing the paperwork that an overnight stay on expenses entailed.

In the morning, after a breakfast less impressive than the Grand's at which Lilley sipped delicately from a glass of mineral water, they went in search of the address Letitia Bandicoot had given them. Cheltenham in the grip of winter was a wonderland. The fountains were frozen and the watery sun dazzled and sparkled on the dripping cascades. Mile after mile of mellow, Cotswold villas spoke of opulence beyond the imagination of the three Yard men. The odd dark faces among the genteel throng also spoke of India. Cheltenham was wall to wall with Pukka Sahibs and Nabobs who had retired here for the saline and chalybeate springs and many had brought their ayahs and syces back with them. A troop of identically clad young fillies in frothy lace and ringlets their mothers would have worn in their day skipped past the bowler-hatted trio and giggled. One of them winked at Dew, who blushed a little and quickened his pace.

They crossed Montpelier Walk, around the Rotunda and on to Queen's Parade. A sharp right brought them into Parabola Road and they rang the bell outside the door of Number Thirteen. There was no reply, but as Lestrade glanced upward at the tracery of wrought iron that graced the balcony, he saw the nets in the window above shiver aside. With that there was a sliding of bolts and a rattling of keys and a hideous old woman stood there. Lestrade was aware of Lilley reeling a little behind him.

'Good morning,' he said, 'we are from Scotland Yard. I am Inspector Lestrade. This is Constable Dew and Constable Lilley.'

The old woman said nothing, but showed them into a vast freezing hall, with the inevitable black-and-white chequered floor. The cobwebs hung thick and white from the aspidistrae.

'I should like to see Mr Lytton,' Lestrade said and his voice fell as the crone raised a knotty finger to her blue lips. In fact, all of her was blue and Lestrade knew why. He couldn't feel his fingers either. It was freezing outside and freezing in.

The old lady left them, padding noiselessly up the stairs. The trio watched her, until she was silhouetted against the light of a huge oriel window, then she was gone.

'Rum place,' whispered Lilley, catching sight of the grotesque elephant-headed statuettes that coiled and leered from each corner.

'Mrs Bandicoot did warn me,' Lestrade murmured.

'Gentlemen!' A young female voice sounded overhead and an apparition in white glided down the stairs. 'I am Cleopatra Lytton. My aunt informs me you wish to see Mr Lytton.'

'Er . . . yes, indeed. I'm sorry, Miss Lytton,' Lestrade said. 'I assumed the lady was your housekeeper.'

'She does keep house,' said Cleopatra, suddenly aware of the cobwebs, 'though not very well. She was once a Trappist nun, Mr . . . er . . .'

'Lestrade, ma'am. Inspector Lestrade.'

She raised her hand for him to kiss it. 'And the rules of austerity are with her yet. It *is* a little trying when one is placing orders with tradesmen. You see, she refuses to write as well. Still, we manage. Gentlemen, you must be frozen. Pray, go into the drawing-room. I will arrange some tea.'

The drawing-room was, if possible, colder than the hall. The three men stood there, looking at each other. The enormous mirror over the black, empty fireplace was cracked from side to side. A spidery plant with pale tendrils was growing through a crack in the wall.

'Now.' Cleopatra Lytton returned. 'Please, gentlemen, do be

seated. I've asked Aunt to make some tea. My cousins will bring it in shortly. We do not get many guests from London. Still less from Scotland Yard.'

'It's about the late Roger Lytton, Miss Lytton. He was . . . ?'

'A tower of strength to us all, Inspector.' She sat quite still for a moment, as though wrestling with an inner problem.

'Quite.' Lestrade was at his most patient. 'But what relation was he to you, Miss Lytton?'

'He was my brother, Inspector.'

'And your parents . . . ?'

'Mama died many years ago. She is buried in her beloved Arbroath.'

Lestrade had been there once. There wasn't much else to do but be buried in Arbroath.

'Papa is upstairs, Inspector. He doesn't normally see visitors, but I realize you must have your reasons.'

'I may have what is good news for him,' said Lestrade. 'The man who may have been responsible for your brother's death is himself dead.'

Miss Lytton pressed her hands together and appeared to be praying silently, 'God keep me from thoughts of revenge.'

Lestrade was becoming less and less comfortable.

'Ah.' Miss Lytton snapped out of her trance. 'Tea.'

At that moment, the double doors swung wide and three teenaged girls flounced in. They were all deathly pale, with red-rimmed eyes and flaxen hair.

'Mr Lestrade, my cousins, Faith, Hope and Charity.'

The policemen stood up and the girls curtsied, clattering down trays, cups and spoons.

'Thank you, girls!' Miss Lytton senior clapped her hands and the three junior Misses Lytton departed, chattering excitedly. Lilley could have sworn he heard one of them say beyond the wall, 'I want the little blond one,' and it brought a lump of fear to his throat.

Now, Lestrade had been around. He had drunk more tea in his time than the whole of the late East India Company had imported, but he had never seen any this colour. It was green and things were floating in it. Mechanically, the three policemen stirred the concoction and one by one, tasted it and put down their cups. Lilley had turned the colour of the marble mantelpiece.

'Have you been to London recently?' Lestrade asked.

'Why, yes, as a matter of fact, I was there yesterday,' Miss Lytton told them. 'You see, we have no servants, Mr Lestrade – you may have noticed that. We are all Socialists in this house.'

'I'm sorry,' Lestrade commiserated.

'Yesterday, I was attending a dockers' meeting at Wapping.'

'Alone?' Lestrade asked.

'Oh, good heavens no. Aunt Sybil – you met her just now – came with us. And my brother Mortimer.'

'Mortimer?'

'Yes, he is my eldest brother. Roger was the middle child. I'm afraid Mortimer is not here just now. He's taking the water at the Pittville Pump Rooms.'

Lilley was beginning to realize he had just taken the waters and was feeling decidedly odd.

'Tell me, Miss Lytton,' Lestrade persisted, 'how did you travel?'

'By train, Inspector. It's too far to cycle in this inclement weather.'

'You are a keen bicyclist, Miss Lytton?'

'Oh, rather.' She sipped her tea enthusiastically. 'The whole family is. In summer and autumn we think nothing of cycling a hundred miles a day.'

'Indeed? Have you been . . . er . . . cycling recently?'

'Now, let me see. I believe we did Hertfordshire this season. Yes, that's right. We tend to do a county a season.'

'I see.' Lestrade smiled, his eyes catching Dew's. It was unfortunate that both men had bent forward simultaneously, but the sickening crack as their heads met did not reverberate too obviously around the chill room. 'And while you were at Wapping, did you travel around at all? By omnibus, perhaps?'

'Why, yes, Inspector. Why do you ask?'

'Oh, idle curiosity. What was the number of the 'bus you caught?'

'Oh, Inspector, I'm afraid I don't remember, they all look rather alike to me. I know it had seats and those stair things and it was pulled by two horses, but other than that . . .'

'Where were you going?'

'Well, we stayed at a small hotel in Paddington. We caught a 'bus that took us through town.'

'Along the Ratcliffe Highway?'

'I really don't know. All those street things look alike to me, Inspector. Why are you asking me all these questions?'

'Force of habit, ma'am, I'm afraid. I wonder if I might talk to your father? Did he accompany you to London?'

'No. He has been confined to his bed for the past year. I'll see if he'll see you.'

The three men got up as she left them. Lestrade looked at the others. 'Right,' he said, 'we've got a connection with London, with a 'bus, with The Sheep and with cycling in Hertfordshire. Dew, talk to the silent old bat. Try to get something out of her.'

'But sir . . .'

'I'm sorry, Dew, you are the only one who went to that sign language lecture. Do the best you can. Lilley, get to those girls. Find out all they know.'

'But, sir . . .'

'Mr Lestrade,' Cleopatra had returned. 'My father will see you now.'

'Thank you.' He nodded in the various directions and followed Cleopatra up the stairs as his underlings went in search of their respective quarries.

Walter Dew tapped lightly on the kitchen door. There was no answer, so he pushed it. Aunt Sybil rose to greet him with a quizzical expression on her hideous features. The door closed on them and Lilley heard no more. He followed a winding passageway that seemed to go on forever, the walls becoming wetter and colder as he went. Then, the parting of the ways. Two doors. He fumbled in his pocket for a tanner and tossed it. Tails. The story of his life. He adjusted the bowler in the crook of his arm and opened the door. It led down two or three steps into a darkened room. Lilley wasn't partial to the dark and he hesitated more than once. But around the corner, he saw daylight again and opened a second door into the garden. Here, in the frozen leaves, swept up from autumn's rout, he heard a plaintive whistling. Climbing the stairs to lawn level, he saw an old man with a muffler wrapped around his head, digging heartily under an elm.

'Good morning,' Lilley called.

The old man stopped, looked up as though scenting the wind and carried on digging.

'I say, good morning,' Lilley repeated.

This time the old man spun round. 'Ah,' he said, 'over there, if you please.' Lilley followed the man's pointing finger and stood there. Unfortunately, the spot placed him in a difficult position and he edged forward.

'No, against the wall,' the old man insisted.

Lilley wiggled backwards so that the top of his head was jammed under a parapet of bricks.

'Well, where is it?' The old man paused, staring wildly around him with rheumy eyes.

'What?' Lilley had lost this conversation a long time ago.

'The shit,' the old man said, and catching sight of Lilley's horrified and bewildered countenance, modified it a little. 'Very well, then, the dung, the manure, the ordure. Well, I did order it!' and he laughed hoarsely, slapping his thigh in a weak sort of way until a paroxysm of coughing caught him and he had to sit down.

'No, I'm not the gardener,' Lilley explained.

'Of course you're not. I am,' spat the old man.

'I'm a policeman.'

The gardener visibly jumped. 'There's no law against it.'

'What?' asked Lilley, emerging now from his cramped position.

'Burying this 'ere dog.' He gestured at the ground. 'He *was* dead, you know.'

'Yes, yes, of course.' Lilley began to retreat. 'I obviously came the wrong way. I was looking for the Misses Lytton.'

'Oh, we're all called Lytton round here.' The gardener drove his spade into the rock-hard earth again. He hauled up a wooden cross and rammed it into the mound he had created. 'Even the bloody dog,' he sighed and Lilley noted the carved marker 'Lytton Lytton of Parabola'. 'Still,' the old man muttered to himself, hammering in the cross, 'the little bastard won't pee over my chrysanths again!'

Lilley returned the way he had come, up the dark staircase and to the other door, the one he had come to wish he had taken in the first place. He adjusted his bowler again and knocked. No reply. He pushed the door and stepped into nothingness. Blackness met his gaze and his legs sawed violently in the air as he plummeted downwards. He was aware of nothing more.

Lestrade stood respectfully bareheaded before the old man in the smoking cap and shawl.

'You'll have to speak up,' Cleopatra muttered. 'He's a little hard of hearing. Papa,' she automatically increased her volume, 'this is Inspector Lestrade. He's come about Roger.'

'Hmph,' the elder Lytton snorted, 'it's a little late, young man. My son is dead.'

'Yes, sir,' said Lestrade. 'I know. I have come on another matter.'

Lytton suddenly drove a sharp cane into his daughter's side. 'He's come about another matter, you blithering idiot. I can't stand people who blither. Especially women! I've been in India, Lefarge. They used to burn the buggers there, you know. Bally good idea. Now, what's all this about Roger?'

'No, sir.' Lestrade closed to the four-poster bed. 'It's not about Roger.'

'Not about Roger?' The old man cupped his good ear. 'She said it was. Eight children – isn't it? – and I'm stuck with the imbecile. What's it about then, Defarge, this other matter?'

'We think Roger was killed by a man named le Mouton.' Lestrade heartily wished he hadn't embarked on this.

'Ah, bloody Frenchman, eh? Can't trust 'em, L'Orange. They're foreign, y'see. Not like you and me. I don't mind tellin' you, when I heard that Frog prince was killed by those damned blackamoors in Zululand, I laughed like a bloody drain. Didn't I, Cleo? You'll bear me out?'

'Yes, Papa,' she said obediently.

'Sir, were you with your son when he was killed? Last year, I mean,' Lestrade battled on regardless.

'God, don't tell me Mortimer's gone too. What's a man supposed to do without his sons?'

'No, Papa,' Cleo comforted him. 'Mr Lestrade is talking about Roger.'

'Roger?' He strained round to face her, staring in astonishment. 'Are you deaf?' he bellowed. 'He's come about another matter.'

The anguish in Cleo's face told Lestrade he was wasting his time. Still, this was a Yard enquiry. No stone must be left interred.

'Does the name Perameles mean anything to you, sir?'

'No.' Lytton was adamant, shaking his head. 'I haven't a son by that name.'

'What about Coquette?' Lestrade was clutching at straws, but Lytton suddenly sat bolt upright in bed. He flung the ear trumpet from him and rammed the rattan cane into Lestrade's navel.

'I have no son by that name either,' he hissed and fell back, deadly white and gasping on the pillow.

'Is he all right?' Lestrade asked as Cleopatra fussed around her father.

'He will be,' she explained. 'Would you leave us?'

'I must be going,' Lestrade said, sensing a wasted journey. 'I'll see myself out.'

Walter Dew's sign language had run out after 'Hello' and a slow stagger through the vowels. He hadn't the courage to tell his guv'nor he had slept through most of that lecture. In any case, Aunt Sybil had just looked at him, bemused. He had finally admitted defeat and left in search of Lestrade or Lilley. The house in Parabola Road unnerved him. It was cold and dark. Ancient Indian gargoyles leered at him from every turn in the corridor and he had a niggling inability to find the hall again. Twice he caught sight of a solitary shadow flitting on a landing above him. It was hunched and twisted and he tightened his grip on his truncheon. The door when he found it came as a relief – an ordinary, everyday object in a house of shadows. He knocked on the mahogany panel.

'Come in,' a female voice called. 'Well, hello.'

At first his eyes could not acclimatize to the room. Then he became aware of a bed facing him and on the bed reclined one of the girls who had brought the tea. A less experienced man might have missed it, but Dew had been married for some years. The girl on the bed was stark naked except for her stockings and she rolled on to her back and kicked her legs in the air.

There was a giggle and Dew became aware of the other two cousins on either side of him. Like their sister they had discarded their dresses and they ran their hands over his Donegal and tickled his ears.

'I'm sorry,' Dew mumbled, flushing crimson in the twilight, 'wrong room.'

'Nonsense,' the girl on the bed crooned. 'We don't have many visitors, especially not men.'

She rolled over again and knelt in front of him, the pert cheeks of her bottom high in the air. Dew swallowed hard and felt fingers loosening his waistcoat buttons and an arm thrusting down the waistband of his trousers. He was aware of a heady scent of perfume and of firm nipples nudging against his chest. They were not his own. He backed to the door but the sight of Hope on the bed and the ministrations of Faith and Charity on each side of him were beginning to have their effect.

'Remember, he's mine first.' Hope ran her tongue over her lips.

'Only until the other two arrive,' Charity said.

'Dew!'

The constable leapt back into reality at the sound of his master's voice and he hauled the girl's arm out of his kicksies. Prising white knuckles off the door, he wrenched it open and collided with his guv'nor, returning from the bedroom of old man Lytton.

'Anything untoward, Dew?' Lestrade noted the high colour, the open waistcoat, the bulge in the trousers. He glanced over the constable's head to the odd, sweetly smelling darkened room beyond and heard the screams subside to a low moan.

'No, sir. I . . . er . . . missed my way, sir.'

'As long as that is all you missed,' said Lestrade. 'Where's Lilley?'

They looked at each other. There was a distant call, as though it came from Hell.

'Down there,' said Dew.

'This way,' said Lestrade and dashed down the stairs. Dew contemplated sliding down the ornate banister to save time, but he wasn't ready for that yet and anyway, there was a much bigger knob at the bottom which would have taken the wind out of more than his sails. He took the more conventional risers.

'Oh, no, it's the cellar!' they heard Cleopatra Lytton cry above them.

Lestrade stopped sharply and Dew hit him again. In a tangle of Donegals and bowlers, the two men rolled over the hall floor. Salvaging what they could of their dignity they struggled upright.

'Cellar?' Lestrade looked up at the apparition in white.

'The floor in the old dining-room. It has a touch of dry rot. And the windows have been boarded up. I fear your colleague has met with an accident.'

Lestrade and Dew followed her to the door through which Lilley had leapt into oblivion. Cleopatra opened it, but held the others back.

'Lilley?' Lestrade called.

'Sir? Is that you?'

'Where the bloody hell are you? Oh, pardon me, Miss Lytton.'

'Down here, sir,' a less than hearty voice called back.

'How the devil did you get down there?' Lestrade roared.

'Oh, it was quite easy, sir, really.'

Lestrade fumbled for his Lucifers, but he couldn't find them. He couldn't find his cigars, either. Obligingly, Miss Lytton struck a match for him. They were his brand, too. She held it out into the void and they all saw Lilley lying against a corner, his coat and face filthy, his hair matted with mildew.

'Are you all right?' Lestrade called.

'I think I have broken my ankle, sir,' Lilley gasped and fainted.

'Oh, God. Dew, get down there. Miss Lytton,' the match went out, 'could you find the constable here a lamp?'

She went in search of one. When it returned, Dew crept gingerly down the slippery stone steps and hauled Lilley over his shoulder in the style of the policeman's lift and brought him up.

'He ought to rest,' Dew said. 'That ankle looks nasty.'

'It'll match the rest of him,' muttered Lestrade, realizing anew how much of a liability his staff were.

'I'll call you a cab,' Cleopatra said. Lestrade settled for that. He'd been called worse in his time and he and Dew lifted the unconscious constable off Dew's shoulder and propped him against a bronze elephant in a corner.

'What do you make of it all, sir?' Dew whispered in the silence.

'As little as possible,' said Lestrade and breathed a sigh of relief when he saw the hansom pull up outside. 'Come on, Dew, it's what your right arm's for,' and he placed Lilley's bowler on Lilley's backside as Dew hoisted him out.

'Thank you, Miss Lytton,' Lestrade said and a sudden movement out of the corner of his eye made him turn. Cleopatra saw it.

'Oh, that's my other sister, Ulrica. She's not quite the ticket, I'm afraid. Lives in the West Wing.'

'Yes, of course,' smiled Lestrade and tipped his bowler.

'I hope we've been of some help in your enquiries, whatever they were,' she said.

He looked at her, a pale, tragic girl surrounded by maniacs. She obviously had more than her share of crosses to bear, the only sane one among them.

'Indeed you have,' said Lestrade. 'Goodbye, Miss Lytton.'

'Oh, Inspector,' she called as he reached the steps and freedom. She held up his matches and cigars. 'Sorry.' She grinned a little sheepishly.

'Ah.' He tried to laugh it off. 'They must have fallen out of my pocket when Dew and I tumbled.'

'Oh . . . and . . .' She produced his half-hunter and its fob chain.

'Ah,' he said.

'And . . . um . . .' His wallet came next.

'Ah.'

'And of course . . .' And the brass knuckles with their secret blade. 'I'm sorry,' she said. 'One picks up rather nasty habits in Holloway, I'm afraid.'

While Dew saw to Lilley's wounds at the local infirmary, Lestrade went in search of the last of the Lyttons. The Pittville Pump Room was an elegant edifice in the Regency style with Ionic columns after the fashion of the Ilissus at Athens. All of which architectural splendour was lost on Lestrade who was shown into a robing room and was told that Mr Lytton may be some time and he could either wait or take the waters. The hot steam was delicious after the cold of Number Thirteen, Parabola Road and he hadn't had a Turkish bath before. He hung his Donegal and bowler on a peg and removed suit and combinations. They gave him a towel which he wrapped round his waist, and he strode out into a fine atrium in the middle of which a steaming pool beckoned.

'Mr Lytton?' he whispered to a lounging attendant.

'Over there,' he was told, 'in the red robe.'

Mortimer Lytton was a tall, elegant man of about Lestrade's own age. He had a finely shaped goatee and a moustache which was clearly used to being waxed and now hung somewhat after the mandarin fashion in the steam.

'Mr Lytton?' Lestrade asked again.

The red-robed man peered through the steam. 'You can call me Coquette,' he lisped.

'I beg your pardon?' said Lestrade after a stunned pause.

'All my friends do.' Lytton patted Lestrade's hand. 'New ones as well as old. What can I call you?'

'Inspector,' said Lestrade.

'Oh, my God!' and Lytton rose as though to bolt. His towel fell off and he seemed in no hurry to pick it up.

'Oh, dear, look at that,' and he preened himself. 'Would you pick it up for me, Inspector?'

Lestrade looked at him. Here was a healthy, apparently able man, yet he could not pick up a towel. Lytton sensed Lestrade's surprise and whispered, 'You daren't bend over in here.'

Lestrade picked up the towel and allowed Lytton to rerobe.

'Look,' Lytton swept the hair back from his forehead, 'I can explain about the incident in the library . . .'

'That's not why I'm here,' Lestrade said.

'No?' Lytton looked furtively around, grateful for the screen the swirling steam provided. 'Oh, it's not that farmer's lad, is it? Because I paid good money to . . . oh dear.'

'Mr Lytton, I am here in connection with the death of your brother.'

'Roger?' Lytton's screech was falsetto. He tapped Lestrade on the shoulder. 'Well, why didn't you say so? Come over here,' he gestured to a huge marble column, 'where it's a bit more private.' He tapped Lestrade's shoulder again. 'You're quite taut for your age, aren't you?' he said, angling his head.

'Why do they call you Coquette?' Lestrade asked, keeping his back firmly to the column.

'Oh, we all have nicknames here. I've had mine for ages, ever since I was a small boy, in fact. See him over there . . .' He gestured to a fat, balding man who sat on a chair under the water. 'He's Myra. And that one over there . . .' He nodded towards one squatting by the poolside. 'He's Alice. We're quite a little fraternity here, you see.'

Lestrade saw and he felt less than at home. 'The man who may have killed your brother has himself been murdered, Mr Lytton.'

'No! Get away! Well, I never!'

Lestrade found that hard to believe. 'Were you in London yesterday, sir?' he asked.

'Good Lord, no. Not since that incident in St Paul's.'

'St Paul's?'

'I used to live in London, Inspector. I sang in the choir. One day – I remember distinctly it was a Palm Sunday – I got . . . quite attached, shall we say, to another choirboy, some years my junior. Well, not to put too fine a point on it, I put my hand up his cassock, only to find another one there already.'

'His own?' Lestrade surmised.

'No, bless your heart, the Dean of St Paul's, sitting on the other side of him. Well, I couldn't go back after that. I gave London a very wide berth, thank you very much. How did you find me?'

'Your sister, Cleopatra,' Lestrade told him, 'who, incidentally, says you *were* in London yesterday.'

'She's deranged, Inspector. You must have noticed. How did you find her?'

'Through your cousin, Letitia Bandicoot.'

Mortimer Lytton's face fell and he broke away from his casual position against the column. 'I see,' he said sourly and his whole demeanour changed. 'What is it you want?'

'Some answers.' Lestrade sensed a raw nerve and went straight for the jugular. 'For instance, Mr Lytton, do you like chocolates?'

The question caught the man off balance but he steadied himself.

'Yes, what of it?'

'Are you familiar with the chocolates of Messrs Rowntree, of York?'

'I don't believe so. I have mine sent by trap from Messrs Cadbury's of Bournville. They too are of the Socialist bent, you see, like we Lyttons.'

Not *quite* like you Lyttons, hoped Lestrade. 'What does the name "Perameles" mean to you? Another of your nicknames, perhaps? Or possibly that of one of your . . . friends?'

'I've never heard the name,' he said. 'Why all these questions? What has all this to do with brother Roger? If you don't tell me, I shall become really vicious.'

'Tut, tut,' scowled Lestrade. 'That would never do. I am conducting an enquiry into a series of murders, Mr Lytton. I believe you may be involved.'

'Murders?' Lytton turned pale in the steam. 'Me?'

'Did you know Archibald Fellowes?'

'No.'

'What about Richard Tetley?'

'What about him?'

'Did you know him?' Lestrade's bonhomie was evaporating with the steam.

'No. Look, Inspector . . . er . . .'

'Lestrade.'

'Lestrade. You mentioned cousin Letitia a moment ago.'

'I did. What of it?'

'What of a man whose old flame is found battered to death in a London park?'

'What?'

'What of a man who has biceps of iron and could kill anybody just by snapping his fingers?'

'Are you . . . are you talking about Harry Bandicoot?'

'The same,' nodded Lytton grimly.

'You seem well informed of recent sudden death, Mr Lytton.'

'I read the newspapers, Inspector. I've known Harry Bandicoot for years. Roger was at Eton with him. I don't know what Bandicoot's been up to with this Marigold de Lacy. But I warned Letitia at the time. I said, "Don't marry him, Letty," I said. "No good will come of it." I don't know what she saw in him. Have you met him?'

'In passing.'

'Well, of course I haven't seen them since the wedding, but we didn't approve. Take my advice, *cherchez l'homme*.'

Lestrade was vaguely sure that that wasn't sound advice and rose to go. 'You hadn't planned to leave Cheltenham for a while, Mr Lytton?'

He looked lugubriously at Lestrade. 'Who'd have me, dear? I'm forty-three.'

'Aren't we all?' sighed Lestrade.

As he reached the door, he heard someone call, 'Where's the soap?' and a chorus of hearty male voices echoed, 'Yes, it does, doesn't it?'

Lestrade didn't usually shop at East India House. His interest in New Art was minimal, and he cared not a jot for the Celtic revival or the Cynuric earthenware and Tewdric pewter that the fashionable were paying small fortunes for. He wandered uncaring and unimpressed through the gorgeous fabrics and sumptuous carpets. At the feet of a vast peacock wrought in bronze lay the object of his visit – a corpse, not three hours dead, and around it, three grim-faced shopkeepers.

'Inspector Lestrade, gentlemen. Who found the body?'

'Gimlet, my nightwatchman,' the eldest said. 'I fired him, of course.'

'Fired him?' Lestrade knelt beside the body. 'Why?'

'What sort of nightwatchman was he, to allow a man to die of a heart attack – and to lie here all night?'

'Heart attack, Mr . . . er . . . ?'

'Liberty. Arthur Liberty. What else? People don't just collapse in a shop, Lestrade, unless . . .'

'Unless they've seen your prices, Mr Liberty?' Lestrade smiled disarmingly.

'Well, really . . .'

'Who are you?' Lestrade asked the second man, rather younger than the first.

'George Lazenby,' he said.

'And you?'

'W. J. Howe.'

'My partners in the firm,' explained Liberty. 'I don't understand why Scotland Yard have been brought in.'

'Dew,' Lestrade turned to his constable. 'Who summoned us?'

'Gimlet, the nightwatchman.' Dew had consulted his notebook.

'There's one reason to reinstate him, Mr Liberty,' Lestrade said, pointing to the body. 'This man has been murdered.'

The three partners looked at each other, Lestrade, the body. They all subconsciously realized there was no point in looking at Dew.

'How do you know?'

'Years of experience, gentlemen. Look here.' He pointed to the tell-tale stains on the shirt and waistcoat. 'Vomit,' he said. 'Were the lights off, you could probably detect a glow. He has been poisoned with phosphorus.'

'Good God!' the partners chorused.

'What will the press make of it?' Liberty asked, bewildered.

'What time did you close yesterday?' Lestrade rummaged routinely in the man's pockets.

The partners looked at Lazenby. 'Six o'clock,' he said, 'as is usual for a Saturday in winter. Next week we shall be open for longer, of course, as it's Christmas.'

'Did anyone see this man in the shop yesterday?'

'We'd have to call our staff,' said Lazenby. 'They don't work on Sundays, Mr Lestrade.'

'Unfortunately, we do,' Lestrade said. 'How is it you three are here?'

'I was stocktaking,' Lazenby told him, 'when Gimlet rushed in with the news of this unfortunate. I immediately contacted Mr Liberty and Mr Howe. Was he a burglar?'

Lestrade fished out a letter from the dead man's inside pocket. It was perfumed and its passages were purple. His eyes widened as he read it. He didn't believe its contents were physically possible. Obviously, his years of experience had been of the wrong kind. 'In a way, he was,' he said. 'But I think we're after much bigger fry, Mr Lazenby.'

He returned to the Grand by late afternoon to talk to Harry about his wife's extraordinary cousins. But the Bandicoots had gone, left suddenly, despite their original intention of spending a few more days at the hotel, and Lestrade was just leaving the elegant vestibule when the bell-boy scurried round calling out, 'Mr Chesney, telegram for Mr Chesney.'

'Here, boy,' Lestrade said on an impulse. It was a name he knew and he had met it too recently and too importantly to ignore. The lad in his maroon stable jacket and cap stood there with his hand out. Lestrade shook it heartily and said to him, 'On your lift.'

He opened the telegram and read the contents: VERY WELL STOP USUAL PLACE NO GOOD STOP ALBERT MEMORIAL STOP TEN O'CLOCK SUNDAY STOP H STOP. He crossed again to the reception counter and the clerk in his pince-nez looked up.

'Since Mr and Mrs Bandicoot have gone, I wonder if Mr Chesney is in?'

The clerk ran his fingers over the pigeon-holes behind him. 'No, sir. I'm afraid not.'

'Thank you,' beamed Lestrade and made for the stairs. He had seen the clerk's fingers come to rest at number forty-two and it was this door he found now, on the second floor. He tried it. Locked fast. He checked the corridor left and right; all clear. He whisked out his brass knuckles, clicked forward the knife blade tucked inside them and inserted it into the door jamb. In a second, it gave under his weight and he went in, careful to close the door again behind him.

The room of the late Mr Chesney, whose corpse Lestrade had left not an hour before on the floor of Messrs Liberty & Co., was neat and untouched. There was no rifling as there had been in the rooms of Hughie Ralph. And Lestrade was convinced that the comparison was valid, since the late Mr Chesney was another in the long line of deceased that began with Captain Fellowes. Murder by the same hand. The inspector checked drawers, wardrobe. Most of the clothes were new; some, he guessed, unworn – as was the suit Chesney had been lying down in at Liberty's. The cases were new as well, and the hat-boxes. Mr Chesney seemed to have acquired a whole new wardrobe recently. His paperwork, however, was older. A particularly interesting bundle of letters caught Lestrade's eye. They were bound in scarlet ribbon as befitted the contents, although arguably purple should have been the colour. The letters followed the same pattern as the one on the body –

written to 'Darling Clementine' and signed 'Ever Yours, H.' What passed between those phrases made Lestrade's hair stand on end. But he was a man of the world and he understood most of it.

It was well and truly dark by the time he had read the correspondence and he peered around the door, checking the corridor to effect his exit. The telegram had said ten o'clock Sunday. Was that ten in the morning? If so, he was too late. Was it ten at night? That seemed more likely, since the bell-boy had been calling for Mr Chesney only a few hours before. He would chance it.

The night was crisp and clear as he plodded through the frost towards the Gothic monstrosity of the Albert Memorial. He looked up at the late Consort, sitting thoughtfully on his bronze throne, gazing wistfully at his Hall across the road. There were few people about, the night being so raw. Here and there, couples laughed and chattered and a foot-weary constable moved some park girls on. Then, as he lit a cigar and wrapped the collar of his Donegal higher around his ears, he saw a dark, top-hatted figure, broad and erect, approach from the far side of the park. He whistled quietly, being as nonchalant as he could, until he heard the clock strike the hour. On the stroke of ten, the top-hatted figure had reached the monument. Lestrade could not make out the face, but the cut of the astrakhan coat said it all and almost certainly explained Mr Chesney's new wardrobe.

'Can I interest you in a light?' Lestrade broke the silence between them.

'No, thank you,' the stranger said. 'I'm waiting for someone.'

'H?' Lestrade ventured. He sensed the stranger stiffen.

'Chesney?' he said. 'Have you the merchandise?'

'Of course.' Lestrade patted his coat. 'Have you the money?'

H reached inside his pocket and produced a large envelope, pale green under the dim gaslight. Lestrade reached out for it, but H withdrew his hand. 'First, the letters,' he said.

'Very well.' Lestrade produced the bundle, but as he looked up he found himself staring into the muzzle of a nickel-plated revolver.

'Give them to me.' H had stuffed the money back into his pocket and was holding out his hand.

'What is this?' Lestrade asked.

'I'm not cheating you,' H told him, checking to see no one was near enough to see and hear the little transaction going on below the disapproving figure of Albert the Good. 'You'll get your money. I just want to check that *you* aren't cheating me.'

He snatched the letters from Lestrade and began to count them. 'They appear to be here,' he said.

'Do they?' Lestrade asked. 'How do you know? How many did you write to Clementine? Twelve? Fifteen? And who's to say I haven't got her letters to you?'

'What?' H levelled the revolver, but Lestrade sensed his heart was not in it. 'Take your hat off.'

Lestrade complied and stood there bare-headed under the stars.

'Y . . . you're not Chesney,' H said.

'No, I am Inspector Lestrade of Scotland Yard. Now, what do I arrest you for? Threatening me with a revolver? Disturbing the public peace? Sending improper material through Her Majesty's mail?'

H dropped the hand that held the revolver and stood staring at the ground. 'My real crime is that I had the misfortune to marry for politics,' he said, 'and to have the temerity to fall in love.'

Lestrade relieved him of the pistol. 'It's Julian Hamilton, isn't it? Member of Parliament for Stoke Newington?'

The *Sun*'s graphic artist was improving all the time.

Hamilton nodded. 'The revolver isn't loaded,' he said. 'I wouldn't know how to shoot it if it were. Where's Chesney?'

'Unless something pretty miraculous has happened, Mr Hamilton, he's at the mortuary. Someone killed him yesterday.'

'What?' The Member of Parliament visibly rocked backwards.

'I think we'd better have a little talk, don't you?'

Julian Hamilton, MP for Stoke Newington, was of little help. If Lestrade had entertained the idea that he had killed all the others for motives he could only guess at, his behaviour that Sunday night had cleared him of the murder of Malcolm Chesney. Why would a man, competent as he would have to be in his use of poisons and sure as he would have to be of their deadly effect, send a telegram to a man he knew to be dead? And further, why should he keep the appointment with a man he knew could not keep it himself?

Hamilton had fallen prey to a blackmailer. He had never loved his wife, who had been forced upon him as an aspiring young politician, eager for success. Instead, he had fallen deeply in love with a lady named Clementine. She too was married and Hamilton declined absolutely to name her further. They had met at Biarritz last year and their affair – for so it became – had blossomed quickly. They met at shooting week-ends and hunting parties and stole what few, sweet hours they could. The rest of it was correspondence.

Then, the unthinkable happened. Clementine wrote a frantic letter saying that his letters to her, which she had bound in red ribbons, the colour of the rose, the colour of blood, had been stolen. She suspected a maid, had dismissed her immediately on a trumped-up charge, but could not prove the theft or reclaim her property without involving her husband. And that she could not do.

Hamilton was then approached by this man Chesney, who had acquired the letters, probably directly from the maid, and was threatening to tell not only Clementine's husband and his, Hamilton's wife, but Hamilton's party leader, the Marquis of Salisbury, Hamilton's constituents and members of Hamilton's club, the strangest in London, the House of Commons. It would have ruined them both. And Hamilton was old enough to remember what fate befell Charles Stuart Parnell and Mrs O'Shea, not to mention Charles Dilke and several ladies. But Chesney had returned one letter at a time and was milking Hamilton of all he had. Hamilton demanded all the letters or he would go to the police.

Instead, the police had come to him.

It was a world-weary Lestrade who collapsed into his chair at the Yard early on Monday morning. It was biting cold and there was no sign of the dawn. He looked at the wall opposite him, hung with its silent testimony of nine deaths, eight by the same hand. He was about to complete the report on Malcolm Chesney, to make the ninth, when his eye fell on a note marked

'Urgent' and written in the languid, scholarly hand of Constable Skinner. Lestrade opened it and read it aloud to himself:

'Missed this before, sir. Sorry. Got lost in the paperwork. Perameles, the name in Rowntree's chocolate ledger at York. It threw me at first because I was thinking of *Peragale lagotis* and *Choeropus castanotis*. It is of course Latin for . . .' and Lestrade's voice tailed away.

He sat there, heart thumping, mouth open, for some time. Then he went into the outer office and was about to wake the snoring Walter Dew, when he thought better of it. He collected a spare shirt and a collar and threw them into his battered old Gladstone. He checked his wallet for money and his pocket for brass knuckles. He held them to the light, flicked out the murderous blade, then placed it quietly on the desk, lest he wake the sleeping policeman.

In the yard below, a constable harnessed up a wagon for him and took him direct to the station. At each rattling mile, he hoped he was wrong, that what Skinner had found was merely a coincidence. But in his heart of hearts, he knew it wasn't. He had his murderer.

And this was the last journey.

11
Omega

Lestrade took the gig at the station and was driven to the village of Huish Episcopi and then to the Hall. At the huge wrought-iron gates with the ornate crest of the wildebeest sejant, he alighted and let the vehicle go, while he took a lane to the south of the estate. It was still early morning and there was a thick frost lying silver on the birches and the mallard droppings through which he crunched. He found the break in the wall he remembered from earlier visits and clambered down through the stiff bracken to the rhododendron bushes that skirted the lower lake.

Here, he was a little startled to hear laughter and peering through the leaves he saw Miss Shadbolt, the nanny, whirling on the ice of the lake with a string of three little children forming a human chain. They were all wrapped in furs against the weather. First, Ivo, laughing hysterically and dragging back on his nanny's hand. Second, his twin brother Rupert, struggling on uncertain skates to keep pace with the others. And last, racing with the wind flying through her long blonde hair, Emma, half a head taller than the boys, her little blades flashing out in the morning.

Lestrade stayed a while, overfond, and did not hear the rattle of wheels on gravel and the snort and whinny of lathered horses. By the time he did, and straightened to face the station wagon of the Somerset Constabulary, it whistled past him on its way to the house and the blue lamp protruding from one corner caught him a nasty one on the temple so that he somersaulted gracefully through the rhododendrons and slid on his back for some yards across the ice.

Nanny Shadbolt *had* heard the arrival of the wagon, but still she was unprepared for the undignified heap of second-rate clothing that rolled to her feet. She gathered the startled children to her.

'It's all right,' shouted Rupert. 'It's only Uncle Sholto.'

And they carried on skating.

'Have you come to join us, Uncle Sholto?' Ivo asked, glancing back over his shoulder.

'Don't be silly, Ivo,' Emma scolded him. 'You can see Uncle Sholto hasn't got his skates on.'

Lestrade looked at her laughing grey eyes. That's my daughter, he thought to himself, ever the copper's kid. She *would* notice something like that. For a fleeting moment he wished he could tell her that he was not Uncle Sholto, but her father. That time would come. But it was not now. Not yet.

'Mr Lestrade,' said Nanny Shadbolt, 'may I lend you some skates?'

The inspector still sat on the ice, the moisture beginning to seep through his trousers.

'I'd settle for a hand,' he said.

'Of course. Children,' she clapped her hands, 'Uncle Sholto must be helped up. Form a circle and rally on him.'

She swept into action, gripping Lestrade's outstretched hand and hauling him upright. Hopelessly wet, hopelessly stunned by his fall and just generally hopeless, he slewed first one way, then the other, supported now by Ivo, now by Rupert. Emma caught hold of his scarf and together, somehow, all four of them hauled him across the ice until he crunched on the far bank. Unfortunately, the sedge had not yet withered and he fetched his other temple a sharp one on the corner of the jetty.

He emerged from the white lagoon, cold, wet, bleeding and furious, and waved through gritted teeth to the chattering skaters below. He realized he'd lost his bowler and caught sight of it at the reedy end of the lake as it disappeared in a crack in the ice. He gave it up as a bad job and made for the house.

That was his first mistake that morning. His second was to be recognized by Dirck, the St Bernard, who had a thing for cold, wet policemen and who loped for Lestrade now. The inspector bobbed through the orchard, vaguely aware of a flurry of blue-coated activity up at the house. The dog bobbed too and trapped him against the bark of an old, gnarled Worcester Pearmain. The beast began contentedly enough by rising on his hind legs and returning circulation to Lestrade's ears with his tongue. Then his loins began to think it was spring and Lestrade's left leg came in for some attention. He managed to haul the amorous monster off and staggered for the house.

'Oh, sir!' A wail made him turn as he reached the shrubbery.

'Maisie?' He recognized a wailing maid when he heard one. 'What is it? What's the matter?'

'Oh, sir. They're taking away the master!' and she blew with the grace of a battleship into her apron.

Lestrade pushed her aside, with rather more force than he intended, and bounded up on to the terrace in time to see a manacled Harry Bandicoot being led to the waiting wagon.

'Sholto!' It was Letitia now who hurtled from the French windows, still clad in nightgown and housecoat. She gripped him. 'Thank God you've come. What's happening?'

'Inspector Guthrie?' Lestrade put her aside a little more decorously than he had the maid, who was rushing away across the fields, screaming.

'What's happening, Lestrade, is that I am executing my duty. What you are doing here I can't imagine, but I trust you will not be attempting to hinder us in the execution of it.'

'Execution?' Letitia was not rational. 'Stop them, Sholto!'

'Where are you taking Mr Bandicoot?' he asked.

'It's all right, Sholto.' Harry's head emerged from the open door, only to be forced in again.

'All right, be damned,' said Lestrade. 'Guthrie, show me your warrant.'

The chief inspector turned squarely to face him. 'You've poked your nose in once too often, Lestrade. Sergeant, arrest this man for interfering with police duty.'

'Sergeant,' Lestrade countered, 'arrest this man for wrongful arrest.'

The sergeant dithered for a moment, but Chief Inspector Guthrie was a big fish in his particular pond and the ditherer finally pounced on Lestrade. The roar of Bandicoot's Purdy broke the pandemonium of the morning and the characters in the mad scene froze, in keeping with the day. In the silence,

Maisie's wailing could be heard echoing back from the woods beyond the lake, but all eyes had turned to the French windows.

'I am not terribly *au fait* with these gadgets, gentlemen,' a tousled old head was saying, drawing a set of beads on the head of Chief Inspector Guthrie, 'but I do remember that Mr Bandicoot said this one had a hair trigger.'

There was a strangled cry and within seconds the only things upright below the terrace were Guthrie's horses, their driver lying along their necks, praying.

'Nanny,' Harry cautiously peered out, 'it's all right. Really. Please. Take your thumb off that metal bit very slowly and point the gun at the ground.'

For a moment, Miss Balsam hesitated, then she relented and stood in her gloved hands feeling rather silly. Lestrade stood up first, followed slowly by Guthrie and the rest. Letitia crossed to the wagon's door and held Harry's handcuffed hands.

'Right!' Guthrie spun on his heel. 'Shooting at police officers,' he growled. 'That old besom will be buried inside!' and he made for her. Letitia blocked his path and with all the force at her disposal, slapped him soundly across the face.

'Striking a police officer in the pursuance of his duty,' Guthrie snarled. 'Sergeant, take this woman as well. We may as well have the whole family.'

'And what are you going to do with *them*?' Lestrade asked, jerking his thumb over his shoulder. Guthrie turned and his eyes bulged under the Homburg. From the woods, two wagons were rolling inexorably, bristling with men. And in the hands of these men, scythes and sickles sparkled in the pale morning sun.

'And *them*?'

Guthrie turned again at Lestrade's voice, to the orchard. A line of men walked abreast, leather-gaitered and woollen-smocked, like harvesters reaping the corn. A white-aproned figure ran from one to the other, weeping and wailing as hysterical housemaids will.

'And of course, *them*?'

Tom Wyatt, the Bandicoots' groom, sauntered around the corner, with a castrating iron carried nonchalantly over his shoulder. Beside him, Nettles, the butler, a man, it had to be admitted, the wrong side of sixty-three, but there was iron in him yet. And flanking him, Maisie's colleagues, starched and resolute, a monstrous regiment of women.

'I count forty-eight of 'em, sir,' the sergeant confided to his chief inspector.

'Thank you,' snapped Guthrie. 'When I need your powers of mental arithmetic, Poulteney, I shall inform you accordingly. Well, Lestrade?'

'Better than I was, thank you, Guthrie,' the inspector beamed.

Guthrie closed to him. So far this morning, he had been slapped, shot at and was now facing the massed agricultural implements of the Bandicoot estate. 'Dammit, Lestrade, what do we do?'

'We?' Lestrade raised an arched brow.

'Everythin' all right, Mr Bandicoot?' one of the labourers called from a halting wagon.

'Yes, Jack,' Harry called, astonished to see his tenants-at-arms ringing the Hall.

'How can we assist, sir?' a voice called from the direction of the stables.

'That won't be necessary, Tom.' Bandicoot leaned further out. 'I'd like you men, all of you, to put your tools away and go home. Please.'

The voice of reason had been heard in the land and Guthrie smiled broadly before turning to the trap. But no one else had moved. He turned back to the mob.

'I'm afraid we can't do that, squire.' It was young Jem, a head taller since Harry had last seen him in the harvest.

'Isn't this marvellous?' Miss Balsam clapped her hands gleefully. 'Just like the fall of the Bastille.'

Guthrie turned on Lestrade. 'You know they're all raving mad here, don't you?'

Lestrade had survived Number Thirteen, Parabola Road. The Bandicoot estate was nothing to him.

'All right, Lestrade.' Guthrie was calmer now, and it cost him dear to say it. 'What do you advise?'

Lestrade looked at him levelly. 'Well,' he said, 'we'll start by going indoors. You, me and Mr and Mrs Bandicoot. Agreed?'

Guthrie looked again at the ring of flashing blades surrounding them all. He nodded. 'Sergeant,' he said, as one final word of bravado designed to restore his own ego, 'if any man tries anything, I want his name. Understand?'

Harry and Letitia went back inside. The table was still full of the breakfast clutter.

'Letitia,' Lestrade said, 'I could manage a cup of your delicious coffee round about now.'

'Of course, Sholto.' She smoothed down her housecoat and a degree of normality prevailed.

'First,' Lestrade positioned himself in front of the fire in the drawing-room, 'the cuffs, Mr Guthrie, if you please.'

'Impossible!' Guthrie folded his arms adamantly on the *chaise-longue*. Harry sat opposite on the sofa.

'Guthrie,' Lestrade said quietly, 'you just heard Mr Bandicoot ask his men to disperse. They refused. If I pop my head out of the window now and imply that you are being less than co-operative, I wouldn't give you or your boys a tinker's damn in the matter of survival of this morning. Let me see, I counted three constables, plus your sergeant of course and yourself. That's five. Armed with truncheons against . . . what was it . . . forty-eight scythes? And as for that thing Harry's groom is carrying . . .'

His sentence was punctuated by a click as Guthrie unlocked Bandicoot's cuffs and the squire rubbed his already chafed wrists.

'Now.' Lestrade felt the warmth of the fire at last counteracting the sodden serge around his nether regions. 'What is the charge against Harry Bandicoot?'

Guthrie unfolded a piece of paper from his breast pocket, cleared his throat and read aloud: 'That the said Mr Bandicoot, of Bandicoot Hall, Huish Episcopi in the County of Somerset, did wilfully and maliciously cause the death of the late Mr Richard Tetley of the same County.'

'I see,' said Lestrade gravely. 'All right, Harry. How did you do it?'

'I poisoned him, Sholto,' Bandicoot said.

Lestrade began to circle the immense room slowly.

'How?'

'I used phosphorus.'

'You see, Lestrade,' Guthrie said, 'he admits it. Just as he admitted to me not ten minutes before you and your rabble turned up.'

'The rabble are not mine,' Lestrade told him. 'I suspect they were summoned by Maisie, the maid. And I am here on another matter. Where's your proof, Guthrie?'

'Proof? When a man confesses, Lestrade, you don't need proof. Don't they do it that way at the Yard?'

'All right,' Lestrade nodded. 'But Harry here had not confessed, I take it, until you arrived with your heavies. I repeat, where is your proof?'

'Very well,' Guthrie sighed. 'The coroner's report . . .'

'The one I never got to see,' said Lestrade, looking pointedly at Bandicoot.

'Quite rightly,' snorted Guthrie. 'It said that Tetley died of phosphorus poisoning.'

'I know,' Lestrade told him.

Guthrie dismissed it as bravado.

'Tell me, Harry, what did you use? Water?'

'That's right, Sholto.' Bandicoot hung his head. 'Please. I know you mean well, but I'd rather get this over.'

'Of course,' he said, 'but why did you use phosphorus? Was it its tasteless, colourless properties?'

'Yes,' said Bandicoot, 'it mixed so well with the water.'

Lestrade took the squire's hands in his. 'Harry, why? Why did you do it?'

The old Etonian looked him straight in the eye. 'I had my reasons,' he said.

Lestrade looked down sadly, then turned to Guthrie.

'You've got to let this man go, Chief Inspector,' he said.

'The devil I will!' bellowed Guthrie. 'He's a murderer.'

'No, he's not,' Lestrade said. 'Where's your motive? Bandicoot here hasn't given us one.'

'I'll get that from him,' said Guthrie, cracking his knuckles with certainty. 'It's the least important.'

'Opportunity?' Lestrade asked.

'The Dower House is on the Bandicoot estate, not a mile away. Wookey Hole is only an hour's ride. Someone of Mr Bandicoot's equestrian inclinations would think nothing of that. He is a free agent to come and go as he pleases.'

'Method?' Lestrade asked. It was the Holy Trinity of the detective.

'He's just told you, Lestrade,' Guthrie yawned. '*Do* concentrate. Phosphorus poisoning.'

Lestrade nodded. 'Is the death of Richard Tetley the first death by phosphorus poisoning you've met, Mr Guthrie?'

'Well, yes . . . as a matter of fact, it is.'

'I thought so. If you'd seen more, you'd know that what Bandicoot just told us is tosh.'

'Sholto!' The squire stood up.

'Sit down, Harry,' Lestrade told him. 'The grown-ups are talking now.' He resisted the temptation of lesser policemen the country over to use his fingers as aids. 'First, the squire tells us he put the phosphorus in water. Unless Tetley was blind, he would never have drunk it. It would leave a lump of nasty stuff at the bottom which would have coloured the whole glass. Second, he said he used phosphorus because of its tasteless property. It tastes revolting, Harry, and can only be ingested in something highly flavoured – like chocolates, for instance. Third, he said he chose phosphorus because of its colourless properties. It's yellower than the Primrose League. Fourth,' Lestrade was in full flight, wearing a furrow in the rich pile of Bandicoot's Wilton, 'Mr Bandicoot's hands bear the marks of a man who has played the Wall Game, boxed and sculled for his school and harvested in due season. What they do not bear is any trace of phosphorus – and even with indiarubber gloves, that is difficult to avoid. No, Harry.' Lestrade turned to him. 'I'm afraid my trap caught you more surely than Guthrie's did outside. The poison I was describing was antimony. I deliberately misled you. Anyone who had *really* used phosphorus would know the difference. Guthrie here didn't because he hasn't seen it used before.'

'Sholto, I . . .' Bandicoot began, but Lestrade's look silenced him.

'Well.' Guthrie got to his feet, fuming quietly. 'I suppose that's it.'

'Not quite,' said Lestrade, lighting up a well-earned cigar. 'You see, Mr Bandicoot is guilty.'

'What?' the squire and the chief inspector chorused.

'Guilty,' said Lestrade, 'of covering up for someone else.'

There was a silence and then a knock at the door. Letitia entered with a tray of coffee for Harry and Lestrade. She had thoughtfully omitted one for Guthrie.

'Letitia,' said Lestrade, 'I'd like you to listen to this.'

'This does not concern Letitia, Sholto.' Harry was adamant.

Lestrade looked at his man. 'I'm afraid it does,' he said. And she sat down. 'As everybody but Chief Inspector Guthrie is willing to admit, the death of Richard Tetley was one of a series.'

'Exactly,' Bandicoot broke in, 'and I did them all.'

'Harry!' Letitia nearly dropped her sugar tongs. She did in fact drop the sugar and it plopped resoundingly into Lestrade's cup, spraying his face as he stood behind the sofa. He put the cup down.

'All right, Harry,' Lestrade sighed. He was prepared to humour him a little further. 'Why did you kill The Sheep? The man on the omnibus? Why him?'

'Er . . . for the wrong he had done Roger Lytton, Sholto. I was at school with him, you know. *Floreat Etona* and all that. There are just some things a chum has to do for a chum.'

'You left it a long time, didn't you, chum?' Lestrade asked. 'Roger Lytton was killed over a year ago. Why the delay?'

'I had to find him first, Sholto. An East End rough in a whole East End full of roughs . . .'

Lestrade nodded. He could see the problem.

'Lestrade,' Guthrie interrupted, 'I don't understand any of this.'

'Of course not,' the inspector smiled, 'you're with the Somerset Constabulary. Tell me, Harry, what did you use?'

'A stiletto,' Bandicoot answered.

'The same one you used on the Mander brothers?'

'Yes, of course.'

'Why did you put the aluminium in the mouth of Cuthbert Mander, known as Sally?'

Bandicoot looked a little vacant at that. No one noticed the difference. 'A private joke,' he said.

Lestrade shook his head. 'Now,' he said quietly, risking his coffee again, 'we come to Howard Luneberg de Lacy. Just what was your relationship with his wife?'

Bandicoot looked at Letitia, whose earnest eyes had not left her husband the whole time. 'I was having . . . an affair with her,' he said.

Lestrade heard Letitia breathe in sharply. 'So when de Lacy killed his wife, you naturally wanted revenge.'

'Yes.' Bandicoot was staring at Letitia, as though no one else were in the room.

'So you gave him phosphorus poisoning?'

'Yes. I . . . that is . . .'

'But you've just said he doesn't know phosphorus from my left testicle – saving your presence, Mrs Bandicoot,' said Guthrie, bewildered and exasperated.

'Poetically put,' said Lestrade, 'but there are one or two other things Mr Bandicoot doesn't know. For instance, that only one Mander brother was killed by stabbing, not both. And the piece of aluminium was found in the mouth of Gerald Mander, not Cuthbert. And, of course, Howard de Lacy was stabbed, not poisoned.'

Everybody looked at everybody else.

'Oh, for a while there,' sighed Lestrade, 'I must confess I had my doubts. Things looked a little black for you, Harry. First of all, you asked Letitia to engage my help in the death of Richard Tetley.'

Guthrie snorted his disapproval.

'For an unworthy moment, it crossed my mind that you did that in the hope that I'd be more lenient with you than the local constabulary, for want of a better phrase.'

'Right.' Guthrie was now following Lestrade's drift.

'And, of course, you also failed to get me the coroner's report on Tetley, which might have established your guilt. And you were in Yorkshire on business at the time that Captain Hellerslyke was killed. You were in London, similarly, at the time when Howard de Lacy met his end. It goes without saying you were there again when The Sheep died. You also knew "Armpits" Parmenter, whose death was almost certainly deliberately caused by the Mander brothers. That gave you a motive for at least two of the murders and the opportunity for three.'

'Then why don't you let Guthrie take me in?' Bandicoot shouted.

'Because you didn't do them, Harry,' Lestrade said. 'Not any of them. What do you know of Mortimer Lytton?'

'Roger's brother?' Bandicoot checked. 'Not much. I didn't care for him.'

'No,' laughed Lestrade, 'not your type, I wouldn't think. Though you were clearly his.'

'What?' Guthrie, baulked of one crime, sensed another.

'Mortimer Lytton is not as other men, Chief Inspector,' Lestrade told him. 'What happened, Harry? Did he make you an offer you could refuse?'

'He certainly did.' Bandicoot raised his head disdainfully.

'What did you do?' Lestrade asked.

'I knocked him out,' Bandicoot and Lestrade chorused.

'I suspected something like that,' Lestrade went on. 'Your rejection of the man must have hit him harder than your fist. Didn't he warn you, Letitia, that Harry wasn't right for you?'

'He did, Sholto. He said the most frightful things about you, Harry. I knew they weren't true. I hit him too.'

They laughed and fell into each other's arms.

'That's enough of that,' Guthrie growled. 'This is a murder enquiry. Isn't it, Lestrade?'

'Letitia, you're a scholar,' said Lestrade. 'What does the Spanish *cherchez l'homme* mean?'

'It's French, Sholto,' she giggled, vaguely recognizing the phrase despite Lestrade's pronunciation. 'It means "look for the man".'

Lestrade nodded. 'Whereas, of course, I should have been looking for a woman.'

Letitia was the first to break the silence. 'Sholto? Do you mean Harry *really* didn't do it?'

Lestrade shook his head slowly. 'No,' he said.

'Oh, thank God!' She held him close. 'Harry, forgive me; for a moment I thought . . . I was about to send Sholto a telegram, to give myself up. I thought it was you.'

'And I thought it was you, dearest heart . . .' Bandicoot laughed. Then he caught the grim faces of Lestrade and Guthrie. It was the chief inspector who crossed the room first.

'I suggest you get dressed, Mrs Bandicoot,' he said.

'Guthrie . . .' Lestrade began.

The chief inspector ignored him. 'Letitia Bandicoot, I am arresting you for the murder of Richard Tetley. You are not obliged to say anything . . .'

Indeed, Guthrie wasn't obliged to say much more. Lestrade expected it. He had seen it before. The flash in the clear blue eyes, the bracing of the back, the swing of the head. And a powerful right hook connected with the chief inspector's jaw as Harry went for him. Guthrie catapulted backwards, carrying the *chaise-longue* with him, and lay with his feet twitching slightly.

Lest the crash of furniture brought inquisitive policemen to the window, Lestrade opened the casement and waved to the sergeant. 'Oops,' he said cheerily, 'there goes Mrs Bandicoot's jardinière. Clumsy me.'

But the sergeant was standing head to head and toe to toe with Tom Wyatt. He couldn't have coped with anything else. Lestrade spun to the couple. 'Harry,' he said and stooped to check the prostrate policeman. 'I'm trying to keep you out of prison, but you're making it damned difficult for me.'

'I'm sorry, Sholto,' Bandicoot said. 'But that oaf is not going to arrest my wife.'

'No, no, of course not,' Lestrade soothed him and then his eyes fell on something dangling from Guthrie's pocket. He picked them up and laughed. 'Harry,' he said, 'come and look at this. You'll never believe it.'

'What?' Bandicoot grinned and bent beside him. Lestrade brought both fists down as hard as he could on the back of the squire's neck and as he crouched, stunned, he flicked out Guthrie's cuffs and clicked one around Bandicoot's wrist and one around the iron ring jutting from the wall below the mullion.

'That's handy,' he said to Letitia. 'Do you suppose that's why it was put there in the first place?'

'Harry!' Letitia had only now realized what was happening and ran to tend her husband.

'He's all right,' Lestrade reassured her. 'At least he'll have less of a headache than old Guthrie. Now,' he lifted her up, 'Harry lied to save you. You were going to lie to save him.' He sat her down on the settee and sat beside her. 'Your confession would have gone something like this. You called me in to sort out the Richard Tetley murder for the same reason Harry might have or because some killers have a compulsion to report their own crimes – a sort of vanity, I suppose.'

She nodded.

'The guide at Wookey Hole – Old Spiggot – said there had been a woman with an ear trumpet there on the morning of Tetley's death. Whoever killed him was presumably the same person who placed the scarab in his mouth shortly after he died. That woman was you.'

She nodded.

'Do you remember when we first met?' he suddenly asked, looking up.

'Why, yes, I do.' She brightened at the memory of it. 'It was at the Openshaw Workhouse in Manchester. I was visiting with Harry . . .'

'Then your intended.'

'. . . Yes. And you were on an assignment, posing as an inmate. Looking back, I remember your face when Harry recognized you and didn't realize the situation.' She laughed in spite of herself. Then her face became serious again. 'Sholto, why are you talking about this?'

'The death of Hughie Ralph,' said Lestrade. 'You see, Letitia, each of the deceased in this case was himself guilty of a crime. The murderer was merely exacting revenge. Hughie Ralph's crime was that he swindled an honest man out of a fortune. That man is now dying alone in a workhouse. His name – or at least one that in his shame and solitude he uses – is George Hypericum Lawrenson.'

Letitia caught her breath. 'Oh, my God,' she whispered.

'I couldn't remember at first where I'd heard the name. Then on the train here this morning, I remembered. When we met at the Openshaw Workhouse you were a widow, weren't you? And your name was Lawrenson.' He smiled to himself. 'It's funny. All the way down, the train rattled on the rails, "Letitia's name, Letitia's name". I couldn't get it out of my head.'

She looked at him.

'He wasn't a relation, I suppose?'

'I don't think so,' she said.

'You were in London, as was Harry, when The Sheep died. And it was you who sent me on a wild goose chase to Parabola Road in Cheltenham. Although the Lyttons proved more useful than you know. Before "Sally" Mander died, he had a visitor. A female visitor, I believe, although there is a confused corporal of Engineers who might call me a liar. And what a neat coincidence for anyone wanting to confess to murder, that old relationship between Harry and Marigold de Lacy. That wasn't true you know – about their affair.'

'I know,' she said and the tears trickled down her face.

'But of course,' he left the settee and stood framed by the window, 'it was your classical education that really gave you away.'

'Sholto?' She sat upright, searching his face in a vague rising sense of panic. He was cold, passionless. Suddenly he wasn't playing a game any more.

'The name you left in Rowntree's ledger. The chocolates you bought and added poison to for Willie Hellerslyke. The name Perameles.'

'Perameles?' she repeated.

'What does it mean?' he asked.

'I . . . I don't know,' she said. 'For God's sake, Sholto, I don't know.'

He crossed the room to her in three strides. It would have taken the fallen Harry one. He held her hand. 'You're a clever woman, Letitia,' he said, looking her in the glistening grey eyes. 'Clever enough, unlike Harry, to be sufficiently vague about murders you were not guilty of to fool me . . . well, Guthrie, anyway. You're also clever enough to use phosphorus – again, unlike Harry – without burning your hands.' He wiped a tear from her cheek, and smiled. 'But I've been talking to murderers for twenty-five years, man and boy. And I think I know a lie when I hear one.'

'It wasn't me,' she whispered, suddenly a little girl again, and afraid.

'No,' he told her, 'I know.'

There was a groan behind them. Lestrade turned to find both men coming round. 'You can let Harry go in a minute.' He threw her the key from Guthrie's pocket. 'You'd better before he pulls this ring out of the wall and the wall with it. As for this one,' he glanced down at Guthrie, 'I think I have the answer,' and he casually dropped a jardinière down on his head. Festooned with roots and potting compost, Guthrie fell back, unconscious once again.

For safety's sake, Lestrade popped his head out of the

window. 'Oops,' he called to the sergeant, 'there goes the other one.'

And he made for the door.

'Sholto?' Letitia held his arm. 'What does Perameles mean?' she asked.

'That's the devil of it,' he smiled. 'That's what brought me here this morning. It's the Latin for Bandicoot,' and he saw himself out. 'I was right to risk your coffee after all.'

'How is she?' Lestrade looked at the prone figure of Maisie lying on the kitchen table.

'Overwrought,' said Miss Balsam. 'We all are.'

'I'm glad you've put the shotgun down, Miss Balsam.' Lestrade closed the door behind him.

'So am I,' she said. 'How are the lambs? What's happened?'

'Well, both Harry and Mr Guthrie will have headaches for a while, but other than that, all is well.'

'Good, good.'

'Perhaps we can have a little chat, Miss Balsam? You see, Harry didn't kill Richard Tetley.'

'I know he didn't,' she said. 'I did.'

'Ah.'

'Walk this way, Inspector,' she smiled. 'I have a capital glass of port put by for moments such as these.'

'Port, Miss Balsam?' Lestrade stopped in his tracks.

She chuckled as he followed her up a little spiral staircase. 'I'll have a glass too,' she said.

Her rooms were cheerful, the December sun of mid-morning filtering through the latticed windows and falling dappled on the chintz of the sofa.

'Please,' she said, 'have a seat. I was wondering how long it would be before you came to see me. Here,' and she poured a large glass for them both.

Lestrade hesitated, checked the liquid in the clear glass and when she had drunk, he did so too. 'Capital,' he said, raising his glass in a toast.

'Well,' she said, 'this *is* nice. I suppose you'd like to know how I did them all.'

'I should caution you, Miss Balsam . . .' Lestrade began.

'Oh, fiddlesticks!' She waved him aside. 'Do you have the time, Inspector?'

He was, of course, the right person to ask and he flicked out his half-hunter. 'It's ten-thirty,' he told her.

'Right. Well, where can I start?'

'Archibald Fellowes?' he prompted her.

'Yes, of course. Archie. Thoroughgoing rotter, he was. I was his nanny for a time, oh, many, many years ago of course, just before I became dear Lettie's nanny, in fact. He was a grizzly, petulant child, always pinching the other children and running away. A dreadful coward, I'm afraid.'

'A coward?'

'Indelibly. You could have knocked me over with a perambulator when I read his commission in the Gazette. All we nannies follow the futures of our charges, you see. I wouldn't have thought Archie would have gone for a soldier at all.'

Rather more Mortimer Lytton's bent, reflected Lestrade.

'Still, there it was. And I read of course of his exploits in the Ashanti War and was still more incredulous.'

'Then?'

'Then, oh, let me replenish your glass,' and she topped them both up, 'then I had a letter from a dear old friend of mine – whose name, by the way, need not concern you – who had been the nanny of Captain Hely, the unfortunate brother officer who died in Ashanti. She was heart-broken and it bothered me. I couldn't sleep, Inspector. My old friend spoke of a letter written to her by young Hely shortly before he died. Some of our charges are very attached to us, you see. Apparently, they found it on the body of the poor boy, after the Fuzzy Wuzzies or whoever they are had finished with him.'

She fanned herself with a napkin at her side.

'It said that Fellowes had led them stupidly into a trap and then fled, claiming to be going for help. Of course, he never returned.'

'Wolseley thought it was something like that,' Lestrade mused.

'Wolseley?' she snorted. 'Useless. Not enough roughage as a child, that's his problem. Perhaps because the envelope was addressed to Nanny . . . never mind; perhaps because the army chose not to investigate, they merely took Archie's word for what had happened – the word of a coward and a liar.'

'What did you do?'

'I decided on something that is sadly all too rare in England these days, Mr Lestrade. I decided on justice.'

'I see. You didn't go to the authorities?'

'Of course not. That would have been a total negation of justice. I found out where Archie was stationed and paid a street urchin to deliver a verbal message to him to meet me.'

'A verbal messsage, so that there was no note for me to find.'

'You're quite clever for a policeman, aren't you?' she smiled.

'And you met in Kew Gardens?'

'Good heavens!' She sat upright. 'How did you know that?'

'A lucky guess,' said Lestrade. 'How did you kill him?'

'Phosphorus,' she beamed. 'I remembered Archie had a very sweet tooth. Most boys do. I gave him three – or was it four – chocolates. Unrobed phosphorus is quite revolting to the taste, you see. Alas, I was rather naïve and totally unused to the stuff.'

'Would you remove your gloves, Miss Balsam?' he asked.

'Tsk, tsk. You forward man! I am old enough to be your mother!' and she complied to reveal the reddish scars along fingers and thumbs.

'I had no idea how long the wretched process took then. I steered the conversation around to Ashanti. To the medal he had not won fairly. To the story he had told. He was carrying the medal in his pocket and he began to stagger.' She closed her eyes and shuddered. 'I was blind with fury as he admitted his guilt and I tried to . . . I don't know, steady him, I suppose. In the struggle he fell on to the towpath beside the river and I popped the medal into his open mouth – like a final chocolate, I suppose. All my boys have to learn to take their medicine, you see. He rolled sideways and fell into the river. I didn't see him struggle and I watched his body float away among the reeds. Well, I waited for someone to rush up and seize me. But no one came. It was broad daylight and yet there was no one around to witness the scene. It was astonishing. I walked away.'

'And Richard Tetley was nearer to home?'

'In every sense,' she said, smiling at the sun on the steaming frost outside. 'It was a curious coincidence that I too received a letter from an old charge, one I cared for for only a short time, Oscar Jones, an American boy. I must have made more impression on him than he on me, I'm afraid, because he wrote to me off and on. His last letter told of fears for his life, that Richard Tetley was jealous to the point of insanity about Oscar's clever find in Egypt and he could not turn his back on a man like that. I was on the point of replying to him when I read in *The Times* of the poor boy's death. And I knew he had turned his back. I should probably have done nothing had not the dig at Wookey come to light. While Arthur Bulleid was at dinner, I suggested he invite Tetley to join him on the excavation. I also suggested to Harry that he offer him the Dower House, which was vacant, at a nominal rent. It all worked perfectly.'

'And you were the lady in the cave with the ear trumpet?' Lestrade asked.

'A rather feeble disguise, I'm afraid. My hearing is perfectly good. The senile old guide wouldn't have noticed if I'd been riding a hobby horse upside-down, but I was on home territory, so to speak, and I couldn't risk being seen. I knew that Tetley worked alone in the mornings or with Bulleid. I chose the former and gave him some of Nanny's delicious chocolates.'

'And the beetle?'

'Yes. It occurred to me after Archie's demise that the placing of something in the mouth was rather symbolic. Naughty boys taking their medicine at last, as I said. I wanted justice, Mr Lestrade. And this was the final touch of poetry about it. I had pretended to Tetley that I was fascinated by archaeology and he was vain enough to show me his collection the night before he died. It was the work of a moment to slip the Amenhotep scarab into my purse and take it, along with the chocolates, the next day. Phosphorus is tricky stuff, Inspector. Archie died too quickly. Tetley died too slowly. I barely had time to pop the beetle in before I heard someone coming. I thought it might have been visitors, but in fact it was Arthur Bulleid. Luckily, there are plenty of hiding places in Wookey for an old witch like me.'

'Which brings us to Howard de Lacy,' Lestrade prompted her.

'What a churl. Married dear Marigold for her money and killed her for the same reason.'

'You know this for a fact?'

'Tosh and nonsense,' she said. 'I realize, dear Inspector, that you police chappies are bound by regulations and evidence and proof and so forth. I have been raising children now for more years than I care to remember. Dear Marigold was a constant companion to Lettie as a girl. She wrote to Lettie saying she was deeply unhappy. Life with Howard had turned bitter. When Lettie told me of her death, I was sure of my path. I caught a London train and waited for my chance.'

'Not phosphorus this time,' Lestrade said, helping himself to Miss Balsam's port.

She slapped his hand. 'Polite boys *ask*,' she said and poured it for him. 'No, I didn't have time to mix up the compound. My "laboratory" is merely this cabinet, Mr Lestrade. I'm afraid it's not very sophisticated.' She opened the doors to show him a box, with pestles and mortars and a little metal bowl stained yellow. 'So I bided my time and used this instead.' She whipped out a knitting needle, stiletto-sharp, and held it glinting at Lestrade's throat. He gently pinged it from his tie knot.

'Oh, I'm so sorry,' she smiled. 'It took me a little while to file that thing to a point. I used a contraption of Tom Wyatt's, the groom here.'

Lestrade nodded. 'How did you get into de Lacy's bedroom?'

'Through the door,' she said. 'I couldn't believe it was that easy. The pig was snoring in his bed. He turned over as I crouched over him and . . .' She shuddered again. 'Oh dear, I haven't really the phlegm for a murderer, Mr Lestrade. He *did* do it, didn't he? He *did* kill Marigold?'

Lestrade nodded. 'I believe he did,' he said. 'But explain something to me, Miss Balsam. You weren't nanny to *all* the victims of those you killed?'

She laughed. 'Good heavens, no, dear boy. My personal involvement ended there. I'm a sentimental old fool you know, underneath this homicidal exterior. I thought it would be fun to meet up with some of my old colleagues, from the days we'd walk our charges in Hyde Park, and talk over old times.'

'The Nannies' Convention in Cheltenham!' Lestrade remembered.

'Yes. Now that Letitia has Miss Shadbolt, I am a free agent these days – though I doubt whether I will be for long. I had the time to travel all over the place in search of my quarries. Oh, I feigned dizziness and senility and tiredness to put people off the scent. It seemed to work. I was dismissed as a harmless old eccentric and that was that. You were looking for what – a bayonet? A stiletto?'

Lestrade nodded, smiling.

'My fellow nannies told me some terrible tales, Mr Lestrade. Tales similar to those I had already heard about Archie Fellows, Richard Tetley and Howard de Lacy. I committed them all to memory and went to work. You know,' she giggled, 'I'm getting quite merry on this port. Still, I suppose it will be the last for a while.' She clinked her glass on his.

'Cheers, Coquette,' said Lestrade.

She tapped his knee. 'You awful boy,' she scolded him, smiling. 'It's been a long time since anyone called me that.'

'Was Mortimer Lytton one of your charges?' he asked.

'Mortimer? No, but the Lyttons were cousins to Lettie. I had to pretend not to remember them at breakfast at the Grand that day so that you wouldn't become suspicious of me. You see, I still had work to do.'

'Did Mortimer take his nickname Coquette from you?'

'Yes, he did. It became a family joke, apparently – although in that family, pray tell me who *isn't* a joke! For some reason, he liked the name and it stuck.'

Could it be his mincing gait? Lestrade wondered, but he wouldn't have shocked Nanny Balsam for the world.

'And Perameles?'

'Ah.' Miss Balsam's gnarled features darkened. 'That was a terrible mistake on my part, wasn't it? A nanny colleague, old Nanny Hardinge – I've forgotten her real name – told me of the tragedy of poor Miss Hardinge. William Hellerslyke was obviously a cad and a rotter. I invited myself to York, told Lettie I was visiting friends, and went along to the open day thing the Hussars had. I introduced myself to the captain as the sender of the chocolates and asked if he'd enjoyed them. He said yes, they were delicious, but who was I and why had I sent them? I explained the whole thing, quietly in the hubbub of people, and he became rather upset and stormed off.'

'You'd got the dose right by now?'

'Yes. It took several hours. Time enough for me to slip away.

I had a delightful luncheon before I left with a charming officer named Daubney.'

Lestrade shook his head. 'Charming, but unobservant,' he said.

'Once again, I'd got the problem of not being able to take my mixture. I had my knitting with me, of course, but that way proved impossible. So I bought some rat poison in York and some chocolates too.'

'And made Coquette's confection,' Lestrade said.

'Quite. But I was rather taken aback when the gentleman asked me to sign his ledger. I thought of the first thing I could which I believed would never be traced. Perameles – the generic name for Bandicoot. Oh, it was wicked of me, Inspector! Wicked! I would not implicate those two dear lambs for the world. I never dreamt anyone would notice.'

'No one did,' said Lestrade, 'unless you count Constable Skinner. It was his rather belated translation that brought me here in the first place.'

'To arrest me?'

Lestrade looked at her from under his eyebrows. His reputation lay in the balance. 'To arrest Harry,' he admitted.

'Oh, heavens!' She covered her mouth.

'Then I realized as we talked that Harry hadn't the motive or the expertise for the job.'

'So you came to me.'

'No,' Lestrade confessed, 'I came to Letitia.'

'Oh, my baby.' She stood up and the glass fell from her hand.

'Calm yourself, Miss Balsam,' he said. 'It was *then* I came to you. How did you kill the bicyclist, Hughie Ralph?'

She sat down, calmer now if a little slurred. 'I knew he had swindled a boy called George Elliott – another colleague's old charge. I discovered, on my sojourn in London, that he took a drug to keep himself fit for his daredevil exploits in the saddle. I was able to doctor his dose while posing as a Salvationist. While he placed his hypocritical pennies in my tambourine on his way to the Tottenham Court Road, I persuaded him that *my* elixir was just the tonic he needed. Odd that such a ruthless businessman should be so gullible.'

'So it wasn't lunch at the Rose, Tewin?' Lestrade said, half to himself.

'No, it was breakfast at Cambridge Circus.'

'And Gerald Mander?'

'I waited for my chance and followed him. He took evening constitutionals near his home in Epping Forest. I must admit,' she turned a shade greyer, 'his death was the most unpleasant. I am not a strong woman, Mr Lestrade, I had to reach up – he was taller than I – and he half turned as I struck him. I shall never forget,' she closed her eyes as though to blot out the memory, 'the look on his face as he went down.'

'The aluminium?'

'The . . . ah, yes, I didn't know what that was. It was in his pocket. I assumed it must have something to do with ballooning, since that was the man's cursed passion. The passion that killed young Parmenter. I had been baulked of my chance to leave my calling card with Mr Ralph. I searched his rooms for some sign of the swindle against poor Elliott – I found none.'

'And you were the . . . lady . . . who visited Sally Mander the night before he died?'

'I was badly disguised again, I'm afraid.'

'Chocolates?'

'Of course,' she smiled.

'And The Sheep, le Mouton? The man on the omnibus? While you claimed to be resting in your room at the Grand?' he asked.

'I was in reality catching the same omnibus and sat behind him, knitting. I got off at the Tower. The rest you know.'

'It must have been difficult to find him,' Lestrade observed.

'Not really. I engaged the help of a private detective . . .'

Lestrade groaned. 'And then,' he said, 'you shopped at Liberty's?'

'Yes. That unspeakable wretch Chesney was the last little job I had to do. I knew of his dastardly game from another old colleague. Her ex-charge was Mr Hamilton's lady friend. She felt terribly guilty about her . . . indiscretion . . . and I felt for her. I contacted Chesney, through her, and invited him to stay at the Grand as I had some business to transact. He obviously smelled money, as I knew he would, and duly arrived. He wasn't much of a chocolate nibbler, but I coaxed him and added some contrived nonsense about Mr Gladstone which I knew a blackmailer could not resist.'

Lestrade's mind boggled. The Grand Old Man was eighty-eight.

'I'm sorry he had to die at Liberty's though. Such a nice shop, don't you think? Well,' she looked at him, 'there it is. My confession. What do you have to say to me, Mr Lestrade?'

'Justice,' he said. 'That's why you did it?'

She closed to him. 'Mr Lestrade,' she said, 'hasn't there been a time in your life when you have seen a man – a really evil man – get away with a crime, be it blackmail or murder, and you couldn't do a thing about it?'

'Yes,' he said slowly, 'I'm afraid there has.'

'Then there you have it,' she said.

'But what gives you the right, Miss Balsam, to be jury, judge and executioner?'

'Claptrap!' she said, 'I am a nanny.' She sat bolt upright. 'And English law has a long way to go before it can match the simple purity of the law of the nursery. Transgress and be punished. It's that straightforward.'

'I suppose to you it is,' he said.

Nanny Balsam rose and crossed to the lattice window that looked out over the covered courtyard and the lake beyond. 'You, Mr Lestrade, in your career, admit you have felt powerless because of the law. There were felons who slipped through your fingers because those fingers were made slippery by the rule of law. You see,' she smiled at him, 'the law really *is* an ass, I'm afraid. Oh, you might have caught Howard de Lacy for the murder of his wife, in time. But the Manders? Hughie Ralph? Willie Hellerslyke? And Archie Fellowes? Not to mention Richard Tetley? No, their crimes were over and done. And yet they were scot free in the eyes of men.'

'But not in the eyes of Nanny Balsam?' Lestrade asked, smiling at her.

She sat quietly in her nursing chair. 'Mr Lestrade,' she said, 'look into those eyes now.'

The inspector did so. His brow furrowed. He edged forward. The grey old eyes were tired. Bright with tiredness and a long day done. But he saw something else. The pupils were small – as all Nanny Balsam's pupils were once small – and they were getting smaller. He threw down his glass and gripped her shoulders.

'What is the time?' she asked him, a little slurred now.

'I . . . don't know. Er . . . eleven, or thereabouts. Nanny, tell me . . .'

She held up her hand. 'In the bureau,' she said, waving towards the corner. Lestrade turned, steadying her swaying little frame with one arm, and found the envelope inside.

'It tells all,' she said. 'My confession. I only wish . . . I only wish Lettie didn't have to know.'

She pitched forward into Lestrade's arms and he gently loosened her collar. The prim, still graceful old lady did not complain. It had been a long time since Coquette had lain in the arms of a man. And now it didn't matter.

'I discovered this . . . other poison,' she said, her breathing more difficult. 'Silly me not to have found it earlier. And only ninety-one years after it was discovered.'

He looked again at the pinpoint eyes and he smelled the opium on her breath. 'Morphine,' he said.

'Look after dear Lettie for me,' she said, squeezing his hand. 'Goodbye, Mr Lestrade. "Look for me in the nurseries of Heaven",' and she slipped sideways, her blurred eyes focusing for a moment. 'Tsk, tsk,' she whispered, 'frayed cuffs. Nanny would never allow that . . .'

He went downstairs as the grandfather clock struck the hour. Eleven o'clock. Nanny Balsam would not be there for Christmas that year. Nor for any other Christmases to come.

In the drawing-room, Harry was sitting with Letitia and Chief Inspector Guthrie was coming round for the second time. Lestrade stood between them. 'It's Miss Balsam,' he said.

'What?' Letitia stood up, shocked by the yellow face and the sad eyes, so weary of the world.

'It must have been the excitement of the morning,' he said. 'I'm afraid she's gone, Letitia.'

The men heard an inrush of breath and gathering her skirts Letitia Bandicoot ran through the house, bounding up the stairs much as her husband had done when Nanny Balsam had slapped the backsides of their boys the day they were born. Harry moved after her, but Lestrade held his shoulder. 'Better not,' he said. 'Leave Letitia alone with her memories. Just for a moment. She'll need you later.'

He patted Bandicoot's arm and the big man sat down. Lestrade crossed to Guthrie and hauled him upright. He pulled a cigar out and forced it between the man's lips. He clamped his on another and for a light he dipped Miss Balsam's letter into the flames and lit first his cheroot, then Guthrie's.

'About this murder,' Guthrie was nursing his neck. 'This series of murders, then.' He had caught Lestrade's surprised look. 'It's Mrs Bandicoot, isn't it? That's why Bandicoot clocked me.' He scowled at the squire. 'Which reminds me . . .' and he staggered towards Harry.

Lestrade placed an avuncular arm around the man's shoulder and led him to the door, shaking his head. 'No, it isn't,' he said, 'and I will go with you to the station now to prove it. You know, Chief Inspector, you were right.'

'You mean it *is* Bandicoot after all?' Guthrie persisted, ever hopeful.

'No, I mean my own incompetence.' Lestrade fanned the burning envelope in the air. 'My own incompetence and, yes, the arrogance of the Yard. Oh, I'll pursue my enquiries elsewhere, of course. We never sleep. No stone unturned, no quarry unpursued, no opportunity missed. But frankly . . . Well, you know how it is . . .'

'A dead end?' The blows to Guthrie's head must have done some good. The man was curiously mellowed.

'You might say that,' Lestrade said. 'Anyway,' he threw the curling brown paper into the fire as he passed, 'we won't find our guilty party here. Harry, go to Letitia now. I must accompany the chief inspector here to the station.'

'Sholto, I don't understand. Are you coming back?'

Lestrade looked at him, at the stairs to Nanny Balsam's room. 'No,' he said, 'there's no need. Merry Christmas, Harry.'

At the sight of their lord and master, the men of the Somerset Constabulary returned warily to the station trap. One by one, Tom Wyatt, Old Jack, Young Jem and the rest broke formation and wandered away across the frosty fields.

Lestrade rode in the jolting Maria alongside the still dizzy chief inspector. At the fork in the road below the old orchard he leaned out to see three little children with their nanny, laughing and squealing as they rolled over on the ice.

'Look for me in the nurseries of Heaven.'

The inspector smiled.

A STEAL OF A DEAL

Order the next volume in the Lestrade Mystery Series:

Volume IX: *Lestrade and the Gift of the Prince*

Have ***Lestrade and the Gift of the Prince*** sent directly to your home for a steal of a deal—20% off plus FREE shipping and handling.

Murder is afoot among the footmen of the Royal Household: a servant girl, Amy Macpherson, has been brutally slaughtered. Ineptly disguised as a schoolmaster, the intrepid Superintendent Sholto Lestrade tries to untangle a villainous web of conspiracy. Following the most baffling clues he has yet unravelled, Lestrade travels from Balmoral Castle to the Isle of Skye to the North British Hotel, where he narrowly escapes an inferno in Room 13. Everyone is convinced this is a case for the local police, but Lestrade of Scotland Yard perseveres to get his man.

Volume IX in the Lestrade Mystery Series will be sent from the publisher—via free expedited shipping—directly to your home at a cost to you of only $15.95. That's a savings of nearly $10 over the actual retail price of the book and normal shipping and handling charges.

And, with the purchase of any book for $15.95, you may buy any of the first four volumes for just $9.95 each!

ALERT SCOTLAND YARD. IT'S A STEAL!

Call 1-888-219-4747 to get your

Lestrade Steal of a Deal!